The Lodeman

A SEA-CHANGE MYSTERY

DOROTHY JOHNSTON

This novel is set in real places, chiefly the town of Queenscliff, Victoria, Australia and surrounding areas. It references actual activities such as, but not exclusive to, the pilot service, the coast guard and the police service. However, all characters are fictitious and any resemblance to any person, whether living or dead, is entirely coincidental.

First published by For Pity Sake Publishing Pty Ltd 2021
Copyright © Dorothy Johnston 2021

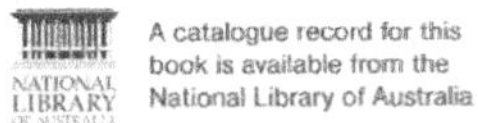

A catalogue record for this book is available from the National Library of Australia

Cover image, cover and internal design by Barbie Robinson – Writing with Light
Ms. Johnston's portrait by Lindsay Kelley – www.lindsaykelleyphotography.com.au
Printed in Australia by IngramSpark

The Lodeman / Dorothy Johnston
9780645040104 (paperback)
9780645040111 (ebook)

Praise for *Through a Camel's Eye*

'The characters and description of the town provide a wonderful sense of place which amplifies Queenscliff in all its glory.'
Ann Byrne, **Sisters in Crime**

'Johnston spins an intriguing tale that keeps us wondering whether the crimes (murder and the theft of a camel) are connected or not — but you'll have to read it yourself to answer that question.'
Whispering Gums

'Move over Miss Fisher and Dr Blake, we have the makings of our own crime series here! There's been a murder and a camel has been stolen from its trainer's paddock. Will the truth be uncovered?'
Gail Thomas, **Geelong's Weekly Review**

Praise for *The Swan Island Connection*

'Dorothy Johnston has delivered an intriguing blend of social observation and crime fiction in her latest novel set in Queenscliff, Victoria. The story is spliced with a sharp sub plot involving the nearby training base for the Australian Secret Intelligence Service. Another strong contribution to the reputation of the nation's novelists.'
Brian Toohey

'Like Garry Disher, Johnston makes evocative and effective use of her setting, bringing the little town of Queenscliff to vivid life.'
Kerryn Goldsworthy, **The Age** and **Sydney Morning Herald**

Praise for *Gerard Hardy's Misfortune*

'Ghost stories turn to murder in Dorothy Johnston's
comic crime novel set in the Victorian seaside town of
Queenscliff… its light humour and sense of place make this
Aussie comic crime caper worth a look.'
The Age and ***Sydney Morning Herald***

'This is a book about how we live with our dead – how we
adjust to the loss of our connection with those who have
been significant to us and have died.'
Janey Runci

Praise for *The Sandra Mahoney Quartet*

'Detective Sergeant Brook, making cheerful capital out of
terminal illness to fast-track police department procedure, is
one of the most unusual and attractive characters to hit the
Australian crime scene in years.'
The Adelaide Advertiser

'An artfully seductive crime story with a denouement which
is chilling, fast and furious.'
The Age

'A class act.'
The Weekend Australian

'A realistic setting, a strong storyline, plausible and affecting
characters and writing of sensitivity and strength.'
The Sunday Age

Praise for Dorothy Johnston's literary fiction

'An awesome talent.'
The Australian

'What I like most about *One for the Master* is its passion and its mystery.'
Australian Book Review

'Johnston achieves the difficult double feat: she creates and maintains a convincing physical world, and yet transcends it through a lovely and original imagination.'
The Sydney Morning Herald

AUTHOR'S NOTE

The Rip, as the entrance to Port Phillip Bay is known, is an extremely dangerous stretch of water, where tidal streams can run up to six knots. In addition to the fast-flowing currents, the shipping channel is narrow. With some exemptions, pilots are required to steer ships out from and into Melbourne through the Rip.

Using a rope ladder, pilots are transferred from small launches which pull alongside the large ships. Other methods have been tried over the years, but rope ladders have been found to be the most reliable and effective. The launches take off in huge swells and howling gales. Some have capsized and pilots and their crews have drowned.

These days, container ships and tankers are of such a size as to leave only the slimmest margin for error, and they do not wait for the pilot launches because to wait would cost the shipping companies money. Thus the pilots often board the large vessels in hazardous conditions.

Chris Blackie, the fictional Queenscliff police officer who is my main protagonist, lost his father in an accident involving a pilot launch. Blackie's father was crewing for a pilot who went overboard. He jumped in after the pilot and was drowned. Chris Blackie's father's body was never recovered.

The first pilot to navigate ships through the Rip was George Tobin, who rowed out to the waiting ships. In 1839 he was appointed as an official pilot.

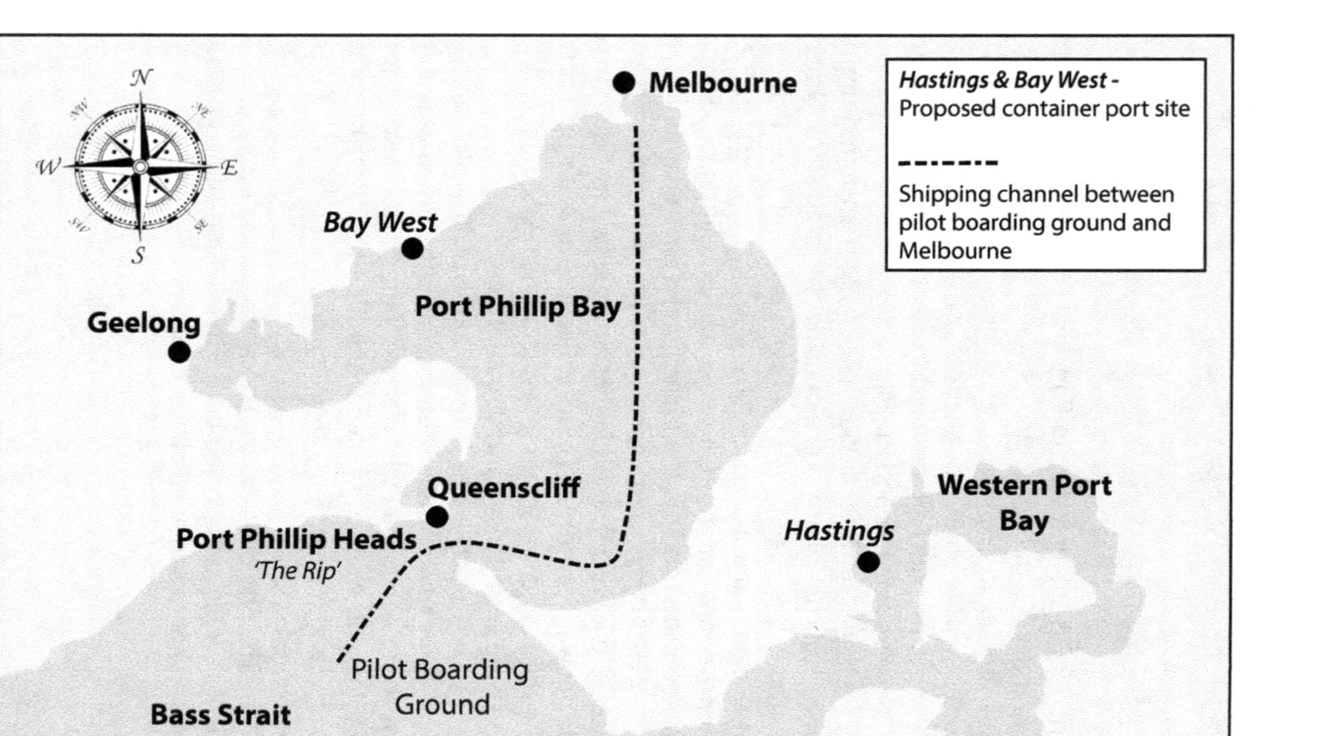

Melbourne
Bay West
Port Phillip Bay
Geelong
Queenscliff
Port Phillip Heads
'The Rip'
Pilot Boarding Ground
Bass Strait
Hastings
Western Port Bay
N
NW
NE
W
E
SW
SE
S
Hastings & Bay West - Proposed container port site
Shipping channel between pilot boarding ground and Melbourne

CAST OF CHARACTERS
In order of appearance

Tom Maloney, volunteer coastguard officer, Queenscliff

Chris Blackie, senior constable, Queenscliff Police

Captain Frederick Delraine, sea pilot

Brian Laidlaw, retired seaman

Camilla Renfrew, friend of Brian Laidlaw

Dr Hammond, pathologist

Sergeant Dawkins, a detective with the Criminal Investigation Unit in Geelong

Michael Travers, a pilot dispatch officer

Rosemary Delraine, Captain Delraine's widow

Alison Delraine, Captain Delraine's sister

Ivan Southeby, chairman of the pilot company's board of directors

John Bennett, CEO of the pilot company

Kerry Holdsworth, Queenscliff resident who lives near the pilots' operations centre

Justin Finbach, Queenscliff resident who lives near the pilots' operations centre

Anthea Merritt, assistant police constable in Queenscliff (on maternity leave)

Olly, Anthea's husband

Aneira, Olly and Anthea's daughter

William, the pilot operation centre's cook

Evan Aldridge, Queenscliff harbourmaster

Alex Stavros, mechanic and boat builder employed by the pilot company

Jim, former mechanic with the pilot company

Bob Sainsbury, former crewman with the pilot company

Scott, Bob Sainsbury's nephew who sat the exam to enter the pilot service but failed.

Hogan, former senior constable and colleague of Chris Blackie

Peter Robinson, former pilot, forced to resign

John Forsyth, launch manager for the pilot service

Captain Trembath, sea pilot

Sergeant Matt Collins, water police

Bobby McGilvrey, boy who was murdered in Queenscliff (See *The Swan Island Connection*)

Max, Bobby McGilvrey's dog

David Anstey, owner of Anstey Limited, an Australian shipping company

George Tobin, first man to be appointed an official sea pilot in 1839

Alistair, in charge of allocating local coastguard volunteers

Robert and Ian Charleton, Rosemary Delraine's brothers

Tony Parry, head of the Hastings Development Group

Minnie Lancaster, Chris Blackie's friend

Eric Finlay, public servant, chair of a consultative committee looking at recommendations for a new container port

Superintendent Walsh, Sergeant Dawkins's superior officer

Thelma Anstey, wife of David Anstey and cousin of Rosemary Delraine

Neil Anstey, Thelma and David Anstey's son

Bryony Langtree, receptionist at the pilots' administration office

Celia Robinson, Peter Robinson's wife

Brendan Hearn, member of the consultative committee

George Norris, Point Lonsdale lighthouse keeper

Bill and **Otto**, crewmen for the pilot company

Julie Beshervase, young woman who owns a camel, friend of Minnie and Camilla (See *Through a Camel's Eye*)

Riza, Julie's camel

Sam and **James**, two boys on the beach

Simon Renfrew, Camilla Renfrew's son

Wal Gilchrist, retired commercial fisherman

Lauren Bloomberg, young woman who fell overboard from Tony Parry's yacht

Nick, a young man who jumped in to the water to save Lauren Bloomberg

Detective Sergeant Flanders, policeman based in the Hastings area

In the Laws of Oleron it was laid down, 'If a ship is lost by default of the lodeman, the maryners may . . . bring the lodeman to the windlass or any other place and cut off his head'.

(From the Oxford Companion to ships and the sea, 2nd edition)

PROLOGUE

'Of course they're an anomaly these days,' Tom Maloney said.

Chris Blackie heard the echo of Tom's voice ringing out across the bay, and only later focussed on the words. They'd joked about being anomalies and anachronisms often enough themselves. Somehow they hung on – Tom in the coastguard office, himself in the police station – withered branches that nobody, in these days of cut-backs and efficiency drives, had got round to lopping off.

Chris had known Tom for over twenty years and thought it strange that they'd never discussed the pilot service before, though Tom lived cheek by jowl with them at the harbour.

He said, 'You mean a closed shop's unusual.'

'Unique.' Tom grimaced around his cigarette and tossed his black fringe off his forehead. He was a rangy man, developing a stoop from years spent leaning over a steering wheel.

'What about the Medical Association?' Chris asked.

Tom made a swift backwards and forwards

movement with his left hand. 'The police force, mate,' he said.

They laughed. Tom stubbed out his Camel Filter and threw the butt over the end of the jetty. Chris bit back a complaint.

He wondered if the proud independence of the pilot service was about to change, then told himself that it already had.

He could not recall any previous occasion when there'd been criticism of the service from the inside; not criticism that he'd got to hear of, which of course was different from it having taken place. But now one of the pilots had been forced to resign.

There must have been disputes in the past, given that the service was over 175 years old. Chris wondered what the disgraced man was doing now. He felt that there was more to the story, but doubted he would ever discover what it was. And maybe this was just as well. Anything to do with the pilot service threatened to unleash old anxieties which, most of the time, he kept under control.

Chris had a sudden premonition that he was about to be plunged back into the past, to thoughts and emotions he would never forget, but managed to control day by day.

ONE

Chris Blackie would have played only a minor part in the investigation into Captain Delraine's death if his old friend Brian Laidlaw hadn't found the body.

It was almost too dark to see where he was going. Chris used a torch to walk from the carpark, but when he got to the bottom of the path, he switched it off. The tide was going out. In the shipping channel, a pilot boat, its lights still on, made for the open water. The heavy pulse of the diesel engines echoed off the dunes.

From humped shadows, a man stood up. Chris knew who it was, but might have recognised him anyway by the shape of his beanie, the way his hair and beard stood out around it, only ever erratically trimmed, by his long-boned frame and braced, watchful stance.

For a long time, Brian Laidlaw had resisted getting a mobile phone. Only the uncertain health of his friend Camilla Renfrew had persuaded him to do so. The retired sailor was often out beachcombing; he spent most of his time on the beaches and the spongy shores of Swan Bay. The fact that Camilla might fall, or otherwise hurt herself and need him, had changed his mind.

When Brian rang, Chris had been asleep and dreaming, the way he sometimes did in the hours before dawn. The dream was still with him, though he shook his head to clear it. Brian had told Chris where he was, and the name of the dead man, Captain Frederick Delraine.

Delraine was lying face down on the sand. Chris

knelt and felt for a pulse. Brian had moved a few steps away and stood staring after the pilot boat, while a dawn the Captain wouldn't see turned the horizon gold.

Delraine might have been in the water six hours or more, though Chris was no expert when it came to estimating things like that. He was wearing a shirt and trousers made of heavy cotton, socks and running shoes. Chris pulled on the latex gloves he always carried with him and felt in the pockets – no keys, wallet, or phone.

There were no obvious signs of injury, but the strengthening sun magnified a fine white froth around his lips. Chris smelt faint traces of vomit and noticed that Delraine's shirt was stained. 'Did you move him?'

Brian didn't turn his head. 'No,' he answered curtly.

Chris stood up. He phoned the Criminal Investigation Unit in Geelong and then for an ambulance.

Brian began to walk away.

Chris called out his name, anticipating the CIU's questions and the old man's reluctance.

'Come back Brian. Tell me what happened. We don't have much time.'

Forty minutes later, a small procession led by paramedics with a stretcher made its way across the sand from the steps. Chris recognised Dr Hammond and felt pleased. He was pleased, too, that nobody had come by while they waited, no early morning joggers or dog walkers.

Chris gave a brief report. After that, the detective in charge, a Sergeant Dawkins, ignored him. The doctor did as well. Brian answered the Sergeant's questions in monosyllables.

Dawkins looked annoyed, as though being got out

of bed early disagreed with him. He was olive skinned, of medium height but broad through the chest and shoulders, dressed in a dark grey crumpled suit.

After asking Brian a few more questions, Dawkins told him to go home and wait there. When Chris offered to ring Camilla so Brian wouldn't be alone, Brian dismissed the suggestion, shaking his head angrily.

TWO

Chris's first impression on entering Captain Delraine's room was that it had been stripped bare. He felt anxious because Sergeant Dawkins had trusted the pilot dispatch officer on duty to lock the room and not remove anything. He wondered, listening to Dawkins giving orders on the phone, who had already been through the Captain's belongings.

Chris stood in the doorway recalling Dawkins' words.

'Have a look round, Blackie. If there's anything interesting, let me know.'

If Chris had been in charge, he would have wanted to examine the room himself. He would have had a forensic team there. It seemed Dawkins had already made up his mind that the Captain's death was an accident, or possibly suicide.

There was no imprint of personality, less than in an ordinary motel room, where, on opening the door, your nose might pick up after-shave, deodorant, sometimes a furtive cigarette.

Chris reminded himself that it was only a few hours since a man had been sitting on the bed, or single chair next to the window, getting ready for the night. The bed covers were pulled tight, not a crease or rumple. Had Delraine smoothed them before going out? Or had someone else? Perhaps it had been second nature for him to set his room in order before leaving it.

Chris pulled his gloves back on and set about

looking for a note, already aware that he would be disappointed if he found one. The bedside cabinet was empty except for a packet of anti-histamine tablets and a box of tissues. A reading light stood next to the bed. The waste paper basket had either just been emptied, or Delraine disposed of his small items of refuse somewhere else.

Chris pulled a plastic bag out of his pocket and placed the packet of hay fever tablets inside it. He stood staring at the label. It wasn't one he recognised. He imagined Dawkins' response should he suggest bringing in a scene-of-crime team.

The obvious place to leave a note would be the pillow or the bedside cabinet. Still, Chris went methodically through pockets, starting with the suit coats and jackets and finishing with the track suit pants.

He emptied drawers. His fingers probed the backs of them. He lifted the mattress and crawled under the bed. Last night hadn't been particularly cold, but still it surprised Chris that Delraine had gone out without a jacket.

He wondered about security cameras. Sergeant Dawkins could ask the pilot dispatch officer. But would he bother? Had Delraine thrown his wallet and his phone away? Chris wondered if the hay fever tablets were a message. But what kind and who for?

Chris's brief conversation with the shocked and white-faced dispatch officer established that Delraine had locked his room before going out the night before. Or at least, Chris thought, nodding encouragement to Michael Travers as the dispatch officer introduced himself, it had been locked that morning when Travers had gone to check.

Travers could not say whether Delraine had taken his phone or wallet with him. The Captain had poked his head around the office door just after eleven and said that he was going for a walk. The dispatch officers worked twelve hour shifts. Chris wondered why this man, who looked exhausted, hadn't been relieved.

When he asked about CCTV, Travers hesitated before replying. Chris thought, you've been through the footage. You know what's on it. He asked to see the film and Travers, after a brief hesitation, agreed.

The film was poor quality, grey and grainy, yet the man leaving the front door of the operations centre was recognisably Delraine. He walked slowly and, to Chris's eye, stumblingly as well.

He'd left the centre at a few minutes past eleven.

Chris turned from the screen to ask, 'Were you worried?'

'A little.' Travers licked dry lips.

'A little?'

'I thought of going after Captain Delraine, but I couldn't leave my post.'

'How many cameras are there at the back?' Chris asked.

There was just one, Travers said, covering the courtyard and the door leading to the laundry and kitchen.

'Could you make a copy, please? Let's say from 8pm last night. Both cameras.'

Travers hesitated and then said he would.

The Captain did not keep a car in Queenscliff.

Everything he'd brought with him was either at the operations centre, on the beach, or in the sea somewhere. Except, of course, if someone had cleaned out his pockets and his room.

'Did anybody ring Captain Delraine yesterday evening?'

'You mean on the office phone?'

Chris nodded.

'No. No, they didn't,' Travers said.

'What about his mobile?'

'I don't know.'

Chris's phone rang.

'Well?' Sergeant Dawkins barked. 'Have you found it?'

'A note, sir? No.' Chris paused, then said, 'I think – '

'You think, Constable? You're not paid to think.'

Chris sighed. He felt – the feeling was like a cold hand clutching his stomach – that something was seriously wrong with Delraine's room.

Pilots died as the result of accidents. Sometimes their crews died with them. Most of Queenscliff knew that Chris's father had drowned attempting to save his master; the town's older inhabitants remembered every drowning that involved pilots, their drivers and their crews.

A pilot who walked into the sea intending never to return was more than an anomaly. It was an event that went against nature. Chris did not believe Delraine had killed himself. He did not believe the pilot had left a note and that someone else, for whatever reason, had removed it.

Accidental death? No, that was illogical as well.

THREE

Brian Laidlaw scorned, for the most part, contact with his fellow men and women. He'd joined the navy as a young man, then worked as a seaman for one transport company after another until he retired. Brian was a night bird; Chris had often come upon him in an otherwise deserted street, in the middle of winter, when a south-westerly was keeping sensible folk indoors.

When Chris knocked on the door of his fisherman's cottage, Brian took a while to answer. He was wearing the same clothes he'd had on early in the morning. His hair and beard looked full of electricity, while his face was bleached and drawn. He glared at Chris, who said,

'A cuppa wouldn't go amiss.'

Without speaking, Brian boiled the jug, poured black, strong tea and set it down on a scrubbed wooden table.

Chris nodded his thanks. He knew Brian was willing him to leave, but there were questions that he had to ask, and Brian had been less than forthcoming on the beach.

'You told me you saw two men talking to the Captain. When was that?'

'A few weeks ago.'

'Did you recognise them?'

'No.'

'Where were you when you saw them?'

'On the beach, wasn't I?' Brian said gruffly, scowling as though Chris had questioned his right to be there.

'And where were they?'

'Round past the pilots jetty.'

It was a convenient spot for a private conversation, screened by bushes on both sides, only visible from certain sections of the beach. But if Brian had seen the men, it stood to reason they'd seen him as well.

'What were they doing?'

'Talking, damn you!'

Brian hadn't poured tea for himself. He turned abruptly from the table so Chris wouldn't see his tears.

Chris said, 'Sergeant Dawkins will be here soon.'

Dawkins will be here demanding answers, Chris added to himself. He won't leave you alone until he's got them. But was this true? Did Dawkins care that much?

Brian said with his back turned, 'Ever heard the expression lodeman?'

'It's an old name for a navigator, isn't it?'

Brian made a choking sound. When he spoke, his voice was jagged. 'That was Captain Delraine. He was a true lodeman.'

'What do you mean, Brian?'

'Some pilots are in it for the money. I'd say that's more than half of them these days.'

'Like who?'

Brian didn't answer. He still had his back to Chris.

'What made Captain Delraine different?'

'In olden times, if a ship was lost, and it was deemed to be the fault of the lodeman, the crew had the right to cut off his head.'

'That's barbaric. What about the men you saw Captain Delraine with? For God's sake, Brian, I need some straight answers.'

'Not now! Just go away and leave me alone!'

The echo of Brian's dismissal followed Chris to the police station. He might have gone on pressuring the seaman, trying to pin down who the men were. But Brian was too distressed. He would have shouted again, maybe thrown him out the door.

Chris sat at his desk to make notes, remembering turns of phrase and the dark, bitter tea. He looked up lodeman in the dictionary, then on Wikipedia. The reference to the gruesome punishment was from laws of the sea probably codified in the thirteenth century. Why had Brian brought it up? What had he been trying to say?

That afternoon, Chris reported to Sergeant Dawkins, who glanced at the anti-histamines and frowned.

Having spoken to Delraine's widow Rosemary, his sister Alison, the staff at the operations centre, the chairman of the board of directors, Ivan Southeby, and Bennett, their CEO, as well as Brian Laidlaw and Delraine's solicitor, the DS was preparing to return to Geelong. Delraine's parents were dead. His sister lived in the UK.

'No surprises,' Dawkins said, getting out his car keys.

Chris would have liked to ask what the Sergeant meant, but he didn't want to be snapped at.

The post mortem was scheduled for tomorrow morning. From the way Dawkins spoke, he sounded as though he wanted to get the formalities over as soon as possible.

Chris guessed he was the kind of officer who avoided the practical, hands-on aspects of detective work. He made phone calls, talked to a few people, and convinced himself that that was enough. He chose the line of least resistance and the easy option automatically. He did not need to think about this process; it simply presented itself to him as the right one.

When Chris suggested door-knocking round the operations centre and the houses bordering the sandhills, asking who'd been out the night before, Dawkins shrugged dismissively, with an expression that said Chris was wasting his time, but told him to go ahead.

Superimposed on Chris's retina was a picture of his father jumping from the launch. He'd kept a lid on it ever since he'd come upon Brian Laidlaw in the dawn light standing guard over Captain Delraine. Now the image came back with the full force of having been suppressed.

The pilots' centre stood on its own at the bottom of a crumbling cliff, topped by a black lighthouse and a water tower, surrounded by scrubby bushes and tussocks of salt-resistant grass. There were no houses adjacent to, or immediately behind it; but a few houses, much older than the centre, overlooked it from the clifftop. Of these, the house belonging to Kerry and Joe Holdsworth was the closest.

The death had been reported on the midday news and Chris avoided the TV crews parked outside the centre.

Kerry Holdsworth came to the door immediately

in answer to his knock.

Chris said yes to a cup of tea. When they were sitting with the tea things on a low table between them, he asked, carefully neutral, 'Were you home last night Mrs Holdsworth?'

Kerry stared at him as though the question might be answered in a dozen different ways. Finally she said, 'Joe's visiting his sister at Apollo Bay.'

'Did you go outside for a breath of air?'

'Who told you I went outside?'

'No one, Mrs Holdsworth.' Chris had seen Kerry was keeping something back from the moment she'd opened the door.

She picked up her cup, then set it down again. She said without looking at Chris, 'I don't like it when Joe's away. I find it hard to sleep. His sister's always on at him to visit. Why doesn't she come here?'

'You heard something?' Chris prompted gently.

'Voices. Down there.'

'Men's voices?'

'It might have been two men, or it might have been a man and a woman.'

'Were they arguing?'

'No, just talking.'

'Could you make out any words?'

Kerry shook her head.

'Was one of the voices Captain Delraine's?'

'I couldn't say.'

'What happened then?'

'I went back inside.'

'Did you get up again that night?' Chris asked, beginning to feel irritated by Kerry's unhelpful answers.

'No,' Kerry said through pursed lips.

'Did you hear anything more?'

'From down there?'

'From anywhere.'

'I heard that Justin fellow coming home. He leaves his car radio on until he's in the garage. It's very inconsiderate.'

'What time was that?'

'I didn't look at the clock.'

'But you did before, when you got up to go outside.'

'I never said that.'

'You knew that it was after eleven.'

Chris understood that Kerry was like many people who had trouble sleeping. She didn't want to check the time, how many hours remained till dawn; but she knew it anyway, by instinct. He was like that himself.

'How long after that did you hear Justin?' he asked.

'Maybe three-quarters of an hour.'

'Have you told anyone else about the voices? Joe?'

'He'd tell me I was imagining things as usual.'

'I'd prefer you kept it to yourself, for the time being at least.'

'I'm not in danger, am I?'

'No, I'm sure you're not. Don't worry.'

The townsfolk accepted the pilots without, for the most part, having much to do with them. Kerry Holdsworth was a typical example. Chris had never heard her mention a single one by name. Apart from Delraine, no pilot currently made his home at Queenscliff. You couldn't exactly say Delraine had made his home there either, though Chris had learnt from the dispatch officer that he hadn't slept at his house in Brighton for the past two months.

Chris thanked Kerry for her time and wished her good-day. He wanted to catch the noisy neighbour Justin before he left for work.

Justin Finbach did not belong in Queenscliff. In mouthing those words to himself, Chris was aware that he had no right to hang onto his old-fashioned conception of the town. He had a right to his private thoughts, but the town was changing all around him and he had no choice but to accept it.

Was Finbach German? Scandinavian? Justin's neighbours on the other side had complained about the late-night music too, and Chris had said he'd have a word. Which he had, but it had made no difference.

Justin smiled his friendly smile as Chris took him through each step of the night before. He'd garaged his car. He'd seen what salt spray did to a car's body-work, so no matter how late and tired he was, he always saw to that. He'd said goodnight to the cat – a stray he'd taken in – and gone to bed.

'Did you hear anything from the pilots' centre, Mr Finbach?'

Justin frowned and shook his head. 'There were lights on.'

'More than usual?'

'I don't know about more.'

There were always lights on in the centre, but surely the man knew that.

'Did you hear anybody talking, voices from outside?'

'No.'

FOUR

Chris made himself a light meal, then sat down to go through the CCTV footage. He wondered what Sergeant Dawkins was doing. Dawkins had given him the go-ahead to look at the film, just as he'd given him the go-ahead to talk to people who lived around the operations centre; but the feeling came back to Chris, stronger now that he was tired and alone, that while the Sergeant had been interested in a suicide note, he wasn't interested in much else.

Chris's eyes glazed over from watching the unchanging scene at the front of the centre – a path that shone in the overhead lights, tussocky grass, a couple of low-lying bushes. Once a rat ran over the path. At 9.12 a thin, dark-haired man left by the front door, walking briskly.

Just after 11, the front door opened again and Delraine stepped out. He walked with his head bent and his shuffling, stumbling gait seemed more pronounced than the first time Chris had watched the film.

The back courtyard was empty. Chris couldn't see, from the viewpoint of the single camera, how anybody could go in and out that way, but he assumed that there must be a gate.

He told himself a walk might clear his head and found his feet taking him towards the coastguard office.

Tom Maloney tossed his cigarette butt off the end of the jetty that ran into Swan Bay thirty metres from the office that was his second home.

'Why, Tom?'

Having asked his question, Chris listened to the silence and decided that Tom wasn't going to reply.

He thought that the sea floor just there, under shallow water, part of the fish nursery and a protected sanctuary, must be covered with butts. He had often reproached Tom with this, and had even, on a couple of occasions, tried to catch one as it fell. But Tom, otherwise careful about littering and protective of the sea, was on this point deaf and blind.

'Maybe he'd had a gutful.' Tom flicked his fringe back off his forehead. In the twilight, Chris noticed the lines around his eyes and that he looked tired.

'Of what?' he asked.

'Life, Blackie.'

Out of long habit, both men turned at the same moment and began walking back along the jetty. They walked in silence, each absorbed in his own thoughts. They were used to this. Tom, half a head taller than Chris, shortened his stride to match Chris's, something he did automatically. Chris was conscious of his neat appearance, even after a long and tiring day. Tom had often teased him about it. He kept his dark hair short, while Tom kept putting off a visit to the barber's.

Chris had seen no signs of violence on Captain Delraine's body, though the post mortem might show something. Dr Hammond had said he wasn't prepared to sign the death certificate without one. The doctor had phoned the station with his preliminary assessment and Chris had heard Sergeant Dawkins' end of the conversation.

It was possible a witness who'd seen Delraine the night before would come forward, but Chris doubted it. The results of his door-to-door had been disappointing.

Dawkins had made Brian Laidlaw angry and upset. A Channel Nine van had been parked outside Brian's house when Chris called back, but Camilla was with him. Camilla had spoken to Chris briefly and told him Brian wanted to be left alone. She'd said he'd called Dawkins an idiot.

If anyone could find out about the men Brian had seen talking to Captain Delraine, then Camilla could. But Brian reacted to stress by closing in on himself, and Chris had little doubt that that's what he was doing now.

Though a generation separated them, Tom and Brian were of a similar type. The day a younger man replaced him in the yellow coastguard launch would be a black day for Tom; but then, Chris reminded himself, people were resourceful. Just when you thought you had them pinned down, they surprised you.

There was a sink at the back of the coastguard office, a small bar fridge, an electric jug which Chris switched on. He knew Tom would have made tea for them both, but he liked to get in first because Tom made it far too strong.

Chris said, lifting two mugs out of the cupboard under the sink, 'You can tip a man out of a boat, knowing it's too far for him to swim to shore.'

'Whose boat?'

'The pilot launch.'

There, he'd said it – a ridiculous idea surely, but one which had been nagging at him ever since he'd looked down at Delraine's body and seen the pilot boat making for the heads.

Tom patted his pocket, but apparently decided against lighting up again. Not out of any consideration for me, Chris thought. Why would any of Delraine's colleagues want to kill him? And why would the driver and the crew comply?

'You always were a suspicious little ferret, Blackie.'

'Thanks.' Chris paused a moment before asking, 'How well did you know him?'

'I knew him by his reputation. Personally, not at all.'

'Which was?'

'He was well respected. Loyal.'

'Why was he living at the operations centre?'

'The rumour was that his wife had left him.'

'Rumour?'

'As I said, I didn't know him personally.'

'Brian Laidlaw did.'

'Ah, Brian.'

'He told me he saw two men talking to the Captain.'

Chris knew he shouldn't be confiding in Tom like this. If Dawkins was still in Queenscliff, if Dawkins hadn't left, he probably wouldn't have felt tempted to seek Tom out. He realised that he did not want to go home to his empty cottage.

'Which two men?' Tom asked.

'Brian wouldn't explain.'

Tom shrugged as if to say, that's Brian for you. He turned suddenly and said, 'I appreciate you dropping by, but to tell you the truth I'm bushed.'

Chris hid his surprise. It was very unlike Tom to ask him to leave.

'If I hear anything I'll let you know.'

Some time during that long day, Dawkins had asked Chris if he played golf. Chris couldn't put his finger on exactly when. Had they been in the office and had Dawkins been in the middle of making phone calls? The question had come out of the blue. The more Chris thought about it, the more certain he became that Dawkins, without any uncomfortable doubts, would recommend that the coroner bring down a verdict of accidental death. This would suit the pilot company better than suicide, and the company was probably already bringing what pressure it could to ensure a satisfactory outcome.

Chris missed Anthea, his assistant constable, suddenly and sharply. They'd learnt to divine each other's thoughts and feelings – a glance or word was usually enough. Chris knew that, by now, he would have discussed those anti-histamine tablets found in Captain Delraine's room with Anthea.

If he rang his former assistant, she would listen, pay attention. But he had no right to interrupt her maternity leave.

Chris wasn't shut out from Anthea's life; he knew he was welcome as often as he chose to visit. But they were a close-knit family, Anthea, Olly and Aneira, and Chris knew that, however happy they were to see him, however welcome they made him, he would never be part of that.

'If we believed in God,' Olly had said, 'we'd make you Aneira's godfather.'

He was Aneira's non-godfather, too much of a mouthful to repeat. Aneira was Welsh for snow. The child had been conceived in the snowfields of the Australian

Alps. Olly had Welsh ancestry, as did Anthea, though further back. Chris wondered how like her mother Aneira would turn out to be. What he did not wonder at was Anthea's desire to enjoy the rest of her leave in peace and quiet.

FIVE

Chris had only witnessed three post mortems in his time as a police officer.

He recalled the photos of Captain Delraine that had been taken on the beach; he'd taken time to study them. The dead man had looked more than usually bloated. Like a puffer fish, Chris had thought. Once the image occurred to him, he was unable to erase it from his mind.

Dr Hammond's gloved hands were small and slight against the Captain's heavy upper body.

There was no doubt about the cause of death, he said. There were no apparent marks of violence.

When Chris asked about puncture marks, wanting to make sure, Sergeant Dawkins cut him off with a scornful remark.

The doctor stiffened ever so slightly. Chris realised that he didn't like Dawkins. The Sergeant hadn't bothered to hang his suit properly so the creases fell out. Chris glanced down briefly at his own neat uniform. It sometimes made him feel self-conscious, but not this morning.

He didn't speak again while the doctor examined organs. Dawkins asked a few questions in an indifferent voice.

Chris thought he might phone Hammond, talk to him on his own.

As they left the morgue, Dawkins told him he had an appointment with the coroner. He made it clear that he felt confident about the outcome.

Dr Hammond answered on the second ring. When Chris asked about evidence of anti-histamines in Delraine's blood, the doctor said he'd let him know the test results. There was a short silence. Chris thought the doctor might say something more, but he didn't.

The station felt very quiet and empty after Chris put down his phone. He chose to sit in the small back office by the kitchen while he made some notes. The front office felt contaminated. There was the faint smell of the Sergeant's after-shave; there was the way he'd re-arranged the computer and moved the chair so that it no longer faced the window.

Chris boiled the jug for tea and arranged some cheese and biscuits on a plate. The neighbour's cat scratched at the back door. Chris was fond of the cat. He let it in and gave it some cheese.

Feeling better, he decided to pay a visit to Camilla Renfrew.

'Hello!' Camilla smiled broadly.

Chris felt a moment of pure gladness that she'd found her voice again.

When he asked how Brian was, Camilla looked over his shoulder as though someone might be hiding in the house. 'Let's go for a walk,' she said.

Camilla had never been able to explain why she'd lost the power of speech, nor why it had returned. She called it an act of grace, though she was not religious.

They walked under the Moonah and found a bench half in and half out of the sun, which was strong for that time of the morning. All around them the acacias were in flower.

'What did Brian tell you?' Chris asked.

Camilla took her time to answer. Finally she said, 'He saw two men talking to Captain Delraine.'

'What did they look like?'

'Brian didn't say. But he spoke to the Captain about it.'

'When was this?'

'Didn't Brian tell you?'

'He clammed up and wouldn't talk.'

'That officer in charge, he – '

'Got Brian's back up?'

Chris and Camilla exchanged a glance in which they agreed that it wasn't hard to do.

Neither spoke for a while. Then Camilla said, 'Brian told me that the Captain hated suicides. A young lieutenant – this was when Brian was in the navy – jumped overboard and drowned. He left a note. There was no doubt that he'd taken his own life. The body was never recovered, though they searched for days. At the end of the search, Delraine assembled the whole crew and gave them a lecture. Suicide was a mortal sin, and even if it hadn't been, it was a coward's way out. Brian was only seventeen but he's never forgotten.'

Chris had often wondered if his father had committed suicide. He'd buried his suspicions when they rose, kept a clamp on them for years and trusted in his ability to go on doing so, to function and to live a decent life as he understood it.

He knew the power his father's death had to drag him down. He respected this power, even as he braced and pushed against it – indeed, the bracing and respect were intertwined. His mother had believed that if only his father's body had been recovered, washed up somewhere, in no matter how decayed and torn a state, then she, they – mother and son together – could begin to recover. Chris had gone along with this view and half believed it.

Did suicide have to have a reason? It was always selfish. Was it more or less selfish to leave a note? With no note, the possibility of accident remained and might give comfort. In his father's case, the coroner's open verdict had been sensible and kind.

Chris saw Camilla back to her house, gently questioning her about Delraine and the two men, what Brian had seen, what Delraine had told him. But Camilla said she really didn't know anything more. She looked tired and twice she stumbled.

Brian Laidlaw, that least duplicitous of men, did not know how to tell a deliberate lie. He'd had no practice, always having been a man of few words which he expected to be taken literally. On the other hand, he knew very well how to keep a secret, especially if it concerned somebody he loved.

SIX

Chris sat facing Dr Hammond across his desk with the packet of hay fever tablets between them.

Hammond made a steeple with his small hands, then looked up at Chris and said, 'You can't buy these over the counter in Australia any more. You used to be able to, but they were taken off.'

Chris realised that he was sitting nervously on the edge of his chair and made an effort to relax. He wondered if Hammond knew he was there without Dawkins' permission. He trusted Hammond not to ask, and he wasn't going to volunteer the information.

'Because of side-effects?' he asked.

'They're almost pure diphenhydramine,' Hammond said in a neutral voice. 'One tablet can make you drowsy and disoriented. More can cause hallucinations.'

'How many had Captain Delraine taken?'

'By the levels in his blood, I'd say possibly three.'

'Why would he do that?'

The doctor stared at Chris with unreadable brown eyes. 'Some people use them as sleeping tablets.' His voice was still calm and non-committal.

'An overdose would – '

'Three tablets might make you sick, but they wouldn't kill you.'

'Where did Captain Delraine get them, do you think?'

'Over the internet probably.'

'He wouldn't take three tablets intending to go for

a late evening walk.'

Hammond gave Chris a sharp look, but said nothing in response to this.

'What if Delraine collapsed on the beach?' Chris asked.

'Then that's where he would have stayed.'

'What if someone dragged him into the water and held him under?'

'I suppose it's possible, but – '

'There'd be signs of dragging, bruising?'

'Yes.'

'Would a man intending to commit suicide by drowning dope himself with diphenhydramine first?'

Hammond frowned as he asked, 'Would you?'

Chris knew he'd pushed the doctor as far as he could. He thanked him and got up to go, replacing the tablets in his pocket.

'I'll email my report to you as well as Detective-Sergeant Dawkins.'

Chris thanked him again, warmly this time.

Chris introduced himself to the dispatch officer on duty at the operations centre and discovered that Michael Travers, whom he'd spoken to last time, had taken a week's leave.

He asked for the key to Delraine's room. Nothing appeared to have changed since his first visit. He made his way through to the kitchen.

The cook was having a smoke in the small paved courtyard at the back of the building. He looked up as Chris walked across. He didn't smile, or say a word of greeting, and his eyes were hard. This was the man who'd been filmed leaving the centre after 9 pm.

Bamboo protected the courtyard on two sides. The cliff rose behind it, slippery and difficult to climb. The yard was neat, uncluttered, the pavers swept clear of sand and leaves. A row of garbage bins had their lids tight shut. Though right next to the sea, the enclosed space had the feel of somewhere inland, sheltered from the weather. Chris noted the single security camera.

He introduced himself and decided to come straight to the point.

'Did you go into Captain Delraine's room on the night he died?'

If the cook, who gave his name as William, was surprised by the question, he didn't show it. All he said was, 'No.'

'Would you mind telling me your movements for that day and evening?'

William took a drag on his cigarette and flicked lank brown hair back from his forehead. He began speaking in a monotone. He'd arrived at the centre just before seven in the morning. The pilots worked around the clock and the kitchen was open round the clock as well, but his hours were seven am till nine pm six days a week. Outside those hours, there were snacks available and dishes left prepared in the fridge for re-heating.

'They're long hours,' Chris said.

William shrugged as if to say, what of it?

It had been a quiet day. Captain Delraine had come in off the launch shortly before four in the afternoon. William had made a pot of tea and the Captain had drunk his in the dining-room. The pilots all had electric jugs and bar fridges in their rooms, but afternoon tea at four was something of a ritual and there was often a freshly-baked cake, or a batch of scones.

'Did you notice anything different about Captain Delraine?' Chris asked.

'What do you mean?'

'Was he tired? Worried about something?'

'A bit tired, but he perked up after he'd had his tea.'

Chris felt that William was hiding something, and that he was too cleverly on guard to be forced into revealing what it was. 'What did Captain Delraine do then?' he asked.

'Went to his room.'

'Did he say anything?'

'Like what?' William's voice was surly, with no pretence at helpfulness.

'Like he didn't want to be disturbed.'

'Who'd be disturbing him?'

Good question, Chris thought, but he didn't say this. Instead he asked, 'Do you know if Captain Delraine made or received any phone calls?'

William threw Chris a scornful look. 'What, like I was listening outside his door?'

'You might have happened to walk past.'

'I didn't.'

Chris wondered if Delraine's use of the drug diphenhydramine was an open secret, but he didn't want to ask about that yet.

Dinner had been a quiet affair. Sometimes the pilots took their coffee into a small room called the lounge, which was really just a room for watching TV, with a sofa placed at the best angle for viewing and a couple of extra chairs. But that night Captain Delraine had been the only pilot sleeping at the centre, and Travers had asked for his dinner to be brought to the office on a tray. Chris wondered if it was unusual for only one pilot to be there overnight. He could ask to check the roster.

By ten past nine, William had finished cleaning up.

He lived in Hobson Street, which was walking distance though he sometimes drove.

'And no one else came in, visited, for whatever reason?'

'Not while I was here.'

'So Captain Delraine had dinner alone that night in the dining-room?'

Chris watched William weighing up his words. 'I ate with him,' he said.

'Was that usual?'

'I thought the Captain might like a bit of company.'

'So there was something upsetting him.'

'I didn't say that.'

'What did you talk about?'

The cook stubbed his butt under a black heel.

'About Mrs Delraine,' he said after another long pause.

'What about her?'

'The captain was concerned about what to do. Look,' William said impatiently. 'Captain Delraine wasn't one to complain, or talk about his personal problems, but he'd been living here for two months. He knew he had to make decisions.'

'Why speak about it that evening?'

'Perhaps because there was no one else here. I don't know.'

'Travers was in the office.'

'I meant no other pilots.'

'What happened after dinner?'

'I cleared up and stacked the dishwasher.'

'Where did Captain Delraine go?'

'Back to his room.'

'How do you know, if you were in the kitchen?'

'He didn't go out the front door because the camera would have caught him.' The cook's eyes flicked up, then down again. Chris wondered if he was thinking of the security camera at the back, and if he had his own way of avoiding it.

'Did you see or hear anything while you were cleaning up?'

'Well, I heard the dishwasher.'

Chris decided to ignore the sarcasm. 'What about voices outside?' he asked.

'No.'

When Chris repeated what Kerry, who lived close to the pilots centre, had said, William shrugged.

'Show me the back gate, please.'

William pointed to a narrow gap in the bamboo. Chris walked across and parted it. A wooden gate was fitted with a simple padlock. It would not be hard to break. The gate was inconveniently close to the cliff. Anyone using it would have to scramble his way in. It would be possible to do so without being caught on film, but then, once in the courtyard, a person would have to use the back door in order to get inside. Again, Chris wondered if the cook had worked out a way to enter and leave the building unseen.

William stood up and placed his cigarette butt in

one of the bins.

'Was Travers surprised when Captain Delraine went for a walk at eleven at night?' Chris asked, returning to stand next to him.

'You'll have to ask him.' William continued after another swift, half contemptuous glance, 'It's not his job to be surprised at anything the pilots do. I should be getting back inside.'

Chris walked to his car. He sat down with the driver's door open and took out his phone. He ought to ring Sergeant Dawkins, tell him he'd been at the centre. Where the hell was Dawkins anyway?

Chris decided to visit Anthea in order to give himself time to think.

Anthea had moved in with Olly a few months before their baby was born, giving up her flat next door. They still joked that, had they not been neighbours, they'd never have had anything to do with one another, and that the saying 'opposites attract' applied to them in spades.

Anthea repeated the words with a calm, secure amusement, but there was a shadow at the back of Olly's eyes when she teased him. Olly would never give up his beliefs and opinions in order to become more like his wife. They both knew this, but Chris guessed that it bothered Olly more than it did Anthea.

On the way there, Chris found himself wishing that he could go back in time, to before he was born. Brian, older by thirty years at least, though he never told anyone his age, had left Queenscliff as a teenager to join the navy. Chris wondered if there was anyone left in the town who remembered Brian as a boy.

Tea tree blossom was coming out along the headland and the walking paths. Soon it would cover the bushes' grey-green leaves. Sometimes the air of expectancy carried by the spring made him feel inadequate. Chris told himself he wouldn't let that happen now.

No one answered when he knocked on Anthea and Olly's door. Chris got out his phone, hesitated, then put it away again.

He wondered if he ought to feel surprised that none of the current pilot crewmen or drivers lived in Queenscliff. At the time his father worked for the company, four of them lived locally. He couldn't have said precisely when the last one had left. They'd kept in contact with his mother while she was alive.

SEVEN

When Chris finally got Dawkins on the phone, the Sergeant sounded pre-occupied. When Chris mentioned CCTV cameras at the harbour, and Dawkins didn't order him to stop asking questions, he interpreted this to mean he could pay a visit to the harbourmaster.

Evan Aldridge, who'd been Queenscliff's harbourmaster for the past eight years, didn't seem to think it was odd to be asked for CCTV footage from the cameras covering the marina on the date Delraine had drowned. His glance at Chris was wary, but not anxious. He said that it would take a few minutes and asked Chris to wait in the camera room.

Aldridge was a big man who'd played for the Geelong Reserves until a back injury had forced him to give up. He had an athlete's grace of movement and, when he was still, an alert, watchful stillness. The few times Chris had dealt with him, he'd been reserved but not unhelpful.

Chris reminded himself that he had no evidence that Delraine had gone out to meet anyone. But he couldn't stop himself from speculating. What if Delraine had been persuaded to get on board a boat? Who was on it? Why had he agreed?

The boat did not need to have been launched from Queenscliff. It could have come from somewhere else on the Bellarine Peninsula, Geelong, or even further away. All this could be a waste of time, and Dawkins would no doubt tell him so when he deigned to make a visit to the station, if and when Chris plucked up the courage to voice his suspicions.

Chris told himself he wouldn't worry about that now. He would start by dealing with the people he knew.

Delraine had been filmed leaving the pilots' centre at eleven, but if a boat had met him, it might have set off well before then. The boardwalks leading to the berths at the marina were gated and covered by security cameras. Boat-owners were issued with electronic discs to access them. But there was only one camera covering the entrance to the 'cut', as the narrow channel joining the berthing sites to Port Phillip Bay was called.

Chris had asked for film from this camera from six pm till four in the morning. He felt relieved to be on his own with something mechanical to do, with nothing but the hum of the monitor to keep him company, and the view outside the small room's window of the marina on an ordinary day.

Two craft had left the harbour before dark, both recreational fishermen who were known to Chris. He made notes, but he didn't believe either of them could be involved in the drowning.

The boats' lights interfered with the infrared cameras, making it impossible, after dark, to identify a craft except by shape and size.

Two craft had left between nine and ten and a third at a quarter to eleven. Again Chris made notes, but could say no more than that they were medium-sized vessels. It was impossible to read any registration details.

A pilot boat, distinctive enough to be identifiable

even with such poor quality film, had left just after nine-thirty.

Chris went back to the harbourmaster's office. When he asked Aldridge why they didn't have a better system for filming at night, Aldridge merely shrugged.

The positions of the cameras would be known to all who used the harbour. If you had a legitimate reason for leaving late at night, what did it matter if you were filmed doing so?

When Chris asked for berthing details for the boats he'd noted, Aldridge printed it off for him without a word.

There were no security cameras at the launching ramp next door to the marina.

Chris had formed the impression years ago that the pilot service operated in distinct layers and that each was allowed a good deal of autonomy. Of course the different sections dealt with each other constantly, the launch drivers and the workshop mechanics, the dispatch officers at the centre and the admin office in Melbourne. The dispatch officers were at the hub, since they negotiated with the port authority, the ships masters who required a pilot, and the pilots themselves.

The pilots were at the top of the pyramid. It was their company; their money paid for salaries and upkeep, and the occasional big capital expense. But it was the drivers who decided when conditions were too bad to take a launch out. This rarely happened – the launches worked in fog, huge seas and howling gales – but when the decision 'no boating' was made, it was the driver on duty who made it.

The pilots knew how to delegate. But, since all

men were different, there surely must be some who were more officious, more interfering than others. Where had Captain Delraine fitted on the spectrum? No one had spoken ill of him in Chris's hearing, but Chris would have been surprised if they had.

Five drivers, five crewmen – was the symmetry co-incidence, or was five exactly the right number?

The workshop did not so much dominate the harbour as provide a solid backing to it: the huge doors, the hangar-like space at the opposite end to the shops and restaurants, were so much a fixture of the harbour that Chris had stopped noticing them years ago. The workshop was plain and unadorned, entirely practical.

The workshop employees effectively managed themselves. There was a mechanical engineer with an IT qualification and two diesel mechanics. One had left several months ago and as far as Chris knew hadn't been replaced.

Chris found it impossible to imagine the power of eight hundred horses hitched to a single boat. He knew this was the wrong way to think about it, but still his imagination tried to encompass the idea and failed. Brian Laidlaw, with his love of ships and everything to do with them, liked spending time in the workshop and was amiably tolerated so far as Chris knew.

Chris decided to drop in for a chat with Alex Stavros. Alex was a skilled boat-builder as well as a diesel mechanic, tall and thin, with prominent elbows, large hands and feet.

When a new launch was commissioned, the fibreglass hull, deck and cabin were shipped to Queenscliff, where they were fitted with engines, electrical systems, radar, VHF and domestic radio, and the most up-to-date rescue equipment.

A few months ago, Chris had stood next to Tom Maloney, watching the unloading of a new beak hull. Tom had been full of admiration mixed with envy. The three and a half million dollar launch would make his coastguard boat look like an antiquated relic.

Alex's concentration had been total, his strong hands shining in the light reflected off the water, his pride in the vessel he was helping to build shining out as well. Chris remembered wondering what it must be like to have that confidence, to experience it every day as part of normal life.

He forced his attention back to the present. Alex straightened up and wiped his hands on a rag.

'Blackie. Constable,' he said warily.

Chris recalled that Alex habitually put people's titles after their names.

'Just a quick word,' he said. 'I won't keep you long. When did you last see Captain Delraine?'

Alex looked from Chris's face to the rag in his hands. The workshop was empty save for the two of them.

'It's not a trick question, Alex. I'm just trying to establish the Captain's movements over the last week or so.'

'I thought – ' Alex began, then frowned and shook his head. 'About two weeks. I called over to the centre with some stuff for Michael Travers. Captain Delraine was coming out the front. We said hello.'

'How did the Captain seem?'

'The same.'

'Which is to say?'

'Polite and courteous.'

Alex threw his rag down, turned his back on Chris and began walking towards the open workroom door.

Chris followed him. 'I'm sorry, but I need to know.'

'Know what, for Christ's sake? He drowned, didn't he? He walked into the bloody sea.'

Chris said quietly, 'Is that what you believe?'

Alex stared at Chris over his shoulder, then said, 'Come into the office.'

Chris followed the mechanic to the back of the building, to a cramped, cluttered space. A narrow desk held a computer, phone and fax machine. Next to it were a pile of receipted bills.

'Do you do your own clerical work now Jim's gone?' Chris asked.

Jim, the other mechanic, had handled the paperwork before suddenly resigning.

'We get copies and keep records, but, well, it's a bit of a shambles as you can see.'

'Have you ever had a break-in?'

'Not while I've been here. But' – Alex hesitated – 'there was one odd thing. Captain Delraine came down here one morning wanting to know about some special maintenance. He said a bill had been sent to head office for some special maintenance. I mean sent from here.'

'Did you know what he meant by special maintenance?'

'No.'

'Did Captain Delraine say who'd told him?'

Alex shook his head.

'What happened to the bill?'

'I don't know.'

Chris was sure Alex was keeping something back. 'Why did Jim go back to Melbourne?' he asked.

'Family reasons.' Alex made a complicated face. 'We miss him down here. Jim was a good egg.'

'When will he be replaced?'

'I don't know,' Alex said again.

Chris asked for Jim's mobile number. After a slight hesitation, Alex told him and Chris copied it into his phone.

He looked up to ask, 'Was Brian Laidlaw here that morning?'

'Brian was often down here.'

'The morning Captain Delraine came to talk to you,' Chris said patiently.

'Over there.' Alex lifted his chin in the direction of the jetty where Tom Maloney often stood.

'Do you think he knew why Captain Delraine was here?'

'How could he?'

One question among many that I have no answer to, Chris thought.

'Were you watching when Captain Delraine left?'

'I was working,' Alex said.

'What about Ivan Southeby?' Chris realised he'd scarcely given a thought to the chair of the pilots' board of directors. 'When was Southeby last here?'

'He came to see the new hull.'

Alex frowned. The silence between them was suddenly tense.

Chris said, 'Captain Delraine was here too, wasn't

he? The hull was special. He would have wanted to see it.'

'Nothing unusual in that. You came down yourself.'

'But not that day. Not the day Southeby and Delraine were here together. What happened?'

'Nothing.'

'Don't do this to me Alex. Not if you care about what happened to Captain Delraine.'

'Why are you asking all these questions? I thought some detective was in charge.'

'What happened?' Chris repeated. 'Did they argue?'

'Not an argument.'

'What then?'

'It wasn't any of my business.'

'Did Southeby warn you to keep quiet about it?'

When Alex didn't answer, Chris said, 'Let's not call it an argument, then. Let's call it an exchange.'

Alex seemed to fall over his words. Now he'd made the decision to speak, it seemed to Chris that the mechanic wanted to get it over with as quickly as possible.

'I didn't hear it all. I heard Mr Southeby say, "I know you're against the dredging". I didn't hear Captain Delraine's reply. Then Mr Southeby said, "You're entitled to your personal opinions, Fred, but you've no right to speak for the company".'

'What did Captain Delraine reply?'

'He said, "You're chairman of the board, Ivan. You have a responsibility".'

'What did Southeby say?'

'He went red and looked annoyed.'

'What happened then?'

'He stalked off.'

'Southeby?'

'Yes.'

'What did Captain Delraine do?'

'He left as well.'

'How did he seem?'

'He looked – angry and upset.'

Chris had another thought. 'Was Brian Laidlaw here that morning?' he asked.

'He was watching from a distance. He didn't come near the workshop.'

'But he might have seen Southeby and Delraine together?'

'He might have. I wasn't paying attention to what Brian was doing.'

Alex turned away. Chris knew he wasn't going to get any more out of the mechanic just then.

'If anyone wants to know what I was doing here, say I was asking about teenage vandals.'

A tiny smile touched Alex's lips. 'All right,' he said. 'I'll do that.'

'And Alex, if you think of anything else, you know where to find me. Or text me and we'll meet somewhere if you don't want to be seen at the station.'

Chris had been looking forward to lunch, a bowl of soup from Salt Bush, or another of Queenscliff's excellent small cafes. He knew they struggled to keep going through the winter, and were grateful for his custom.

He thought back to when Alex had first come to Queenscliff. Though Alex worked at the harbour, he lived on the other side of town, in a 1960s brick veneer of a type that had replaced many of the cottages and beach shacks.

Chris remembered Tom pointing out the house to him one day, saying, 'Bored to the back teeth.'

Tom had been referring to Alex's wife, who hadn't wanted to leave Melbourne. Chris hadn't asked how Tom knew this, or why he spoke with such certainty. It was the sort of thing Tom did know, or rather concluded from a few bits of gossip. Not for the first time, Chris reflected that Tom would have made the better policeman, but Tom would hate the hierarchy, and he would hate even more being stuck on land.

Alex had two sons at university. Perhaps his wife hadn't wanted to be separated from them. Melbourne was only two hours away, but it often seemed to Chris much further than that.

He wondered how she spent her time. Someone would have told him if she'd upped and left. He toyed with the idea of dropping in. But Alex would be angry when he got to hear of it, and any hope he had of getting more information out of him would be gone for good.

Chris phoned Jim, who said he was at work and couldn't talk. There was machine noise in the background.

Bob Sainsbury, former crewman for the pilot service, raised cautious eyes when he answered Chris's knock. Chris recalled him as a sensitive man, who'd called on his mother and sent flowers, but hadn't pestered her. He'd been retired for perhaps ten years.

Chris accepted the offer of a cup of tea and sat looking out the kitchen window while Bob made it. He approved of what he saw. Bob was a widower whose wife had died young and who'd never re-married. Since retiring, he spent a lot of time in his garden. His spring seedlings were doing well.

When Chris asked if Bob kept in touch with anyone from the service, he said, 'That's a bad business about Captain Delraine.'

Chris agreed that it was.

'Of course it's very different now,' Bob said.

'How different?' Chris asked.

Bob gave Chris a swift, appraising look, then turned his attention to his mug of tea.

'Used to be the crews were taken on from anywhere. You had a seaman's ticket and good references, chances were when a vacancy came up you'd get the job.'

'Like my father,' Chris said.

Bob nodded and then frowned. 'Now you have to sit an exam.'

Chris doubted his father would have passed. 'A man can be an excellent seaman, and not much good with pen and paper.'

'Very true,' Bob said. Chris remembered something about him coaching his nephew. 'Is that what happened with – '

'Scott never made it, did he? Always wanted to crew for a pilot. Same as me.'

'Where's Scott now?'

'Williamstown. Got a wife and son. I'm a great-uncle.' Bob offered Chris a proud, half defiant smile. 'He's not done badly for himself.'

'Why don't the crews live here any more?'

'I've got a theory about that,' Bob said.

When Chris phoned Jim back that evening, Jim was reluctant to talk. When Chris asked why he'd left Queenscliff, he replied, 'Personal reasons', and would not say anything more. When Chris, careful not to mention Alex's name, but afraid that Jim would know where the information came from, asked about a bill for special maintenance, Jim said, 'Look, I've got nothing against Captain Delraine, but – '

'But what?'

'Suicide's a coward's way out, and a mortal sin.'

Jim ended the call.

A Saturday night fight on the Blues Train seemed to come out of a clear sky. The train ran from the railway yard along the shore of Swan Bay. People paid for dinner and music, and sat in old, restored carriages.

The fight had broken out over seating and should have been resolved quickly. Customers made mistakes over bookings; event organisers sometimes did as well. Compromises were usually reached, and storms deflected. Not this time, the organiser told Chris in a harried voice, wiping his sweaty forehead with a large blue handkerchief.

Two men, old enough to know better, were already drunk when they arrived with their female companions at the railway station. The organiser had taken note, had been wary rather than worried. He often had to deal with problems caused by alcohol. But this time, he told Chris, before you knew it there were shouts and bloody noses, screaming women.

Chris made sure the warring parties, now subdued, stayed separate. Apologies had been made for the delay and the train had continued on its journey. In the intense darkness that followed the last of the twilight, he sat in the police station's front office taking statements from the principal couples and witnesses. One man loudly demanded his money back, and Chris said that could be arranged, without knowing whether or not a refund would be possible.

The night outside seemed to gather strength. Chris had closed the blinds tight, but still he felt it. He glanced around the room. Now the drama was over, the people involved sat half stunned, concentrating on their statements. Chris found himself envying them, envying the intensity of argument, however messy, followed by release. He couldn't see such a trajectory, such an outcome, for his efforts with regard to Captain Delarine.

He spent the first two hours next morning catching up on routine work, berating himself for letting it fall behind.

EIGHT

Former Senior Constable Hogan had got a Sworn Police position at the new forensic lab in the grounds of Latrobe University. Chris could have dusted the packet of tablets for fingerprints himself, and told himself that he should already have done so. But he wanted someone with greater expertise than he had; he wanted another pair of eyes. On the long drive to Melbourne, he told himself that Dawkins ought to be that other person, repeating it like a mantra, as though repeating it would somehow change the way the Sergeant behaved. Dawkins hadn't responded to his phone calls or text messages, and Chris knew nothing about his visit to the coroner. Dawkins would say it wasn't his job to keep a uniformed constable informed. Well bugger that, Chris thought.

He met Hogan in the lab cafeteria.

'Not a way I'd choose,' Hogan said, adding four teaspoons of sugar to his coffee. He was a skinny man, stronger than he looked, his grey hair a defiant stubble and his eyes a pale, clear blue.

'Drowning?' Chris asked, careful to keep his voice neutral.

'Too much time to reconsider. Not a way that you'd choose either.'

'No.'

'This wouldn't be to do with your Dad, would it?'

'Not directly.'

They went back to Hogan's office and Chris handed over his small plastic bag.

While Hogan worked, taking his time, Chris filled him in on what Dr Hammond had said.

Hogan raised his head to say, 'There's one clear print.'

The two men compared it to a photograph of Delraine's fingerprints.

'It's his all right,' said Hogan, then went back to his task of dusting and comparing.

'Nope.' He looked up and shook his head.

'Are you sure?'

'I'm sure.'

Chris was preparing to leave when Hogan asked suddenly, 'Who had keys?'

'If you mean who had access to Captain Delraine's room, that's difficult to say. There were no keys on the body, but his wallet and his phone are missing too. There's a spare set of room keys in the office, but the dispatch officer on duty the night he died said no one asked for them.'

'What do you think?'

'I think someone rang him after he was settled for the night.'

'He used those anti-histamines as sleeping tablets?'

'Partly, yes. I think so.'

'Someone pretty persuasive then.'

Chris agreed that it must have been.

'The room key could have been taken earlier and a duplicate made.'

'Or the dispatch officer could be lying, or he could have been the one to clear the room. But it hardly matters because, according to him, Delraine often didn't bother to lock his door.'

'What do the rest of the staff say?'

'I'll talk to the cook again. He's keeping something back.'

'Good hunting,' Hogan said.

Chris thanked him, feeling grateful for the solidarity of senior constables, and that Hogan hadn't asked why he was going behind Sergeant Dawkins' back. His thoughts returned to Delraine. Was his diphenhydramine addiction the scandal that was brewing, that would have seen him forcibly retired?

On the drive home – Chris called by the station only briefly then continued on to the operations centre – he re-lived that early morning on the beach, how Brian had stood stiffly erect beside the body of his friend and mentor. By the time Dawkins had finished his preliminary examination – even then, Chris had noted how cursory it was – and Dr Hammond had examined the body, Southeby, the chair of the pilots board of directors, was on his way to Queenscliff.

'You knew Captain Delraine suffered from hay fever.'

'It wasn't a secret,' the operation centre's cook replied.

'And you knew what he took for it.'

William ground his cigarette butt under the heel of his black shoe. Chris recalled the action from the last time they'd spoken. The cook was avoiding having to look up, buying time while he thought of a reply.

His response when Chris had said he had a few more questions had been sullen, bordering on hostile. Without a word, with barely a nod in Chris's direction, he'd led the way out to the back courtyard.

'Had the captain increased his dose?'

William stared at Chris, his expression challenging with a hint of derision.

'Captain Delraine couldn't sleep. Sometimes he managed a few hours at night, but he couldn't sleep during the day. Lately, for a while now, the dispatch officers have only been giving him day shifts.'

When Chris asked, 'Why would the captain dose himself on anti-histamines and then go for a walk on the beach?' William replied curtly, 'I don't know.'

His brown hair had fallen forward. Chris thought it must annoy him when he was cooking and wondered why he didn't get it cut.

'Was it Captain Delraine's marriage causing the insomnia?'

'Captain Delraine didn't complain about his personal problems. I already told you that.'

'Was Mrs Delraine having an affair?'

William raised cold, unfriendly eyes. When he spoke, his voice was hard.

'I wouldn't put it past her.'

'You've met Mrs Delraine?'

'Once.'

'What did you think of her?'

'I thought she was a stuck-up bitch.'

Chris let the echo of the words hang between them and told himself he shouldn't be surprised. William was furious and grieving.

'What about phone calls to the captain's mobile?'

'What about them?'

'Did he take any calls that upset him in the last few

days? While he was in the dining-room, for instance.'

William thought for a moment before saying, 'I can't recall that happening.'

'Did the other pilots know about the antihistamines?'

'What do you think?'

'I think everyone who worked here was protecting Captain Delraine, but it wasn't enough.'

William's rudeness was a mask; but what was he hiding? Could he be protecting someone else?

He said suddenly, 'Captain Delraine could be angry with fools, with greedy fools in particular.'

'Such as?'

'Those who'd wreck the bay for short-sighted gain.'

'Those were Captain Delraine's words?'

'More or less.'

'When did he speak to you about it?'

'It was late at night. The Captain – I sat with him sometimes when he couldn't sleep, made him herbal tea. He hated it!'

William smiled at the memory.

'Those who'd wreck the bay,' Chris repeated. 'Did Captain Delraine name names?'

'No, but he talked about the dredging.'

'He was against further dredging to accommodate bigger container ships?'

William's expression changed and his face gained a bit of colour, making Chris realise how blanched and pinched he'd looked. 'The Captain believed that Melbourne could still be an important port, but with smaller ships and more emphasis on Australian coastal trade.'

'Ships that needed pilots?'

'Not all of them, but enough.'

'Was Captain Delraine thinking of resigning from the pilot service?'

'He never said so. I think he would have considered that a cop-out.'

'Like suicide,' Chris said softly.

'That's the stupidest idea I ever heard! The Captain would never, ever – '

'You must know what's being said.'

'By idiots!'

'Idiots?'

'Those who should know better, your Sergeant for one.'

Chris thought that it was time to change the subject. 'Who pays the bills for food here?'

William lit another cigarette and blew smoke sideways, looking as if, of all the questions he might have expected, this one was bottom of the list.

'Head office,' he said.

'You don't have a separate account?'

William shook his head, concentrating on his cigarette.

'Who orders the food?'

'I do.'

'Are the bills sent to you first, to forward on?'

'No.'

'So you never see them?'

'Why should I?'

'Has it always been done like that?'

'Since I've been here, it has.'

Chris felt as though he was wasting time. What was

he looking for? Opportunities for embezzlement on a small scale, bills for food and 'special maintenance' that included a cut for someone at head office? If William was telling the truth, the bills were sent straight from the suppliers.

The cook did not strike Chris as dishonest, at least not in that way; not guilty of stealing from his employers.

On his way out, Chris asked the dispatch officer on duty if he could have a look at the roster sheets for the last two weeks. The officer, who looked tired to the point of exhaustion, first of all said no, but then, in response to Chris's quiet persistence, relented and printed off a copy.

Chris asked how long he'd been on duty and was told fourteen hours. Pressured, over-tired people made mistakes. That didn't just apply to pilots, but to the whole of their support staff.

On impulse, he drove past where the cook lived, 12 Hobson Street, which turned out to be a small block of flats.

Some of Queenscliff's older houses were being knocked down and replaced by units. They looked ugly to Chris, but he resisted this judgement, knowing that it was only by good luck that he'd inherited a cottage near the harbour.

He thought of the flat Anthea had rented when she moved out of Melbourne to take up a position that she didn't want. At the time, Anthea had wanted to stay in the city, close to her boyfriend. The flat had been in a double storey cement block like the one in Hobson Street, but with a balcony and a view over Swan Bay. The memory made him wish again for a good long talk with his assistant. Suspended assistant, he should call her; that might make her smile. He should just ring. She wouldn't mind.

Two of the dispatch officers lived in Queenscliff,

including Michael Travers, who'd been on duty the night Delraine had drowned. Of the other three, one lived at Collendina, fifteen minutes away by car, one at Barwon Heads and the fifth at Drysdale. Given that they worked twelve hour shifts, all had found it expedient to buy or rent within at most a twenty minute drive of the operations centre.

The cook had told him Travers had a young family, which must make shift work doubly difficult, Chris thought.

He'd hoped, when he rang Travers, that a few personal questions might ease the tension, but Travers made it clear that he regarded them as an invasion of his privacy. He also made it clear that he'd already answered Sergeant Dawkins' questions and had nothing more to say.

'You knew Captain Delraine was in the habit of taking anti-histamines at night, to help him get to sleep. Yet you weren't concerned about him walking on the beach?'

'I was concerned, but how could I – look, Captain Delraine was his own boss. He didn't even come into the office. He just poked his head around the door and told me he was going out.'

'How did he seem?'

'How was I to know that – '

'Did he say how long he'd be?'

Travers shook his head.

'Captain Delraine had only been on day shifts for weeks. You arranged that for him, you and the other dispatch officers, because you knew he wasn't fit to work at night.'

Travers coughed. When he spoke again, his voice was shaking. 'I did what I could,' he said.

NINE

Sergeant Dawkins looked well fed and rested, while Chris was conscious of fatigue dragging at his limbs.

As he read Chris's report, Dawkins' face hardened and turned the colour of wet sand.

Chris stood to attention underneath a pile of insults and said, 'Sir,' whenever there was a space for him to say anything. He breathed slowly in and out and told himself that it might be worse.

When he heard the station's front door slam, he sighed and willed himself to relax. He walked slowly to the kitchen and filled the electric jug.

Sipping his tea on the back veranda, listening to the baby magpies, Chris thought that if he'd been in the habit of attending to gossip, he'd know what rumours were being passed around Geelong's Criminal Investigation Unit. If Dawkins was as incompetent as Chris believed he was, then there'd be stories, jokes.

Chris knew the value of gossip and had made use of it when it suited him. But he hadn't realised how narrow his focus had become, fixed on one small town and its surrounding farms. He'd been beneath the notice of the CIU, unless they needed something from him. He wondered if Dawkins had been given the drowning in order to get him out of someone's hair. If that were the case, the DS showed every sign of wanting to finish up as quickly as possible and get back to Geelong.

It was more than six months since Peter Robinson had

been forced to resign from the pilot company. Chris sat down to read about it and refresh his memory.

Robinson had been charged with negligence, resulting in the overturning of a fishing boat. The coastguard boat had been close by and the fishermen had been rescued.

The dispatch officer who'd reluctantly copied the time sheets had given Chris Robinson's number. Chris knew Melbourne suburbs by their phone numbers. Robinson's was beach-side and expensive, the same suburb the Delraines had lived in before separating. Chris had heard Dawkins talking on the phone about searching the house for a suicide note, as though the Captain had, for some unaccountable reason, left it there.

He wondered who'd replaced Robinson, and who would replace Delraine. There might be a waiting list.

Chris rang Robinson's number and arranged to see him the next day. He didn't tell himself that he was doing this in defiance of Sergeant Dawkins, but, recalling Dawkins' scornful dismissal of his report, he understood that something close to defiance was behind it.

Resources were stretched to the limit. Chris had read in the police newsletter a couple of months ago that uniformed officers were reluctant to call detectives to a crime scene because the detectives were already over-worked. At the time he'd thought it an extraordinary admission to make in public, to be up on the Police News website for anyone to see. Wasn't it an invitation to criminals and those contemplating crimes? Now he thought he might use the shortage of manpower as an excuse.

On the night Delraine drowned, the launch manager who usually drove for him had been at a birthday party in Geelong. John Forsyth had been working for the pilots for over fifteen years, and wouldn't hear a word said against any of them. They were all splendid, courageous men.

When Chris rang to ask if they swapped shifts, John said, 'Sometimes.'

'For what reasons?'

'If one of us is sick.'

'Did you swap shifts with any of the other drivers in the last few weeks?'

'After – ' John's voice broke.

'I understand that things have been topsy-turvy since Captain Delraine died. I was wondering about the week or two before that.'

'There were a couple. Captain Trembath had a medical appointment.'

'Was that unusual?'

'What? That Captain Trembath had to see a doctor suddenly? It happens.'

'But he's back at work? He's not in hospital or anything?'

'No.'

'Who swapped with him?'

'Does it matter?'

'I'm just trying to build up a picture.'

After another pause, John said, 'I did.'

'Were you driving for Captain Delraine on the day of Captain Robinson's collision with a fishing boat?'

'It wasn't – ' John began, then changed his mind and said simply, 'Yes.'

'How did he seem?'

'The same as always.'

'Did anything unusual happen on the way out to the boarding ground?'

'What do you mean?'

'Did Captain Delraine take any calls?'

'It was months ago.' John paused again. 'Actually there was something. Captain Delraine was on the radio to the ship's captain when another call came through. I don't think he was expecting it. He went white and lost his balance for a moment.'

'What happened after that?'

'He boarded and I brought the launch back.'

'Could the call have been about the accident?'

'It could have. I don't know.'

'After you brought the launch back, what did you do then?'

'It was my last run. I went home.'

'Who rang to tell you what had happened to Captain Robinson?'

John named one of the other crewmen before saying abruptly that he had to go.

He was conveniently alibied by thirty people for the night Delraine had drowned. But why should John Forsyth need an alibi?

Chris decided it was time to pay another visit to Tom Maloney.

'Tell me what happened with Robinson and that fishing boat,' he said.

They were sitting in the small, draughty coastguard office. Freezing rain thrust itself against the single window. Spring had flounced off again after making an appearance. It often happened that way.

'You want the statement I made to the inquiry?' Tom asked, his voice a mixture of reluctance and suspicion.

Chris wondered what was bugging him. 'Later, yes,' he said. 'That would be good. For now, just what you remember.'

'I was over by Corsair. A Netherland Line container was in the channel, Melbourne bound. No room for anything else with one of those buggers around. Then this stupid Haines Hunter cuts straight in front of it.'

'That's what you saw, Tom? There's no doubt about it?'

'Don't trust my memory, I'll get you the report.'

Tom stood up and rummaged in his desk.

'Not here,' he said after a few minutes. 'It'll be on that thing.' Tom waved a hand at the computer he didn't like and had never got used to.

'But why?' Chris asked.

'Why do recreational fishermen do daft things?'

Tom's views on the subject were well known, and often colourfully expressed.

'Why did Peter Robinson take the rap for it?' Chris asked.

'The ship's master told him to keep on course. Robinson ignored him. It was a close thing. Could have been a disaster.'

'The fishermen could have been killed?'

Tom nodded. 'Or the container could have run aground. You know how narrow the channel is there.'

'The ship's master's always in charge, that's the

rule?' Chris said.

Tom nodded, looking wary.

'Can you remember any other instances when the pilot disobeyed the master?'

Tom sat quite still for the space of five seconds, then he slowly shook his head.

Chris left him cursing as he searched for the report he'd made to the inquiry. It would be on his laptop somewhere, but it might take an IT specialist to find it. It had always surprised Chris that Tom, who was meticulous and knowledgeable about so many things, should turn into a helpless baby when dealing with computer files.

Sergeant Collins of the water police had also given evidence to the inquiry. He and the young constable assisting him had taken statements from everyone involved. The water police often had to carry out work similar to the CIU, dealing with complicated accidents and sometimes loss of life, but Chris had found them to be without the automatic assumption of superiority which irked him in the land-based detectives he'd come across. He'd dealt with Matt Collins before and had found him to be straightforward and unpretentious.

'We've got a bit of a flap on here at the moment,' Collins explained when Chris was put through to him. 'I'll refresh my memory and call you back.'

'Right,' Chris said, and thanked him.

Collins was as good as his word and rang back within an hour.

'Robinson had an argument with the master. Shouted at him, called him names. Pretty heated stuff.

All recorded naturally.'

Chris knew that all conversations on the bridge were recorded. Could Robinson have forgotten that when he lost his temper? Had he been so angry that he didn't care?

Collins said, 'The master made an official complaint and Robinson lost his job.'

'Let me make sure I've got this straight. Robinson disobeyed the master and altered course. What would have happened if he hadn't done that?'

'Maybe they would have hit the fishing boat. We'll never know.'

'It was the fishermen's fault. If they hadn't been in the channel none of it would have happened.'

Collins snorted and Chris was reminded of Tom Maloney.

'Robinson hated boaties,' Collins said. He often rang me to complain about them.'

'And boaties hated him?'

'Why would they? A pilot's got to do his job.'

'Why did Robinson lose his temper?'

'I thought at the time there might have been something else going on.'

'Like what?'

'I don't know.'

Chris searched through old newspaper articles at the historical centre and maritime museum, but found no controversy the pilots had spoken about openly, though controversial matters to do with the management of Port Phillip Bay came up all the time.

Tom got on well with the various authorities; it

was one reason he'd managed to hold onto his position as coastguard officer for so long. And his membership of the environmental group Our Bay didn't seem to have damaged his reputation.

Once the press got their teeth around the bone of port development, it was hard for them to let go. Beware the promises of politicians, Chris muttered to himself as he mulched around his bean and lettuce seedlings, waiting for Sergeant Dawkins to return his calls. He was hoping for a truce between them; but, on the other hand, while Dawkins shouted at him then ignored him, Chris felt justified in going his own way.

There was no true dormant season here on the coast. The temperature seldom dropped below ten degrees; frosts were rare. If you stayed out of the wind, it wasn't all that cold. But it would be a month or so before the ground was warm enough for his vegetables to flourish. Some said it was a waste to plant them early, but he didn't think so.

The ibis were flying across the sky in their ragged 'vs'. They weren't neat in formation like the swans were. All spring the ibis flew from their islands in Port Phillip Bay to the paddocks where they grazed, then flew back to feed their young. Chris often watched them scattered by strong winds then re-forming, patient, undeterred.

There were three islands where birds nested, at least fifteen species, Tom had told him once. Chris had visited them years ago, in a water police launch. He'd been sea-sick and anxious, and all of his energy had gone into not letting it show. Funny how he'd forgotten the reason for the trip, but remembered the feeling all too well.

Some ibis would be injured, weary, old, possibly making the trip for the last time. They weren't neat and fast-flying, but all spring achieved their purpose, fed their young. How would the islands be affected if further rounds of dredging went ahead?

The sight of swans rowing on their great wings had always calmed Chris, made him feel better. One early morning, not long after his mother died, he'd gone out into the back yard. Four swans had been flying low over the cottage, so low that he'd heard their wingbeats, steady and reliable. He'd often wondered why so low, why that morning of all mornings.

TEN

Peter Robinson's grey beard was well trimmed and neat. His hair had streaks of brown alongside the grey. His eyes, a very light brown, looked past Chris, who was standing on his porch. Chris wondered if he was checking for someone in the street, or possibly a car.

The ex-pilot held out his hand. He had an air about him of a man who was past being surprised. He asked if Chris would like something to drink and Chris said yes to coffee.

On the drive to Melbourne, he'd had plenty of time to think about why he was taking the step of interviewing Robinson. It was one thing to go around Queenscliff, where people knew him, or knew of him, another thing to travel for two hours to question a stranger. Chris knew that Dawkins would be furious when he told him – and he would tell Dawkins – he'd make himself do that. He hoped he'd learn something that would make it worthwhile. But all he could come up with, as he crossed the Westgate Bridge, appalled by the traffic around the docks, was that he wanted to hear Robinson's side of the story.

'That fishing boat veered into the shipping channel, right into the middle of it,' Robinson said when they were seated with their coffee in the living-room.

'But who would risk their lives for – '

'Money,' Robinson said sharply. 'The fishermen were paid. That was part of the deal.'

'Whose deal?'

Robinson's pale brown eyes took on a gleam that to Chris suggested some kind of obsession.

'It was bloody obvious that we'd hit them if I didn't alter course.'

'Tell me about your disagreement with the ship's master.'

'He was paid as well.'

'Do you have any evidence for that?'

'Evidence!' Robinson spat the word out. 'That's all you coppers think of.'

'What did the master say?'

'Haven't you listened to the recording?'

'Not yet.'

Robinson's lip curled in a sneer, meaning that he expected incompetence and lack of preparation from the police.

'You're here about Fred Delraine, right?'

'I'd like to find out what happened.'

'And you expect me to tell you? How would I know?'

'We'll leave that for now. I want to hear about the incident with the fishing boat. Why did you lose your temper?'

'I was set up!' Robinson's face and neck were mottled red. He leant forward, fists clenched.

Chris involuntarily drew back and repeated his earlier question. 'What evidence do you have for that?'

'Look, the pilots bring the ships through the heads, then the channel, then into dock. And bloody hazardous it is. The masters don't believe it till they see it for themselves. They're theoretically in charge, but most of them have the good sense to realise that the pilots are the ones with the local knowledge and expertise. This master was different. He was domineering and up himself from the word go.'

'Why was that do you think?'

'Because he knew what was planned.'

'Did Captain Delraine take your side?'

'Fred was sympathetic, but – '

Chris waited.

'He wasn't a well man.'

'What did Captain Delraine do?'

'He spoke to Southeby.'

'The board's chairman?'

Robinson nodded bitterly. 'Southeby didn't lift a finger.'

'What could he have done?'

'Spoken up for me at the inquiry.'

'What about the other pilots?'

'Nothing. Sod all.'

Robinson relaxed a little, but his eyes shone with the brilliant, unwavering light of paranoia.

Chris felt out of his depth. It was all very well to jump in his car and drive to Brighton, but at the very least he needed a colleague with him, as witness and corroboration. The steps that had taken him to the ex-pilot's sitting room seemed shaky at best, at worst a deliberate and foolish flouting of the rules.

He decided to concentrate on more practical matters. 'What about the money you invested in the company? Have you got it back?'

'Not yet.'

'Does that bother you?'

'It's only money. My solicitor's handling it. What I

care about's my reputation and I'll never get *that* back.' Robinson paused and stared at Chris, who waited in silence. 'There was an audit after I was fired. Ostensibly it was to review safety procedures, but there was a full financial audit.'

'Who did it?'

Robinson named a well-known accounting firm.

'It was an independent audit and the pilots, as the subject of it, were kept at arm's length, but the results were made available to Southeby.'

'How do you know, if you'd already left?'

Chris had guessed the answer to this, and was pleased to have his guess confirmed.

'Fred thought there were questions that needed answering. I gave twenty-five years of my life to the company. What did they do when the going got tough? They dumped me.'

'But not Captain Delraine.'

'Fred made inquiries,' Robinson said bitterly.

'And?'

'Then he died, didn't he?'

'Do you believe someone killed him?'

'No. Fred walked into the sea. He'd had enough. God knows, I've thought about doing it myself.'

'Because of his marriage?'

'Our wives used to be friends. If you knew them, you'd know what an irony that is.'

'Where's your wife now?'

'What do you want with her?'

'Just her mobile number,' Chris said mildly.

Robinson's expression implied that phoning his ex-wife wasn't something normal people did unless they had a very good excuse. But he gave Chris the number and Chris copied it into his phone.

'Who paid the fishermen and the captain?'

'I don't know.'

'You must have some idea or suspicion.' Chris realised he'd gone back to asking tricky questions against his better judgment.

'Suspicion?' Robinson repeated with an ugly twist to his mouth. 'I suspect the men who were my friends and colleagues for more than two decades. Don't you think I haven't been over and around it till I thought I was going mad?'

'Wasn't anybody on your side?'

'Apart from Fred? Not really.'

'Do you have a letter from your solicitor about the money?'

When Robinson said he did, Chris asked if he could see it.

There were two letters. The first was short and dated five months previously. It requested the return of $347,500, the sum of the shares Robinson had invested, plus his superannuation and final dividend payment.

Robinson had also brought the accountant's reply, which was brief as well. It stated that the money would be paid into his bank account.

The solicitor's second letter began as a repeat of the first, then queried the delay.

Chris asked who worked out the dividend payments.

'The accountant. To say we buy shares can be a bit misleading. The cost of joining in 1980 is obviously different from the present time.'

'So what is it now?'

'One fifty.'

'One hundred and fifty thousand? That's what your replacement paid?'

'I don't know if anyone's replaced me yet. That's what he would have to pay.'

'And Captain Delraine's shares and superannuation?'

'They'll be paid to his widow.'

Chris could think of one reason for delaying payment. Robinson would be relieved when he finally was paid. If the payment was slightly less than he expected, he wouldn't be inclined to quibble. Would the same apply to Rosemary Delraine?

'Normally a pilot's retirement would be known in advance, prepared for. He'd take his 'share' as a lump sum and his superannuation as a pension. Is that right?' Chris asked.

'Yes.'

'You've asked for two lump sums.'

'I don't want any more to do with them.'

'And the money, once you get it?'

'That's my business.'

'Did Captain Delraine speak to the accountant on your behalf?'

'He offered to, once he found out how long I'd been waiting. I said no – he had enough troubles of his own, but – '

'But Delraine went ahead? When was this?'

'Six weeks ago? I can't recall exactly. He said he'd get it sorted out.'

'What happened?'

'Nothing so far as I know. I didn't ask. I didn't want to pester him.'

'Would you expect Captain Delraine to leave a suicide note?'

'No.'

'Why not?'

'Because it leaves it open to conclude that his death was accidental.'

'And that's what he would have wanted?'

'Yes.'

'For the company's sake?'

'For his sake, and – and for the sake of the people he loved.'

'Captain Delraine had been living at the operations centre for months, yet his room was practically empty. Why do you think that was?'

Robinson shook his head and sighed. 'Fred lived as though he was still in the navy. He was like that for as long as I knew him. Never lost the habit of confining his belongings to the smallest space.'

'Which belongings?'

Robinson shrugged as if to say, what difference does it make?

'What else did you and Captain Delraine talk about?'

'Marriage,' Robinson said, his face set once more into hard, vengeful lines. 'And divorce.'

Safety was in everybody's interests. How could it not be? Tom wasn't alone in blaming recreational fishermen for disregarding the regulations and half the time not even knowing what they were. Every week during the summer there was an incident involving a recreational craft of some kind straying into, or failing to get out of, the commercial shipping channel.

Responsibility for policing breaches of this kind rested with the water police. Sometimes the offenders were let off with a warning. Sometimes they were fined. There'd been a public awareness campaign eighteen months ago and Chris had been involved. New notices had been put up around the harbour and the launching ramps; there'd been articles in the local press. Chris had spoken at a public meeting, emphasising how long it took for a container or bulk carrier to turn. Common sense should tell you to stay out of their way. But the campaign had made no difference. Speed boat enthusiasts and weekend fishermen continued to behave as though the bay belonged to them.

Why was Robinson convinced there'd been a plot to get rid of him? It seemed too indirect a method, just as likely to backfire as to succeed.

Chris bought coffee and a pastry from a cafe not far from Robinson's house. The coffee was good, strong and restorative. He got out his phone and scrolled through the pilot company's website, looking for the names of clerical staff. They weren't listed. Maybe this was odd, but on the other hand, maybe it wasn't.

Profits for the last financial year were just under 18 million, shared by the pilots according to their charter. What about the rest of the staff? Chris assumed that they were on fixed salaries. There was no copy of the charter on the website. He wondered exactly what it said.

He suddenly wished he'd heard Fred Delraine's

voice and wondered if there was a recording of it somewhere.

Chris phoned Peter Robinson. If the former pilot was surprised to hear from him again so soon, he didn't say so.

'How often does the company pay dividends?'

'Every six months.'

'When did you receive your last one?'

'I can't remember the exact date. I'd have to look it up.'

Chris said he would wait.

'It was five weeks before the inquiry,' Robinson said when he came back on the line.

'Are all the pilots paid at the same time?'

'I assume so.'

'Did you compare your payment with anybody else's?'

'No.'

'Was the amount what you were expecting?'

'Roughly speaking.'

'Roughly?'

'I wouldn't know to the exact dollar unless I had all the figures in front of me.'

'If you thought the amount was out by a few hundred dollars, what would you do?'

'Nothing, probably.'

Chris said carefully, 'When you were working for the company, let's just say you suspected there might have been a clerical error, what would you have done then?'

'Rung up the accountant, I suppose.'

'What if the accountant said there was no mistake,

but six months later it happened again?'

'What are you getting at? I wouldn't suspect a discrepancy of a few hundred dollars.'

'Do you know if anyone queried a payment in the last year or so?'

'No, I don't.'

'Is it something you discussed with Fred Delraine?'

'I –'

'Yes?'

'I – actually, I just remembered something Freddie said. If each of us was paid $300 less than he was owed, then this amounted to $9,000 every six months. When I asked him what he meant, he said nothing, to forget about it.'

Chris asked if Robinson had a copy of the company charter. When Robinson said he had one somewhere, Chris asked for it to be faxed to him and gave the station's number.

According to Robinson, Delraine had been his only loyal supporter from within the company. Had Delraine's loyalty been something of a mixed blessing? Might it have been better for Robinson if he'd made a clean break, left Melbourne and sought employment in another state?

Chris guessed that something had bound Delraine and Robinson together – more than Delraine's support over the fishing boat incident. Had their marriage problems been a bond? Chris wondered why neither man had children. Was it a co-incidence, or was there a particular reason?

One of the inquiry's recommendations was that the state government should be given the power to revoke pilots' licences. A phone call confirmed that this recommendation was still under consideration.

Chris rang the accounting firm and asked about the company's financial audit. He received the answer he'd expected, that the information was commercially sensitive and could not be released.

There was no one currently working in the fraud squad whom Chris could claim as an acquaintance. He knew there was a huge backlog of cases. A recent article in the Melbourne Age claimed that victims were being forced to wait for over a year. So long as the coroner's report was pending, Chris told himself that the best he could do was to proceed one step at a time.

ELEVEN

The police station was cold, with the peculiar coldness of a building that has been left uninhabited for weeks. Chris half expected to see cobwebs hanging from the ceiling. He shivered, unable to shake himself free of the illusion. He switched on the heater and listened to messages on the answerphone. There were two inquiries about lost pets, but they could wait.

Tom's message sounded jubilant. 'I found it!' It might have been a life he'd saved.

Chris considered dropping by the coastguard office, but it was late and he was tired.

He spent half an hour on the internet, where he discovered that Australian-owned shipping companies were a thing of the past. The Australian National Line – a patriotic name if ever there was one – had become a subsidiary of French CMA, CGM in 1998.

Anstey Ltd was a transport company whose ships travelled from Melbourne to Tasmania each day. They had a dedicated terminal at Webb Dock, but shipping was only a part of their operations. The ships' masters, Chris noted, were qualified to pilot their own ships in and out of Port Phillip Heads. Anstey's Melbourne office was around the corner from the pilots admin building. Was this an interesting co-incidence, or was there a reason for it?

Chris bought fresh rolls and fruit on his way to the coastguard office next morning, knowing that Tom would probably not have had any breakfast.

He read Tom's evidence to the inquiry while Tom made tea and clattered plates.

Nothing jumped out at him that was different from what Tom had already said. From the coastguard launch, Tom had seen the fishing boat cut in front of the container. He'd rescued the fishermen, none of whom was injured.

'Here.' Tom dumped a mug of tea in front of Chris. 'Get that into you, old woman.'

Chris looked at the tea, which was black as tar. 'You'd never eat unless I fed you.'

'Bullshit. There's a problem with the regulations,' Tom went on. 'The pilot's task is to bring the ship safely in to port, but the master has the authority to over-ride the pilot. The inquiry was charged with looking into safety procedures, but they didn't recommend a change.'

'In this case the master and the pilot argued, the pilot went against the master's orders, and the master made a complaint which ended with the pilot being sacked.'

Tom nodded, took a sip of tea and grimaced. Chris felt like asking why he made it so strong, but he knew Tom had no answer. It was just what he did.

'Robinson claims he was set up.'

Tom made a face, raising his eyebrows and lifting both hands. 'The man's all bitter and twisted, I expect.'

'What if he's right?'

'Did he tell you why he thinks that?'

'He said Delraine was the only one to back him up.'

'And now Delraine's dead.'

'Do you think there's a connection?'

'I don't know.'

Chris knew he shouldn't be talking to Tom like this, using Tom as a sounding board. I'll stop in a minute, he said to himself.

'What do you know about the financial audit?' he asked, thinking this was safer ground.

'It was in the inquiry's recommendations.'

'A copy was sent to Southeby, but Robinson doesn't know any more than that.'

'Well, he wouldn't, would he? He was out on his ear by then.'

Chris had studied Southeby's photograph on the pilots website, but it had told him nothing. The board's chairman wore his hair very short. He looked neat, clean shaven, dressed in an expensive suit. He looked like a man who would be good at hiding his emotions.

Chris had never felt comfortable sitting underneath the photograph of Bobby McGilvrey and his dog Max that occupied the wall above Tom's desk. When they were together in Tom's office, Tom didn't look at the photo, but Chris knew he was aware of it, that his grief never really left him.

Tom had loved Bobby as only a man with no son of his own can love a neglected child. Bobby had been killed in the railway yard next to the harbour. He'd been strangled with Max's lead. Chris knew that Tom believed they'd both failed the boy. Tom never alluded to their failure directly, but the judgment was there, underneath their dealings with each other.

Chris had brought a newspaper with him. He spread it out on Tom's desk and pointed to an article about the need for more channel dredging at the heads.

Tom snorted and made a disgusted face.

He'd been opposed to channel dredging from the start. This opposition had marred his usually friendly relations with the water police, whose job it had been to keep protestors from sailing or paddling too close to the dredger, whose name, Chris recalled, had been Netherland Queen.

Tom had remarked at the time that it was a good thing he was a volunteer and couldn't be sacked for speaking out.

Chris had stayed out of the dispute. The protests had all taken place on the water and his involvement as a police officer had been minimal. He wondered now if Tom had resented his silence. Tom had joined the coalition of groups opposed to the dredging, which hadn't just included conservationists and environmental activists, but a multi-millionaire trucking magnate, and David Anstey, owner of Anstey Limited.

Chris said, 'There's no doubt that deepening the channel makes it easier for the pilots, getting those behemoths up the channel and safely into port.'

Tom frowned and busied himself blowing smoke at the ceiling. 'It's a joke,' he said.

'Are you aware of any pilots speaking out against it?'

'Fred Delraine you mean?'

'Anyone.'

'Nope. The Netherland Queen was paid half a billion dollars for the job.'

The figure was well known, but Chris still caught his breath every time he heard it.

'Let's get out of here,' Tom said, throwing his cigarette butt in the bin.

Usually they headed for the jetty, but this time Tom turned the other way. They hardly spoke until they'd come up behind the fort and black lighthouse overlooking the pilots' centre.

'Remember all those estimates of size and tonnage?'

Chris knew from experience that talking to Tom was sometimes like peeling back the layers of an onion. He said quietly that yes, he did remember.

'Remember how we thought they'd over-estimated?'

'Where did Captain Delraine stand?' Chris asked.

'Don't know. Said nothing publicly, but you wouldn't expect him to. They could have dredged half a metre,' Tom continued. 'It would have been enough for the containers coming through now. But that wasn't what the port corporation wanted. They have to be ready for the next generation of giants, compete with Sydney and Brisbane. I can't believe we're going to have to go through it all again.'

'I haven't forgotten about tomorrow,' Chris said quietly. 'Will we take some flowers to the railway yard?'

Tom snorted again, but he didn't say no.

'Do you think it will make a difference if any of the pilots speak out against further dredging?'

'Probably not. Perhaps if they act together – but what makes you think the pilots are against it anyway?'

'Delraine was, according to a couple of the people I've spoken to.' Chris recalled the paved back courtyard of the pilots' centre, the line of bins and the cook

squashing his cigarette butt under a black heel.
He was thinking of who confided in whom, and who might have betrayed a confidence.

Back at the station, he found the original decision to dredge the bay online and began reading through the Environmental Effects Statements. There were lots of them. He sighed, wondering if his conscience would allow him to print them out, or whether he should force himself to read on the screen.

The board's chairman, Ivan Southeby, had submitted a statement saying that dredging was necessary for Victoria's commercial future and he was satisfied all the necessary steps were being taken to protect the bay.

An article on the Crikey news website claimed the port corporation had spent millions of dollars soliciting statements favourable to dredging, but the ploy had back-fired because many of the statements did not stand up to scrutiny.

The article went on to say that the Our Bay coalition had tried to take the port corporation to court over what it called 'trail dredging', but had had to back down because they couldn't afford the legal fees.

TWELVE

The two men met in the middle of the morning, hardly speaking as they gathered grevillea and tea-tree blossom on their way to where Bobby McGilvrey's body had been found.

'I don't like cemeteries.' It was what Tom said every time.

'Me neither.'

'I wouldn't mind my ashes being scattered here.'

'I'll do that for you, Tom.'

'What makes you think you'll outlast me, you conceited bugger?'

They performed their small ceremony, Chris glad the railway yard was empty except for them, then retraced their steps to the coastguard office.

Tom put the jug on for tea.

Suddenly the great expanse of sea and sky that was so often a burden to Chris shrank to the proportions of the small, draughty room. Tom never mentioned his fear of the sea. Chris felt glad that there was no need to explain.

'Did anyone from Our Bay talk to Ivan Southeby, explain your opposition to the dredging?' he asked when they were sitting with their tea in front of them.

'Waste of time,' Tom said.

'Did you ever meet him?'

'Not meet. I saw him once. He came down here. Did a tour of the harbour.'

'Was that to see the new beak hull?'

Tom looked thoughtful. 'That wasn't when I saw him. It was before that. We watched them unloading the hull, you and me.'

'We did. That was a good day. Southeby doesn't pilot ships any more,' Chris said.

'Too much paper-work, I guess.'

'But there's a CEO and clerical staff.'

'Maybe he's had a gutful of the sea, climbing up and down those ladders.'

'It doesn't strike you as odd?'

'A lot of things strike me as odd about them, Blackie. I already told you. Secretive bloody bunch.'

'But successful. And proud of their history.'

Chris thought of George Tobin, who'd won a licence to pilot sailing ships in and out of Port Phillip Heads. He thought of Tobin sleeping on the beach in a tent and getting into his rowing boat to face the Rip in a howling gale.

He shuddered and said, 'Tell me what you remember about Southeby's visit.'

'Saw him arriving in a white Mercedes.'

'On his own?'

'He had a driver and a couple of guys with him.'

'Did you recognise them?'

'No. Actually the driver looked a bit familiar. I thought I might have seen him somewhere before.'

'Where?'

'Does it matter?'

Chris didn't try to answer. If Dawkins would reply to his phone messages, even if it was to bawl him out again, Chris thought he might regain some kind of balance, give up his one-man crusade.

'Trail dredging,' he said, taking a sip of dark brown tea, 'explain it to me Tom.'

'A trailing suction hopper dredger. Think of it like a giant vacuum cleaner, trailing its suction pipe.' Tom mimed the action with his arms outstretched. 'When the hoppers are full, it empties them. In our case, right outside the heads.'

'Will they do the same again?'

Tom shrugged. It wasn't indifference, Chris knew, more a kind of desperation.

'The dredging was always going to go ahead. We were never going to be able to stop it. But this new scheme is something else. The amount of rock and sand and silt they'll have to get rid of is forty-five times as much.'

Chris imagined the hopper dredger like something from a science fiction movie or a horror story by Stephen King. It would gouge and dump and swallow till there was nothing left.

He wondered how he might find out if Southeby had been paid to submit a statement favourable to the dredging. If the Crikey article was accurate, and he had been paid, it made him one of many.

'I've been reading the submissions that were taken when the first round of dredging was being planned. You'd be familiar with Our Bay's submission.'

Tom grimaced around his mug of tea. 'The whole thing was a charade,' he said. 'The government had already made up its mind to go ahead. The Environmental Effects Statements were a joke. It wasn't only our group that said so. Did you read the submission by that civil engineer? Caused a bit of a kerfuffle in the press at the time. But like I said, it made no difference in the end.'

'The engineer's submission's very detailed – '

'And damning.'

Chris nodded. 'From an economic as well as a technical point of view.'

Tom thumped his mug down and said morosely, 'Don't know if I'll be here much longer.'

'What?'

'Young blood, Blackie. Alistair phoned up.'

'To say what? Come on, Tom.'

'To warn me to prepare for a change.'

Chris had never directly queried Tom's occupancy of the coastguard office, though he'd joked from time to time about Tom's skill in seeing off potential rivals. Though they'd had their ups and downs, Tom generally got on well with Alistair, who was in charge of allocating volunteers.

They'd talked about how redundancy hung over them, but while Chris had often pictured his station being closed down, he hadn't really thought of Tom as expendable in that way. He was liked and respected. He'd saved lives.

'You know what I'll miss most? My old yellow bucket. I wonder if my replacement will get a new launch.'

'Don't be so defeatist, Tom. That's not like you.'

'Why should I hang on like an arthritic spider?'

'Where will you go if you leave here? What will you do?'

Chris realised too late that these were the wrong questions, and that Tom had no answer to them.

Back at the station, he made a few phone calls. He was given a number for the author of the Crikey article, who sounded pleased to hear from the police. His source was his own business, and he made this clear.

The journalist wanted to talk about how the port corporation's scheme had back-fired.

Chris listened patiently. When he thought about dredging, he thought about it in Tom Maloney's words, with Tom's gift for mockery and scornful turns of phrase.

'What if this new round doesn't go ahead? What if the government says no?' he asked when the journalist paused for breath.

'The threat is that the new generation of ships won't come to Victoria. Melbourne will fall behind.'

'Have you spoken to Ivan Southeby?'

'This is because of Captain Delraine drowning isn't it? That's why you're asking questions.'

'What do you know about that?'

'Only what I read in the mainstream press.'

'Have you spoken to Southeby?' Chris repeated.

'Once. There was an incident, a pilot was sacked.'

'I read about it,' Chris said.

'I thought there was a story there, I mean about what really happened, so I rang him up. He refused to comment. I rang the pilot who was sacked and he gave me an earful, most of it defamatory.'

'What did he say about Southeby?'

'It was all off the record. Why don't you ask him yourself?'

When Chris didn't reply, the journalist changed tack and began talking about the new container port proposals, how if dredging was a controversial issue, then where to build the new container port was a controversial issue multiplied a hundred fold.

Chris had a general idea of the different proposals, one at Hastings, another inside the bay and much closer to Melbourne.

'Which one is the government backing?' he asked.

'With an election coming up? They'll back the one that'll bring them the most votes.'

Chris asked for some links and thanked the reporter for his time.

If Hastings were chosen by whichever party won the next election, that port would need dredging too. Hastings was on Westernport Bay, seventy-two kilometres from Melbourne. Bay West, the other option, was much closer to the capital, half way between Melbourne and Geelong. If that proposal won, Geelong would become an important commercial port again. It was how the city had begun, first with the gold rush, then shipping wool to the northern hemisphere, then textiles as Geelong became the Bradford of the south.

Those days and that prosperity were long gone. Geelong was a depressed industrial has-been. Unemployment was high and the Labor Government had been elected on a pledge to do something about it. Voters were sick of empty promises, and Chris could sympathise with that.

But was Bay West a suitable site for a container port? Ships would still have to go in and out through Port Phillip Heads. Then there was the Point Henry sandbar which, as often as it was dredged away, silted up again.

Chris went outside to stare at the station's back

fence and give his eyes a rest from the computer screen.

He got out his phone and pressed Tom's number.

'I've been reading about Hastings. There'd need to be dredging there too, a lot of it silt, which is harder to get rid of.'

It was as though Tom had been waiting for his call. 'But not nearly so much,' he said. 'Twenty-five to fifty cubic metres compared with sixty-six to eighty-four for Bay West. This bay, ours Blackie, that we're responsible for, has had as much as it can take!'

'Have you heard from Alistair again?'

'Not yet. It's too late anyway,' Tom said crankily.

'For what?'

'For Victoria to stay in the race. Melbourne's a disaster. Bay West will be worse. Portland, now there's a good deep-water port. In a comparison with Bay West or Hastings, Portland ought to win hands down. Would the government listen to that argument? Of course not.'

'Imagine the cost of trucking all our imports from Portland to Melbourne.'

'Not trucks, Blackie. Cabotage. Smaller ships designed for local distribution. The Europeans do it. Why can't we?'

Chris went back to his reading.

Was there a better alternative? Just thinking about the complexity of it, the port of Melbourne a vital cog in the wheel of commerce powering the state of Victoria, gave him a headache. He despaired of ever getting his mind around it all. But he had a hunch that, in the tangle of competing interests, lay the reason why Captain Delraine had drowned.

Costs would go up in order to pay for the new port, including the cost of dredging. If costs went up too much, then shipping companies might stop coming to Melbourne.

The Victorian opposition favoured Hastings, predicting that Melbourne would wind down in the decades ahead as Hastings outgrew it in size and activity.

The former chief executive of the Port of Melbourne Corporation supported the opposition's plan and criticised Bay West which seemed on balance to be supported by the Labor Government.

Fred Delraine had been on a consultative committee appointed to advise the government on the container port proposals.

Chris read the sentence, re-read it, then read it for a third time. His eyes were tired and could be playing tricks with him; but no, the words were there.

THIRTEEN

Normally Chris avoided funerals. Once he'd got over his initial anger with his mother for refusing a memorial service for his father, he'd been glad of her decision. He should have told her that, should have found a way to tell her she'd been right. Standing back from the church, watching the mourners arriving, the men in suits, the well-dressed women moving like a dark wave, Chris felt a sharp moment of regret.

He spotted Tom slouching along, his eyebrows clamped together as though he was in pain. Chris smiled and lifted his hand in greeting but all he got in return was a nod.

He went inside and looked for a suitable place to sit.

A cloth with the pilots insignia was draped over the coffin. Spring wild flowers lay on top of and around it.

Bobby McGilvrey's coffin had been achingly small. Chris had a sudden startling memory of Bobby's mother, dressed in the same rusty black she'd worn every day since her son's death, smoking outside the church, his older sister and two small brothers holding hands. He wondered if Tom was remembering Bobby.

He recognised Captain Delraine's sister, Alison, from a photograph. Brian Laidlaw was sitting near the front, but not so near as to presume on the rights of Delraine's family. Camilla Renfrew was next to him. Chris thought, though from behind he couldn't see, that they were holding hands.

Brian turned and raised his head, the gesture like a startled kangaroo. Rosemary Delraine was walking slowly down the centre aisle with two men, one on either side of her. Rosemary's fair hair stood out against her black suit. The men were tall, well-built; she looked very small between them. Chris recognised the men from photographs as well; they were her brothers, Robert and Ian Charleton.

Sergeant Dawkins stood for a moment at the door, looking blank, then lifted his chin in Chris's direction. His suit, one Chris hadn't seen before, looked shiny, made of some cheap material. The church was filling up. A lot of the townspeople had come to pay their respects.

The pilots' CEO, John Bennett, and Southeby, the board's chairman, took their places near the front. Southeby was tall, with broad shoulders and an athlete's build. That hadn't been apparent from his photograph. His very short fair hair shone in the church's subdued light.

Chris looked round for Peter Robinson and found him at the back, staring fixedly ahead. He nodded hello to William, but the cook turned away. William was sitting next to Michael Travers, the dispatch officer on duty the night Delraine had died. The pilots were by far the most impressive group. Apart from those actually on the water, Chris didn't think a single one was missing.

The service began, but Chris hardly paid attention to it; his mind was busy sorting through the people.

Six pilots balanced the coffin on broad shoulders. Leaving the church, Rosemary and her brothers walked as one person, the men matching their stride to hers.

Alison Delraine stood in shadow, to one side of the doors, shaking hands with her brother's former colleagues, occasionally nodding and smiling sadly, as though reminding herself of what was expected.

Chris watched her from a distance. She looked six to eight years younger than her brother. He wondered how long she was staying in Australia and thought it was time he introduced himself.

'My name's Chris Blackie. I'm sorry for your loss.'

Alison stared at Chris as though she scarcely took in what he was saying. Then she shook his outstretched hand and asked him to repeat his name.

Alison's hand was freezing. She shivered, though she looked warmly dressed.

But when she spoke, her voice was firm and calm. 'I want to talk to whoever is in charge of the investigation into my brother's death.'

'I'll find Sergeant Dawkins,' Chris said.

Half an hour later, at the pilots' centre, Chris watched William taking around trays of food and drinks. He had a young helper, whom Chris had never seen before. More food was laid out on tables along one wall of the dining-room. Most of the tables and chairs had been removed. The room was full of people, the atmosphere solemn.

Chris found Tom, who grabbed hold of his hand and held it, shaking his head to let Chris know that, as far as his job was concerned, he had no further news.

Chris returned the pressure of Tom's hand, then looked towards a short man with a straggly beard and hair to match, who was standing near the door that led from the dining-room to the kitchen.

'Who's that?'

'David Anstey,' Tom said, as though Chris should have recognised the shipping owner for himself.

Chris wondered if Anstey cultivated a garden gnome appearance, or if the effect was unintentional.

He shifted his glance sideways. 'And the man talking to Southeby?'

'That's Tony Parry, head of the Hastings Development Group.' Again Tom sounded surprised at Chris's ignorance. 'He's often on TV.'

'He looks rich.'

Tom shrugged. 'There's a lot of rich men here.'

Chris supposed Parry had been at the church. Perhaps he'd come late. He was a man you'd notice in a crowd, as tall as Southeby, and as well turned out.

Tom wandered off and Chris continued watching the guests, noting who was grouped together. There was plenty of alcohol, but nobody was drinking much. The pilots were all in uniform, which was one way of presenting a united front.

Alison Delraine looked unhappy, out of place.

Chris wondered who would notice. As he was thinking this, William walked across and, bending down, spoke to Alison with his mouth close to her ear.

A little colour came into Alison's cheeks and she smiled gratefully.

Along one side of the dining-room, windows faced the sea. The sun came out and shone on the waves, which were rough, irregular. The south-westerly was gaining strength. By tonight, Chris thought, we might be in for a real blow. He wondered where Alison was staying, and had a sudden premonition that she might not be safe.

Approaching Chris in his shiny suit, Dawkins looked like a bookie or a spiv. Chris felt embarrassed for him, then reminded himself that his own suit wasn't much better. He could have worn his uniform: he would have felt more comfortable; but he wasn't on duty, and his uniform would have made the kind of statement he didn't want to make.

'Come with me while I talk to them.' Dawkins indicated Rosemary and her brothers with a sideways movement of his head. His usually irritable expression had changed to a determined one.

Chris gave his jacket sleeve a tug and followed. He wondered if Dawkins had spoken to Alison yet and what she'd wanted to tell him.

Robert Charleton looked Dawkins up and down and barely glanced at Chris, his eyes taking in everything about the Sergeant, from his badly cut hair to the cheap glitter of his clothes.

'Thank you for coming, Sergeant.'

The other brother, Ian – close up he looked to be at least three or four years younger than Robert - managed a small smile.

Dawkins shook the brothers' hands, then, after hesitating fractionally, took Rosemary's as well. Rosemary looked exhausted. Her eyeshadow and lipstick had run. Her eyes stared blankly straight ahead.

A grieving widow might not care about her appearance, might go through the forms, knowing how she ought to look and what she ought to say, while all the time she felt like screaming and throwing things at walls. But did that apply to Rosemary? Chris doubted it.

Robert's dark hair was greying at the temples. He was heavy through the chest and thighs, Ian slimmer and more lightly built.

Robert said, 'I thought it went off well, don't you?'

'Very well,' said Dawkins.

Chris looked towards Ian, thinking he might add something. But Ian was staring at the glass of fizzy water in his hand. Chris felt a shudder pass between him and Rosemary, some sort of unspoken warning.

'We'll be leaving soon,' Robert said evenly. 'We've a long drive back.'

Chris was suddenly sure Robert had argued with the coroner, and possibly with Southeby as well. Out of the corner of his eye, he caught sight of Southeby still talking to Tony Parry.

Dawkins seemed about to ask Robert a question, but the pilots' CEO, John Bennett, moved suddenly in front of him, holding out his hand to Rosemary and mouthing condolences.

Bennett's expression was the right mixture of sympathy and sadness. He was dressed impeccably for a funeral, as indeed was everyone associated with the company.

Rosemary took the CEO's hand after a second's hesitation, but did not raise her head or meet his eyes.

Ian's expression remained impassive, but Robert didn't trouble to hide the small curve of satisfaction round his mouth.

Others came to pay their respects. Dawkins, with a slight twist of his head in Chris's direction, moved away.

If Delraine had been murdered, his killer might be here in the dining-room. Chris looked around again, to fix faces and figures in his mind.

Brian hadn't come, but Chris hadn't expected him to. Camilla hadn't come either. She'd been at the church to support Brian, who would probably by now be on his own somewhere, walking along the beach or the spongy shore of Swan Bay.

Chris knew he should find Brian and insist on talking to him, if not today then tomorrow. Brian was holding back something, either out of respect for Delraine's memory, or because Delraine had asked him to.

William was back by the doorway, upright, eyes narrowed. The cook might have made a good detective, Chris thought, if he wasn't so single-minded. Was single-mindedness a good quality or a bad one, in a detective? Chris felt he didn't know the answer to that.

His eye caught Ivan Southeby and John Bennett in conversation in the corner furthest from the door. Their heads were close together. It looked to Chris as though they believed they were the only two men in the room, such was their absorption in each other. There was nothing unusual in those two having a private conversation, yet there seemed more to it than that.

Bennett lifted his head and Chris turned around in order not to be caught staring. His eye caught Alison's. He gave her a brief, sympathetic smile. Alison had come from the other side of the world to attend her brother's funeral, made the journey alone. She had a look about her – it had been apparent on the church steps – of having had to take all of life's important decisions alone. In this she stood in sharp contrast to Rosemary Delraine.

Chris watched as Alison approached Rosemary and the Charleton brothers. Alison held out her hand, and Rosemary, after what seemed too long a hesitation, took it.

In the navy, Fred Delraine would have been surrounded by other people, living with them closely, almost all of them men. And then in the pilot company. But Chris was sure he'd been a very private man. William knew that, and Brian Laidlaw, both themselves solitary men. Chris would have been surprised to find that William had a partner, or shared his flat with anyone.

This solitariness, Chris said to himself, which was distinct from loneliness, could be a person's strength. It meant they had to rely on themselves. But Chris understood that it could also be a person's weakness. Vision could become distorted, through not having another's thoughts and opinions to take into account, another's observations and perceptions to consider.

He watched Rosemary and her brothers leave the centre, aware that quite a few pairs of eyes were turned towards them, William the cook's included. Rosemary hesitated and looked over her shoulder. Robert took hold of his sister by the elbow. From that distance, Rosemary's expression was difficult to read, but her smudged make-up stood out, and her demeanour was that of a person anxious and afraid.

Chris and Dawkins sat in the upstairs bar at the Brewhouse.

Chris's friend Minnie had served them, raising an inquisitive eyebrow. Chris had shaken his head slightly in response, knowing Minnie wouldn't take offence at not being introduced.

It wouldn't have been an awkward introduction. Minnie got along with people. From the age of ten, when he'd first set eyes on her, Minnie had had the gift of getting on with people, liking them and being liked and respected in return.

She would be curious about the detective from Geelong. And why not? But Chris didn't feel up to coping with introductions. He had to concentrate on Dawkins. He'd hidden his surprise when the Sergeant had asked him to come for a drink. He didn't say that he would never have chosen the Brewhouse.

Dawkins had ordered one of the hotel's craft beers and Chris had followed suit. Dawkins took a long swallow, sighed then said, 'That's better.'

He leant forward, his shoulder and arm muscles prominent under his white shirt. He'd taken off his jacket and hung it on the back of his chair. It was much warmer in the bar than it had been at the pilots' centre. A burly man, Chris thought. Dawkins might have been a rower, or might have built those muscles in a gym.

'The widow and her brothers, what did you make of them?' he asked.

Chris took a moment to think before replying. 'They were very composed.'

'Composed?' Dawkins seemed to chew over the word.

'They'd planned how to behave. But – '

'Yes?'

'Rosemary Delraine's make-up was smudged. I thought she would have repaired it, fixed it up.'

'A quick trip to the Ladies between the church and

the reception?'

Dawkins smiled around his beer. Chris forced himself to smile back, though he'd meant the point seriously. He didn't believe Delraine's widow was the sort of person who would willingly appear in public with her make-up smudged.

He recalled Rosemary's expression as she'd been leaving the pilots centre, the way she'd turned to look over her shoulder, almost stumbled. Robert had moved swiftly, hand at her elbow, to assist, or to force her to move on?

Had Dawkins noticed? Chris hadn't looked to see. Should he raise it now, tell Dawkins how Robert's behaviour had made him uneasy? He needed time to think about his impressions.

Chris felt a space between him and Sergeant Dawkins that had not been there before. He was suddenly aware that he did not know what might fill it. He thought that he had never seen the man so clearly. Dawkins had been a blur of authority, a voice barking instructions; but most of all an absence, refusing to communicate at all.

Was Dawkins going to refer to all the times Chris had phoned and he hadn't bothered to phone back, the angry response to his report? It seemed not. It seemed as though a line had been drawn and the Sergeant had stepped over it. But what lay on the other side?

Chris imagined what it might have been like if he'd stayed in Melbourne and done his detective training, as his old supervisor had wanted him to do. He would have had colleagues to work with, who were trained in investigation, and would have learnt how to work with them; some bad, patronising, bossy, or worse. Maybe there would have been one like Sergeant Dawkins. Chris had dismissed Dawkins as a man who'd be swayed by powerful interests, the arguments of those in power, in the pilot service and the government, not to mention wealthy landowners like Rosemary Delraine's brothers. Now, in front of his eyes, or so it seemed, Dawkins was changing into a different kind of man.

Chris asked, 'How did Rosemary Delraine seem when you talked to her on the phone the day Brian found the body?'

'Upset,' Dawkins said, taking another appreciative sip of beer.

'Do you think her brother was listening? I mean Robert.'

Dawkins thought about that. 'Possibly. I think Mrs Delraine had been waiting for me – for the police to ring.'

'She already knew the Captain was dead?'

'Not that so much. I'd say probably not that. But she was expecting the kind of bad news that comes with a call from the police.'

Chris nodded, digesting this. 'What did Alison Delraine say?' he asked.

'She's coming to the station tomorrow morning. I want you to be there too.'

Chris nodded again, hiding his surprise. He felt light-headed, partly the result of drinking alcohol on an empty stomach. He hadn't been hungry all day. He hadn't felt like eating at the pilots centre.

Dawkins said, 'I spoke to Delraine's solicitor again. He left everything to his widow. I asked him if Delraine had said anything about changing his will. His reply was interesting. He said Delraine had phoned and asked to make an appointment.'

'When was this?'

'A couple of weeks before he died. He never kept the appointment. His will wasn't changed.'

'I wonder if Robert Charleton contacted him about it.'

'I asked about that. He admitted that Charleton did phone, but he wouldn't tell him anything.'

'So he says.'

'Why would the solicitor lie about it? Why would he divulge that kind of information to Delraine's brother-in-law?'

Because Robert intimidated him, Chris thought.

Dawkins lifted his eyes from his glass and stared at Chris, his expression focussed and at the same time with an openness about it, a willingness to discuss the point.

But Chris wasn't sure what was wanted of him.

Dawkins wiped his mouth and leant back in his chair. 'Not bad beer they have here, eh? Delraine's will wasn't changed. His widow's a rich woman.'

The Sergeant wasn't fat, but burly. Burly was an adjective that had gone out of fashion, but Chris thought it suited him.

FOURTEEN

'Fred wrote to me,' Alison Delraine said.

They were sitting in the station's front office, Alison upright with her knees and feet together. She took a letter out of her bag and handed it to Dawkins.

The Sergeant took it from her but didn't open it immediately.

'Who else has touched this besides yourself?' he asked.

Alison looked confused.

Dawkins re-phrased his question. 'Have you shown it to anybody else?'

'No,' Alison said, confirming Chris's impression that she was a solitary person, with no one to confide in.

'Did you reply?'

'No – I – I thought about it. I tried to ring him.'

Dawkins handed the letter to Chris with instructions that he make two copies.

Chris read quickly, standing by the photocopier. Delraine began his letter by recalling their childhood, growing up on the south coast of New South Wales, his love of boats and the sea.

Chris's eyes fixed on a phrase near the end – 'corruption in the committee'.

'I was never any good at working out the time difference.' Alison spoke as though she expected to be criticised for all kinds of practical matters. Criticism made her more nervous, less likely to get the calculations right, but that didn't stop it happening. Chris had a sudden vision of her as a small, timid child.

'And then Fred's shifts – ' Alison put her face in her hands. 'I feel so terrible. If I'd made more of an effort. If I'd kept on ringing - '

'You tried,' Dawkins said. 'What number did you ring?'

'The centre. I left messages. And his mobile.'

'Were you worried when your brother didn't respond?'

'Of course. I should have kept on trying.'

'Did you contact Rosemary Delraine?'

'Oh no. Fred wouldn't want Rosemary to know he'd written to me.'

'Did you talk to anyone about the letter?'

'There was no one I could have – no.'

'An old friend of your brother's lives here in Queenscliff. His name's Brian Laidlaw. Did Captain Delraine ever mention him?'

'An old seaman? Whom Fred knew from the navy? Yes, he did mention him from time to time.'

'Recently?'

'Not that I recall. You think I should have contacted the police, don't you? I should have phoned the police here in Australia and told them I was worried.'

For the last five months I have been on a committee advising the government on the future of the port of Melbourne, and the alternatives for a second container port. I don't need to tell you how complicated it all is, from an economic and an environmental point of view. When I was asked to join the committee, I wanted to refuse. I've never been much of a one for committees. I know that very soon I must make decisions, and that these decisions will determine how I live the rest of my life. My marriage has placed on me obligations and burdens I could never have foreseen.

Delraine's writing faltered and Chris wondered if he'd written the letter late at night, after he'd dosed himself on anti-histamines.

We in the pilot service have kept our own house in order for a hundred and seventy-five years. But now I fear that the service I hold dear has become corrupted, rotten from the inside. A colleague found himself in trouble and as a consequence of this a financial audit was ordered by the court. The results have not been released to us, though I have repeatedly requested them.

I know you understand the meaning of loyalty, that loyalty, once pledged, must be kept. I have often thought about my years in the navy, and have wished I'd remained in that service, rather than choosing one which gave me more opportunity for financial gain.

And now this committee. I have told the chairman that I wish to resign, but have yet to write a letter of resignation. There is too much conflict and I find I'm not equipped to handle it. I overheard something one day which made me suspect that the recommendation process is open to bribery and corruption – more than that – that the committee itself is corrupt.

I told Rosemary about my suspicions, what I'd overheard. Perhaps that was a mistake. The chairman said that resigning was my decision, that it was up to me. His name is Eric Finlay. He's a senior public servant with the

Infrastructure Department. He told me to think about it and to take my time.

Delraine's handwriting deteriorated even more towards the end of the letter. His signature was practically illegible.

'The corruption your brother refers to, what do you know about that?' Dawkins asked.

'Only what's in the letter.'

'Had your brother mentioned it before?'

'No. You should understand that Fred is' – Alison realised her mistake and tears came to her eyes – 'was a very private person. He hated talking about his problems. He felt he should simply overcome them.'

'But you were close to one another, in spite of living so far apart?'

'Oh, yes.'

'So you may have picked up hints, a sense that Captain Delraine wasn't happy with his work on the committee?'

'I'm sorry. I can see that it's important, but no, there were no hints.'

'You brother doesn't name names apart from the chairman. Had he mentioned him before?'

'He did say something once. He said that Mr Finlay was very experienced.'

'What do you think he meant?'

'I'm not sure. It was months ago, during one of our phone conversations. But the way Fred said it, it didn't sound like a compliment. It didn't sound as though he respected Mr Finlay very much.'

Dawkins indicated the letter again. 'Do you think

your brother was saying goodbye?' he asked gently.

'I didn't read it that way, not until – well, not until I found out he was dead.'

Alison stared out the window, at the new leaves on the rose bushes. Her eyes filled with tears again and she reached for her handkerchief.

'Do you think your brother killed himself?'

'By drowning? Never!'

Dawkins waited.

'I think Fred was putting his house in order,' Alison said in a calmer voice. 'Not because he intended to commit suicide, but because he was about to make an important decision. Or perhaps he'd already made it, and was waiting for the outcome.'

'A decision to do with his job as a pilot?'

'It could have been that.'

'His marriage?'

'Fred didn't want a divorce, but – '

'Yes?'

'I think he may have accepted that it was inevitable.'

'What about your brother's will?'

'He didn't talk to me about that.'

'His widow's a rich woman now.'

Alison shrugged as if Rosemary's financial situation didn't interest her.

'You don't like Rosemary Delraine?'

'She always acted as though Fred wasn't good enough for her. Whereas the truth is he was worth a hundred of her.'

'Did you speak to Rosemary yesterday?'

'I said hello. I wasn't obliged to chat and I didn't want to.'

'Rosemary's brothers seem very protective.'

Alison said nothing to this.

Chris thought that if he'd been the one framing the questions he would have asked for Alison's opinion of Robert's behavior and character.

Alison said, 'I'm sorry but I'm very tired. The trip, the jet lag.'

'Write down your contact details please and the time and date of your return flight. I'll need to talk to you again.'

After Alison had left, Dawkins made a series of phone calls, then turned to Chris to say, 'We need to find out what the Charletons' financial interests are, any campaign donations they may have made, who to and when. If you could do a bit of digging round?'

Chris said that he would.

'We'll head down there tomorrow. Phone and say I want to speak to all three of them. Today I'd like to visit David Anstey and Peter Robinson.'

'Sir. Detective Sergeant – '

'Dawkins will be fine. Blackie and Dawkins. It has a certain ring to it, don't you think?'

Chris wasn't sure what he was being asked to agree to or confirm. What's come over you, he wanted to ask. Why the sudden change?

'I spoke to the coroner again,' Dawkins said, ignoring Chris's discomfort. 'And the coroner spoke to Superintendent Walsh. A week of asking questions. That's what I've been given. No more manpower and certainly not an official homicide inquiry. You and me, Blackie. Seven days.'

'The coroner?' Chris asked.

'I think Robert Charleton pissed him off. Apparently he's been ringing every day.'

'And you?'

'I thought it was straightforward. Now I'm not so sure.'

Dawkins smiled again. He had a versatile smile. This one was wolfish, with a hint of satisfaction.

FIFTEEN

Chris made sandwiches and packed biscuits, fruit and drinks. He wasn't sure if they would find a place or time to stop for lunch.

On the long, straight highway to Melbourne, Dawkins seemed disinclined to talk. He stared out the window, his expression thoughtful rather than disgruntled or annoyed.

Chris finally broke the silence to ask, 'Did you speak to David Anstey at the funeral?'

What he really meant was, why are we going to see him? Why Anstey in particular?'

'Said hello,' Dawkins replied.

'You know Anstey then?'

'By reputation. He's a patriotic shipping owner, one of a dying breed.'

Chris could have said he knew that much, although he hadn't until Tom had told him.

'Why was he at the funeral?' Dawkins asked. 'Did he know Delraine personally? If so, how well? That's what I'm hoping to find out.'

'I saw Anstey scowling at Tony Parry,' Chris said. 'You know, the head of the Hastings Development Group?'

'I know,' Dawkins said, not in a reprimanding voice, more one of acknowledging that he'd checked out some of the funeral guests, or else knew them by their reputations and made mental notes of who'd been chatting with whom.

'Anstey seemed to be keeping to himself,' Chris said.

'Another reason why I wondered why he'd made the trip. And I looked up the submissions to that consultative committee. Most of them are publicly available. Anyone can read them. But not his.'

His father would have liked David Anstey, Chris thought. He would have looked past Anstey's unkempt appearance to the man behind it. They would have recognised something in each other which there was no need to put into words. They would also have recognised a difference – Chris's father having remained all his life an able-bodied seaman – Anstey having risen from that position to chief engineer, then owner of a shipping company.

Anstey hadn't bothered dressing up for a visit from the police. And his hair, Chris guessed, was the type that sprang into untidy tendrils five minutes after it was combed. He thought of Brian Laidlaw and smiled to himself.

They were sitting in the pleasant, airy front room of a Federation cottage, within walking distance of the pilots administration building.

Dawkins said, 'Your submission to the consultative committee on the new container port proposals hasn't been made public.'

Anstey looked at Dawkins as though he'd just made a statement to the effect that the sea was salty.

Dawkins ignored his expression and asked why he'd put in a submission.

'For Thelma. For my wife's sake.'

'Did Thelma ask you to?'

'Thelma's dead. She was Rosemary Delraine's cousin. I thought you knew that. Why else would you be here?'

It wasn't a good beginning. Chris wondered why Dawkins hadn't asked a few general questions, eased his way in.

'Who gave you permission to make a confidential submission?' Dawkins asked.

'The committee chair, Eric Finlay.'

'Why?'

'That's my business.'

'Not if it's part of the inquiry into Captain Delraine's death.'

Anstey stared at Dawkins. When he spoke, his voice was cold. 'My late wife was an environmental activist, which, if you'd done your homework, you would already know. It was in her memory that I made my submission.'

'Then why not make it public?'

'As I said, that's my business. It will be part of the public record, only not just yet.'

'Did Eric Finlay understand your reasons?'

'He accepted them.'

'Do you share your wife's views Mr Anstey?'

Chris expected a quick reply to the question, but Anstey took his time before saying, 'With some qualifications, yes.'

It was another house without a woman, the difference being that evidence of a shared life was everywhere – in a tapestry wall-hanging, in the smell and essence of the place. Anstey looked to be retiring age, but perhaps he would resist retirement for as long as he could.

Anstey took a deep breath, then began delivering a lecture about the sorry state of coastal shipping, how the number of Australian flag ships had shrunk almost to zero, how indifferent and short-sighted governments on both sides had allowed a valuable industry to be destroyed.

Australian coastal shipping companies had nothing to gain from the construction of a big new container port, either at Hastings, or half way between Melbourne and Geelong. Anstey added that his ships were small enough to get in and out of the heads without further dredging.

Dawkins waited politely till he'd finished before asking, 'Which proposal do you think the government will back?'

'The Coalition's already come out in support of Hastings.'

'And Labor, if they get back in?'

'I'd say 50/50 at the moment, but leaning towards Bay West.'

'What sort of a person is Rosemary Delraine?'

If Dawkins expected Anstey to be disconcerted by the change of subject, then he was disappointed.

'Tough,' Anstey said composedly. 'Ambitious, independent.'

'She didn't look like that at the funeral.'

'I paid my respects for Thelma's sake. To tell you the truth I didn't really notice what she looked like.'

'Did Rosemary and your wife get on?'

'Well enough.'

'Why didn't the Delraines have children?'

'It wasn't something Rosemary talked about, or not to Thelma anyway.'

'Rosemary would have spent a lot of time alone?'

'She often went home.'

'What do you think of her brothers?'

'I never had much to do with them.'

'Who have you spoken to about Captain Delraine's death?'

'My son and daughter.'

'Other relatives?'

'No one from my wife's side of the family. I put up with Rosemary for Thelma's sake. Now I don't have to any longer.'

Was that the reason why Anstey had gone to Delraine's funeral? Chris thought it was what he wanted them to believe.

'She'll be a rich woman,' Dawkins said.

'I doubt if it will make her happy.'

'Why do you dislike Tony Parry?'

Anstey looked uncomfortable. He blinked rapidly and two patches of purplish red appeared below his cheekbones.

'Parry's a development cowboy,' he said.

'Did you speak to him at the funeral yesterday?'

For a moment it looked as though Anstey wasn't going to reply, then he said, 'Tony Parry has no shame and no conscience. He insulted Thelma. When he learnt of her involvement with the environment groups opposed to the Hastings development, he rang her up and abused her. He called her a gullible fool. He insulted our son Neil as well. That didn't matter. Neil could take it, but Thelma, she – she'd already been diagnosed.'

Anstey's voice broke, then he rallied. 'I rang Parry back and gave him a piece of my mind.'

'And yesterday?' Dawkins repeated.

'I stayed away from him and he stayed away from me.'

When Dawkins thanked Anstey for his time and said he might want to talk to him again, Anstey's response was an indifferent shrug.

Dawkins rang Eric Finlay from the car. Somewhat to Chris's surprise, he was put straight through.

Dawkins introduced himself, then asked, 'Why hasn't David Anstey's submission to your committee been made public?'

The Sergeant listened to Finlay's reply, then asked, 'At whose request?' Then, 'Are there others?'

He was silent for a few moments before putting another question. 'When will that be?'

After he'd ended the call, Dawkins turned to Chris.

'He said that it was Anstey's request and he could see no reason for refusing.'

'But it's unusual, surely, when all the other submissions are publicly available.'

'We don't know that.'

'What did Finlay say when you asked him?'

'That it wasn't any of my business. Once the committee's finished taking submissions, then they'll all be published.'

'Why didn't you ask about Delraine's resignation?'

'I was going to, then I decided that question would be better asked face to face.'

So you can tell if he's lying, Chris thought, but he

didn't say the words aloud.

When Dawkins asked Chris what he'd thought of Anstey, Chris replied, 'He's an impressive man.'

'Do you think he's telling the truth?'

'About what?'

'His involvement with Rosemary Delraine and her family.'

After a moment, Chris said, 'I think he knows more than he's letting on.'

The receptionist at the pilots administration office let the two police officers know by her tone of voice and flicker of her large blue eyes that their visit was unwelcome. She told them the CEO was in a meeting.

Dawkins had said to Chris, while they walked round the corner from David Anstey's house to the office, 'We've got a bit of time before meeting Robinson. Why don't we just turn up?'

Chris had hidden his surprise.

'While we're waiting,' Dawkins told the receptionist, 'I'd like to ask you a few questions, please.'

The receptionist frowned, pressed a button on her desk, and said, 'George. Can you take over for – ' she shot Dawkins another swift, assessing glance – 'five minutes?'

Chris thought the receptionist was very self-possessed, since she could not be more than twenty. She took them into a small office, bare except for two chairs and a table, a water jug and several drinking glasses. She had a model's haughty stride. Perhaps modelling classes had preceded a receptionist's course. He couldn't help comparing her to Anthea, also tall, long-legged. But there the likeness ended.

Dawkins said, 'Let's start with your name, Miss - '

'Langtree. Bryony Langtree.'

'Miss Langtree. When did you first hear that Captain Delraine was dead?'

'When I got to work in – the morning after. Mr Bennett called us all together for a meeting in his room.'

'When was that?'

'About ten-thirty.'

Bryony explained the CEO's instructions that all calls regarding Captain Delraine's death be put straight through to him, and that on no account should any of the staff attempt to answer questions from the media.

'So between nine in the morning, when you got to work, up until ten-thirty, you were answering the phone and passing on the calls?'

Bryony nodded.

Bennett rang before Dawkins could ask any more questions.

'I find this very irregular, Sergeant,' he said, after he'd led the way to his office.

Bennett was again immaculately turned out. Chris told himself that he'd expect the CEO of a company with a proud tradition to look the part, but there was something more to Bennett's appearance than that. Chris was reminded of the board's chairman and their private conversation in the pilots centre dining-room. Though the two men weren't similar to look at – Bennett was shorter and more lightly built – something in their appearance and demeanour was the same.

Bennett didn't invite them to sit down, or

offer them anything to drink. 'You should not have interviewed my receptionist without my permission,' he said sharply. 'And frankly, I don't know what you're doing here.'

Dawkins could have argued. Instead he asked where Bennett had been on the night Delraine had drowned.

'Of what possible relevance can that be?'

'Just answer the question, please.'

Bennett seemed to realise that being obstructive would only prolong the interview and said he'd taken his wife and mother-in-law to dinner.

'It was her – my mother-in-law's - birthday.'

Convenient, Chris thought, keeping his expression neutral, though Bennett, after a brief introductory nod, ignored him.

When Dawkins asked what he thought of Captain Delraine, the CEO looked affronted all over again.

'What do you mean?'

'Your opinion of him.'

'His death was a tragic accident. Captain Delraine will be sorely missed.'

'How often did you and Captain Delraine meet?'

'We'd met once or twice, that's all.'

Dawkins asked for details and was told about the last AGM.

'He wasn't one to drop into the office?'

'No.'

'Which of the pilots do that?'

'I don't see that that's any of your business.'

Dawkins persisted and was told that the CEO had met Delraine at the operations centre. It had been a

Sunday, not long after Bennett's appointment. Delraine had just come off a launch.

'I nodded to Captain Delraine and we said hello.'

Dawkins kept his voice mild and uninflected. 'That's all, just hello?' he asked.

Bennett looked as though he was going to object again, but he shook his head and replied, 'I might have mentioned the weather, how it was a bit rough.'

'What did Delraine say to that?'

'I can't remember.'

'How did you know he'd just come off a launch?' Dawkins continued evenly.

'I saw the Captain through the control room windows. They look straight onto the jetty.'

'The dispatch officer told you who it was?'

'He said, "That's Captain Delraine coming in."'

'Did he sound relieved?'

Bennett stared at Dawkins. 'What do you mean?'

Dawkins stared back. Chris noticed that he was standing squarely on both feet as though ready for a physical challenge. His hands were by his sides, not clenched, but Chris could see the tension in them.

'What was his tone of voice?'

'I don't see the point of your question,' Bennett said.

'But you knew Captain Delraine was living at the centre.'

'Temporarily.'

'And the reason why.' Dawkins's voice was steely now, unwilling to give an inch.

'I wasn't told the details.'

'Had there been complaints?'

'What kind of complaints? Who from?'

'From the other pilots.'

'No.'

'The board's chairman?'

'Of course not!'

'Outside the service?'

'Nobody complained.'

'Do you get on well with Ivan Southeby?

'Of course I do.'

Bennett's expression remained superior, but he was beginning to get rattled.

'Would you have expected Captain Delraine to leave a suicide note?'

'Why are you asking me?'

'For the coroner's report.'

'I suppose there are plenty who don't leave a note,' Bennett said.

'About seventy per cent.'

'There you are then.'

'Why didn't you like Captain Delraine?'

'I never said that!'

'But you don't deny you're angry.'

'I'm angry with your line of questioning. Why bring up matters that can't possibly be relevant? It's in everyone's interests to get this tidied up as soon as possible.'

Chris thought the CEO's choice of words was interesting. Who was 'everyone'? What did 'tidied up' mean?

Bennett's phone rang. He looked up and said, 'This is an urgent call.'

And you arranged that too, Chris thought.

The rest of the administrative staff seemed a pretty ordinary bunch. They could have worked for any medium-sized company, anywhere in Melbourne. Chris got no sense of that personal involvement and loyalty he'd felt at the operations centre and from Alex at the workshop. Perhaps you had to be on the spot, by the harbour, watching the gales blow in from the south-west, the swell that could grow from negligible to mountainous in the twinkling of an eye. Perhaps you had to watch the pilots take off in all weathers, with their drivers and their crew.

The young clerical officers stared at Dawkins incredulously when he asked them what they'd thought of Captain Delraine. None admitted to having met or spoken to him.

The IT specialist was too busy to spare more than a few minutes. He said of course the company's systems were secure. The accountant was conveniently on leave.

They could come back, but Chris knew what the accountant would say. The company's books were perfectly in order. Captain Robinson's final payment was underway.

On his second trip to Brighton, Chris noticed more than he had the first time, or perhaps it would be more accurate to say that he noticed different things. He noticed the way the clouds hung on 'his' side of the bay, and the way the heads were the very faintest pencil line, disappearing then appearing again on the horizon. Port Phillip Bay was a huge tilting silver plate – he'd read that somewhere – he thought an artist might have said it. A person could sit and watch the light all day, how it travelled, where it stopped.

It was ironic to think that this vast expanse of water was too shallow for tankers and container ships, except for a narrow, winding channel that followed an ancient glacier. And even that wasn't deep enough. It was a kind of cosmic joke, if you believed in such things, which Chris told himself he didn't.

During the drive across the city, Dawkins had commented on the pilots' CEO.

'A slippery customer.'

'But very well turned out.'

'Oh, he knows how to put on a performance.'

Chris thought again of Bennett and Southeby with their heads together and said, 'Maybe it comes with the job.'

They ate their lunch sitting at a picnic table overlooking the bay. It was Dawkins' choice. Chris sat with his back to the sea and hoped Dawkins wouldn't comment on this.

The park he'd chosen was a long narrow strip, mainly grass and bushes, with a few sorry-looking eucalypts. Port Phillip Bay, this side of it, seemed tame. No doubt storm waves crashed against the pylons and the jetties, but on a day like this, practically windless, it seemed the mild shorebreak would never have any more force behind it than it did at present.

Chris noticed that the Sergeant's eyes were the same grey-green-blue as the water.

When they'd finished, he surprised Chris by pulling a set of keys from his pocket and saying, 'We're still early for Robinson. Let's have a look at Delraine's house.'

Of course, if this had been a murder inquiry, a

scene-of-crime team would have been through the house. Dawkins had arranged for someone from the nearest police station to look for a suicide note, but as far as Chris was aware, there'd been no more systematic search than that.

He reminded himself of this as he walked from room to room, getting the look of them fixed in his mind. The house had been completely cleared. Situated one street back from the sea, and a fashionable address, no doubt it would fetch a good price, but it hadn't been put on the market yet.

Not only were there no papers, letters or personal items of any kind; there was no desk, bureau or cupboard in which they might have been kept. Chris noticed scratch marks on the dining room floor that looked as though they'd been made by dragging something heavy.

Had the marks been made by removalists? When exactly had the furniture been taken?

In the kitchen, Chris opened built-in cupboards one by one, wondering if the Delraines had done much cooking. Somehow he couldn't picture Rosemary with a recipe book and three pots on the stove. He recalled William at the pilots centre, William's pride and grief.

Chris drank water from his cupped hands while Dawkins checked drawers, searching for some small item that had been overlooked.

They locked up behind them and walked out to the car.

When Chris asked what he thought had happened to the furniture, Dawkins said gruffly, 'In storage. Or she's taken it to Hastings with her.'

Peter Robinson led the way down a narrow corridor to a sitting room at the back of his house.

When Dawkins had introduced himself, Robinson had looked at him soberly and given Chris the briefest of nods.

The house was darker than Chris remembered. In the dimness, he was aware of the way Dawkins squared his shoulders and his stumpy walk.

'What do you think of the proposal to build a container port at Bay West?' Dawkins asked as soon as they were seated around a low coffee table.

Robinson looked relieved, as though he'd been expecting a different question altogether.

'It has some merits,' he said carefully.

'Which are?'

'Easier access to the south and west of Melbourne. Cost.'

'Cheaper than the Hastings option?'

'Considerably.'

'And the dredging?'

'Both developments would require dredging.'

Robinson pressed his lips together as if trying to contain himself, then burst out in an angry voice, 'There'll be plenty of jobs building the bloody thing. But what if the new generation of container ships don't come? What if the companies decide Australia's too far away and the markets are too small? Billions of dollars will be wasted, and the bay wrecked for nothing.'

'Wrecked?'

'Port Phillip Bay's had as much as it can stand, and Hastings would be ruined.'

'What was Captain Delraine's opinion?'

Robinson blinked a few times, looking as though he regretted his outburst. When he spoke again, he had his voice under control.

'Fred was concerned about environmental damage.'

'Which option did he think would be worse?'

'Hastings, probably.'

'Was Captain Delraine under pressure from anyone on the consultative committee?'

'To do what?

'Pressure from Eric Finlay?'

'Well, he's chair of it. Fred wouldn't have told me if he was under pressure. That wasn't his way.'

'Did you get the impression from talking to Captain Delraine that he had problems with the committee?'

'What problems?'

'I'm asking you, Mr Robinson.'

'Fred didn't mention any.'

And you were too self-absorbed to notice, Chris thought. You only think about yourself.

Dawkins asked what effect it would have on the pilots if Hastings went ahead.

'Pilots are compulsory for any commercial vessel over thirty-five metres, except for those whose masters are exempt.'

'What about their personal lives?'

'They'd build an operations centre down there.'

'Some might not like being so far from Melbourne.'

Robinson's expression changed. He smiled and looked much younger. 'I wouldn't have minded,' he said. 'It would have been a relief.'

'Did Captain Delraine tell you he was intending to

resign from the committee?'

'No.'

Was Robinson's reply too abrupt, too sudden? Chris wished the interview was being recorded.

'What about pressure from Rosemary Delraine?' Dawkins asked.

'What pressure?'

'Her family comes from the Hastings area.'

'Fred wouldn't bow to pressure like that.'

'Not even if he was desperate to save his marriage?'

'No.'

'Captain Delraine must have known his health problems made him vulnerable to criticism.'

'Fred wouldn't have minded leaving the service, but he wanted to do it in his own way and in his own time.'

'By walking into the sea?'

'Maybe. I don't know!' Robinson's reply came out like a strangled cry.

When Dawkins asked what he'd been doing on the night of Delraine's death, he said he'd been at home.

'Did anybody ring or call in?'

'No one,' Robinson replied after a slight hesitation.

'Did you know that Ivan Southeby submitted an environmental impact statement in support of another round of dredging?'

Robinson shrugged as if to say, what of it?

'Might he have been paid to do that?'

Robinson's lip curled in a sneer. 'Bribed, you mean?' he said. 'It wouldn't surprise me.'

'You don't have a high opinion of Southeby?'

'Would you, in my position?'

'What about David Anstey? Where does he fit in?'

'Anstey wants to promote Australian coastal shipping. A true David among the Goliaths.'

'Do you know him well?'

'No, but Fred did. They've known each other for years.'

'How did Rosemary and Captain Delraine meet?'

At a party at the Queenscliff marina. Rosemary's brothers are keen sailors, particularly Ian. They had a big party down there and invited the pilots. Fred went along.'

'Was that unusual?'

'What do you mean?'

'The impression I've gained is that Captain Delraine wasn't a party-goer.'

'Not in recent years. He was different then. We all were.'

'Did you go to the party?' Dawkins asked.

'I was invited. Like I said, it was a general invitation. But no. I can't remember why now. I was probably working. I remember the occasion because Fred fell in love.'

'What went wrong?'

'It's impossible to tell, really, from the outside. I mean, who understands a marriage except for the people in it? Even they don't understand it half the time.'

'You must have some idea.'

'They weren't able to have children and I think that divided them. But Fred had very little experience with women. I don't think he'd ever really had a girlfriend before he met Rosemary. He'd been in the navy since he was sixteen. Duty and service were what mattered to him, and leaving an heir behind him, fathering a son.'

By the time Dawkins asked Robinson about the fishing boat incident, Robinson had worked off some of his angry energy. He responded more calmly than when Chris had talked to him on his own.

'If I hadn't altered course I would have hit them. I was punished for disobeying the ship's master, but at least I haven't got dead men on my conscience.'

'Punished?' Dawkins asked mildly.

'I'm sure your Constable here has told you that I was set up.'

'You didn't have to lose your temper with the master.'

'What would you have done?'

'I don't know.'

Dawkins' voice was still mild, low pitched. Chris thought he was telling the truth. He couldn't imagine what he would do, faced with Robinson's dilemma.

'Did any of your colleagues back you up?'

'Fred did.'

'No one else?'

Robinson frowned and shook his head.

'What did Captain Delraine do on your behalf?'

'I already told *him*.' Robinson's nod in Chris's direction was brief and dismissive.

'I'm asking you to tell me.'

'Fred spoke to Southeby, who did bugger all.'

'Did he speak to other pilots too?'

'I think he did. He – Fred didn't name names. He didn't have any good news for me and he didn't want to give me more bad news.'

'Meaning?'

'Meaning none of the bastards backed me up. They were happy to get rid of me.'

The paranoid glitter came back into Robinson's eyes. He leant forward and glared at Dawkins, who responded calmly. 'Did that worry Captain Delraine?'

'Of course it did. Fred liked to believe the best about people, but they disappointed him.'

'And what about his wife's family?'

'He'd given up on them.'

Dawkins seemed to be giving this comment careful thought, but instead of following up with more questions about Rosemary's brothers, he asked Robinson about his payment from the pilot company.

Robinson brought out his solicitor's letters and the accountant's replies. There'd been no progress. He told Dawkins he was annoyed about it, but not worried.

When they were walking back to the car, Dawkins said, 'You suspected that Bennett, or Bennett and the accountant might be taking a cut before dividends were paid?'

Chris wondered why Dawkins hadn't asked Robinson about this directly. 'I don't have any evidence,' he said. 'Robinson's final payment seems to be a long time coming. And there's – I put it in my report – there was also a bill for some "special maintenance" at the pilots' workshop which Delraine came down to ask about.'

Dawkins nodded. 'Thanks for that,' he said. 'I mean those reports.'

SIXTEEN

Dawkins made himself comfortable in the car's passenger seat and wound the window down. He switched his phone to speaker before ringing the board's chairman.

'I've already made a full statement to the coroner,' Southeby said. 'Captain Delraine's death was a tragic accident and he'll be sorely missed.'

Chris pictured Southeby sitting back in his chair, perfectly relaxed. He'd be wearing a well-cut suit. Chris imagined a row of them hanging in a linen press.

'Was Peter Robinson forced to retire from the pilot company?' Dawkins asked.

'The inquiry found against him.'

'That isn't what I asked.'

'Mr Robinson abused the ship's master, swore at him repeatedly.' Southeby's voice went up a notch. 'Once the inquiry had made its decision there was nothing I could do. Will that be all Sergeant? I'm due at a meeting.'

'Just a few more questions,' Dawkins said, with a lift of his chin in Chris's direction. 'Why did you submit an environmental effects statement supporting the need for further dredging in Port Phillip Bay?'

There was silence on Southeby's end. Perhaps he was adjusting to a question he had not expected.

'Dredging's necessary in the shipping channel. Everyone knows that.'

'Who asked you to submit a statement?'

'That's none of your business.'

'When a man dies in suspicious circumstances, then it is my business.'

'Suspicious circumstances? Is that what the coroner's calling it?'

Chris felt sure that Bennett would have phoned Southeby as soon as they left his office. But why wouldn't Southeby welcome a proper investigation into Delraine's death? What did he have to hide?

'About the container port proposals,' Dawkins asked, stolidly determined, 'which option do you prefer?'

'There are arguments for and against both.'

'But Hastings is much further from Melbourne. You'd have to move your operations centre.'

'We could build a second one.'

'What if both proposals are rejected?'

'That won't happen.'

'Who'll replace Captain Delraine on the consultative committee?'

'It hasn't been decided yet. Now I'm sorry, Sergeant, but I really have to go.'

Dawkins looked up another number.

'Tell me this,' Celia Robinson said in answer to his question, 'would you stay in a marriage that was hell every minute of the day?'

Dawkins asked, 'When did you and your husband separate, Mrs Robinson?'

Celia named a date.

'Why then?'

'Let's say something occurred – the straw that broke the camel's back.'

'What was that?'

'It's personal and I'm not obliged to tell you.'

'I understand that you and Rosemary Delraine were friends.'

'Friends?' Celia laughed. 'We spent time with one another because our husbands were friends.'

'Why don't you like Mrs Delraine?'

'Within five minutes of meeting Rosie, she'll tell you her family's one of the oldest in the Hastings region.'

'Why did she marry Captain Delraine?'

'Maybe she was in love with him. Why don't you ask her?'

'Do you believe your husband was responsible for the accident with the fishing boat, Mrs Robinson?'

'He said it was a set-up and for all I know it was.'

'But?'

'My guess is he had it coming to him. My ex is a giant pain in the arse.'

Dawkins ended the call, then he sighed and said, 'Maybe she knows more than she's letting on.' He turned to Chris and brightened, his voice becoming lighter.

'Delraine's phone may be at the bottom of the Rip, but his phone records aren't. I'll put in a request to the phone companies when we get back. I should have thought of it before.'

'Good idea,' Chris said.

Dawkins suggested that they return to the street where the Delraines had lived and try speaking to their neighbours.

Chris had had enough of Melbourne, but he nodded, not wanting to object.

More than half of the doors Chris knocked on were

opened by a man or woman of retirement age. It clearly wasn't one of those streets that stood empty from eight till six on weekdays.

One neighbour, who'd watched Rosemary Delraine's furniture being loaded, recalled the name of the storage firm printed in big letters on the side of the van. He also recalled the approximate date, which was a week after the Captain began living at the pilots' centre. Rosemary hadn't wasted time.

'I guess Mrs Delraine had a lot of furniture,' Chris said mildly.

'I was never in the house.'

'You didn't get along with your neighbours?'

'I didn't say that.' The man pressed his lips together, then appeared to relent. 'If this is about that unfortunate drowning, you'd better come inside.'

The man walked ahead of Chris to a sunroom opening onto an attractive garden.

'My wife's over minding the grandchildren,' he said, as though needing to supply an explanation for her absence.

'I said we were never invited to their house, and it's true, we weren't. They were a cut above. Or she was. The Captain would smile and say hello if he passed you in the street. She never did. My wife went there, collecting for the Red Cross. She told me about it afterwards. She knocked on the door. No one came to answer it, but she heard shouting from inside.'

'When was this?'

'Six months ago? Red Cross month is March.'

'And your wife was sure it was Captain and Mrs Delraine arguing?'

'Quite sure.'
'Did she hear what they were arguing about?'
'Money,' the neighbour said.

SEVENTEEN

Chris had time to reflect on Rosemary Delraine and her brothers during the long drive from Queenscliff to Hastings on the shores of Westernport.

They talked about what they hoped to get from Robert and Ian Charleton and Dawkins said he would play it by ear.

When Dawkins changed the subject and began speaking about their interviews of the day before, Chris raised his suspicions about Bennett and Southeby. He spoke hesitantly, realising that he had little more to go on than a delay in Robinson's payment and the feeling he'd had watching the two men deep in conversation after Delraine's funeral.

He reminded Dawkins about Southeby's payment for making a statement favourable to dredging.'

'If it's true,' Dawkins said.

'The Crikey journalist seemed pretty confident.'

'Did Bennett submit an environmental effects statement?'

'No. I checked.'

The night before, Dawkins had spoken to as many of the pilots as he could get hold of. They'd been saddened by Fred Delraine's death and had expressed their sadness appropriately. They'd either said they were neutral with regard to dredging, or considered it necessary.

Bennett was an employee of the company. If Southeby had accepted a bribe to submit a statement favourable to dredging, then Bennett was hardly in a position to complain. But Chris had the feeling – so strong as to be a conviction – that Bennett was the kind of man to use this knowledge to benefit himself.

How did this tie in with Captain Delraine drowning? Chris recalled again the bill for special maintenance Delraine had asked about at the workshop. He still had no idea how Delraine had got to hear of it.

He concentrated on negotiating traffic, then the long highway with farmland on either side, the half dead mining towns, the sea that he fancied he could smell, but didn't have to look at.

After a long silence, Dawkins asked, 'What did you find out about the family?'

'The pastoral property goes back three generations. Rosemary's father died a couple of years ago and left a substantial share portfolio as well as land. He invested in companies with interests and holdings in the Hastings area such as Bluescope Steel and Esso Australia.'

'What about the mother?'

'She died quite young. Of cancer.'

Chris's voice caught. Dawkins glanced at him, then away. He said he'd spoken to the officer in charge at Hastings police station and told him they'd be making the trip. The officer had said that wouldn't be a problem, but Dawkins had got the feeling that their presence wouldn't be welcome. Relaying the conversation to Chris, the Sergeant's voice hardened, and his grey-green eyes took on an expression both of wariness and determination.

The real estate agent looked affronted. The Charleton property wasn't for sale and never would be.

'How can you be sure?' asked Dawkins.

'I know the family.'

The phone rang on the agent's desk and he turned away pointedly to answer it.

Dawkins cocked his head towards the door. They had no authority to demand answers to their questions. Officially, any inquiry into Captain Delraine's death had to be explained as gathering information for the coroner.

Chris drove a few blocks then parked again, noting the prominent sign of the Hastings Development Group and its colourful shopfront.

There was a great deal of industrial development around Hastings. It was one thing to look at Google maps and another to be there on the ground. The development stood on what would once have been farming land, claimed by settlers and squatters in the nineteenth century, pushing out, perhaps murdering the original inhabitants.

Some businesses had made submissions to the inquiry into the new container port. The Hastings Development Group had made submissions on behalf of local businesses as well.

They ordered lunch at a small café and opted to sit outside.

'How many estate agents did you say there were?' Dawkins asked while they waited for their food.

'Eight. Seven in High Street.' Chris raised his head and looked along it. 'And one out on the highway.'

'Helluva lot for a town this size. And they all

said the same thing over the phone? The Charleton property's not for sale?'

'If it was for sale it'd be listed online.'

'I know that Blackie, but it doesn't hurt to check.'

Ian Charleton owned an ocean-going yacht. Chris had looked up the registration details and recorded them on his phone. He'd also downloaded a photo, not of Ian's boat, but a similar one.

Dawkins leant across and let out a soft hiss.

'How much did you say that's worth?'

'I didn't, but about three million.'

Chris felt a sudden warmth for Dawkins. They were both out of their depth with that degree of wealth, but the consciousness of this made them stubborn.

The slanting light of High Street stopped at the Sergeant's suit, stopped more decidedly, Chris thought, than at the clothing of another man. Would you pick them for detectives? Chris was not wearing his uniform. He gave his jacket sleeve a surreptitious tug.

Inside his suit, Dawkins sat solid and four-square, munching on his sandwich. He gave a particular meaning to the verb 'to munch'.

Light slanted down between the buildings much as it did in a city, creating shadows at noon on a mild spring day. Chris pictured High Street Hastings with twice, three times the number of restaurants and cafes, Hastings prosperous and shining. People would be sitting at outside tables eating fancy lunches; music would be playing; there would be a well-fed air, and perhaps, to those who knew how to look for it, an air of having won a race.

Chris studied the Hastings Development Group

shopfront. Large photographs filled the window, in the centre a smiling group of men and women surrounding the director, Tony Parry. Chris had stayed up late reading the submissions the group had made to the consultative committee.

The submissions were impressive, not least because they spoke for a community, a collection of businesses and farming people, making a plea – Chris did not think the word exaggerated – for their future.

On the other side, the environment groups were just as sincere and just as impressive, in their way. But the environment groups were in something of a quandary, in that one or other of the proposals would be chosen. For them, Chris guessed, it was a matter of picking the lesser of two evils. Tom Maloney understood that and it caused him anguish.

In the submissions Chris had read, there was nothing comparable to the Hastings Development Group on the side favouring Bay West. Geelong should benefit economically, but the more Chris thought about it, the more he realised that in terms of economic benefit for the people of Geelong, there was no guarantee.

They were early for their appointment with the Charletons, but Dawkins ate as though eating was some kind of obligation, a chore to be got through as quickly as possible.

There was no feeling of homeliness about him, no feeling that he came from a home and returned there in the evenings. Chris would have liked to ask, but was aware that personal questions would be unwelcome. He didn't want to upset the fragile balance they'd found at the Brewhouse, and maintained through a day together in Melbourne.

They were going to meet, for the second time, a family of three adults tied to one another – a widow who had just lost her husband, and two brothers who, Chris guessed, were guarding her.

About to face the Charletons on their home ground, Chris was aware that Dawkins had made a personal commitment, a solitary commitment that yet included him.

As they approached the front door, there was a sudden chorus of barking dogs, followed by a shout from the back of the house.

When Robert Charleton answered the door, he allowed himself to look mildly annoyed. They were meant to notice his good manners in masking this, Chris thought.

'It's good of you to come all this way, Sergeant,' he said in an even voice, 'but I really don't know what more we can say.'

Robert led the way to a living-room where Ian and Rosemary were sitting on a couch, near enough to touch, but not touching. Rosemary was carefully made up. Ian shot her a quick worried glance, which Chris felt sure he and Dawkins were not meant to see.

The house was beautifully proportioned, its wide verandas covered with wisteria so old its main stems were as big as tree trunks. Spring had made a tentative beginning on the Bellarine Peninsula, but here, a little inland, where the soil was rich and there'd been good winter rains, everything was an emerald green seldom seen in Australia. Sheep and lambs filled the paddocks;

daffodils and jonquils lined the gravel paths.

Now he was there, Chris understood how proud all three might be of their inheritance, how selling land in order to take advantage of rising prices might be the last thing on the brothers' minds.

It was cold inside. Both Robert and Ian wore jackets and Rosemary a woollen suit.

Dawkins greeted Rosemary and Ian, then asked, his eyes on Rosemary, 'What do you think happened to your husband's keys?'

Robert smiled as though this question was one he might expect from an unintelligent plodder. He answered for his sister. 'Does that matter now?'

Dawkins ignored him. 'The keys weren't on Captain Delraine's body, or in his room. Where do you think they might be?'

Rosemary said, in a voice just above a whisper, 'I don't know.'

'I don't believe there's any mystery, Sergeant,' Robert said smoothly. 'They fell out of my brother-in-law's pocket when he was in the water.'

Again Dawkins addressed Rosemary. 'How did Captain Delraine seem to you the last time you spoke?'

Rosemary blinked. 'He seemed – distressed, as I told you on the phone the day he – the day my husband's body was found.'

'Do you believe your husband killed himself Mrs Delraine?'

'It's terrible to think of, but – '

'It's inappropriate to interrogate my sister at this time,' Robert said sharply. 'She's been through enough.'

'Did you and Captain Delraine leave your Brighton

home together?'

'Not – 'Robert began.

'I asked Mrs Delraine.'

'Freddy left first. I stayed behind to – I wasn't sure – I didn't want to wait there on my own so I came here.'

'How long did you wait?'

'I – 'Rosemary glanced at Robert, who said, 'I can't see that that matters now.'

'You arranged for your furniture to be moved a week after Captain Delraine left.' Dawkins glanced from Rosemary to Robert, and said, 'Or perhaps it was you who did that.'

Robert said coldly, 'My sister did. Not that it's any of your business.'

'How long do you intend to remain here, Mrs Delraine?'

'My sister will stay as long as she likes. As you can see, there's plenty of room.'

Dawkins ignored this and changed the subject. 'Which option do you favour for a container port, Hastings or Bay West?'

'We grow crops and raise livestock,' Ian said. 'The port facilities at Hastings are perfectly adequate for our needs.'

Chris thought it was interesting that Robert let his brother answer that question. Perhaps they'd anticipated it and decided in advance.

'Do you have a preference?'

'There are two sides to it. There's financial gain in terms of land values. Local businesses and industries will benefit if Hastings goes ahead. But the whole region will change dramatically. Think of the massive increase in road transport, for one thing. The destruction of important wetlands and other environmental damage.'

Chris was worried that Dawkins was showing his hand and getting nothing in return.

'I understand your boat's berthed at the marina. What's it called?'

'The *Aeola*. She's in dry dock at the moment.'

Robert and Rosemary were both watching Ian. If there'd been any evidence that Fred Delraine had been on board recently, it wouldn't be there now.

With mention of his boat, Ian became more lively. He began to speak about the Hastings marina and the history of the port. Chris felt sure he was on first name terms with every boat-owner who berthed there. A shadow passed across Robert's face. He didn't interrupt, but it seemed to Chris that the digression wasn't part of his plan and he was willing Ian to shut up.

When Ian said. 'Sailing is my passion,' Rosemary winced ever so slightly, but Chris caught the movement.

'What do you think of the chairman of the pilots board?' Dawkins asked Robert.

'He seems a capable man.'

'Did you ever speak to him about Captain Delraine's problems?'

'What problems?'

'Personal. Family.'

Robert looked affronted. 'No.'

'What about you, Mrs Delraine? Did you speak to Mr Southeby?'

'Oh, no,' Rosemary said. It seemed to Chris that she was hanging on by a thread.

'Did Captain Delraine talk to you about his work

on the consultative committee?'

'He – Fred did say that he thought it was getting too much for him.'

'Did he say he was intending to resign?'

'He said he was thinking of it, yes.'

'Did he say why?'

'The travelling was getting too much.'

'The meetings were only once a month.'

'What are all these questions in aid of?' Robert snapped.

'They help to build up a picture of Captain Delraine's last few weeks.'

'But surely the matter is straightforward.' Robert's expression was hard and domineering. 'My brother-in-law drowned himself.'

'Why do you think he did that?'

'Fred had problems, but – '

'But what?'

'I thought he'd cope with them, come through it.'

Dawkins and Robert Charleton held each other's gaze. The interview had become a contest between them. Everyone else in the room was practically forgotten.

Rosemary's expression was closed in, frozen. Ian looked anxious, his lips a thin line.

Robert would stick to his story of suicide and neither of them would say anything to counter or to question it.

Dawkins changed the angle of his questions once again.

'I noticed the pilots' CEO, John Bennett, paying his respects to you at the funeral.'

Robert opened his mouth to speak, but this time Rosemary was quicker. 'Mr Bennett was kind. All of my husband's colleagues have been very kind.'

'Mr Robinson?'

'Poor Mr Robinson. He has troubles of his own, but he's very sad about what happened to Fred.'

Robert asked, in a voice of controlled impatience, when they thought the coroner's report would be ready.

'I don't know,' Dawkins said.

Suddenly he gave a sharp nod at Chris and they got up to go.

Chris wanted to ask about the hasty departure, but he knew the question would be unwelcome. He started the car and negotiated the driveway in silence.

'What did you make of them?' Dawkins asked after they'd turned onto the highway.

It was the same question he'd asked on the evening of the funeral, but this time the Sergeant's intonation was completely different. That night at the Brewhouse he'd been relaxed, pleased with himself, and pleased to have a drinking companion. Now he bit down on the question.

Chris decided on a relatively safe reply. 'Robert didn't like Ian talking about boats. His boat.'

'Do you think we should go and see it?'

'They'll have thought of that. There won't be anything to see. I think *Aeola* must be the feminine form of Aeolus. In Greek mythology Aeolus was the keeper of the winds.'

'A man of many talents.'

Chris went red. He hadn't meant to show off his

knowledge. He was interested in Greek myths. It was unfair of Dawkins to take out his bad mood on him.

'The bastard was laughing at me,' Dawkins said.

'He was laughing at us both.'

'But I was the main target. He's got the other two under his thumb. He wanted to make it obvious that we were wasting our time.'

'Not entirely,' Chris said. He was thinking that it didn't really matter if Robert believed he'd won the round. What mattered was to find physical evidence. They'd already spent two days of the seven talking to people. For all he knew, half of them were lying.

He recalled how slight and scared Rosemary had looked sandwiched between her brothers in the church and the reception afterwards. She would have been told to look natural and relaxed in Robert's house. She'd tried, but hadn't pulled it off.

What had happened to the woman Celia Robinson and others had described? David Anstey had called her 'tough, ambitious, independent'. He'd claimed to have cut off contact with her after his wife died.

'Robert pissed the coroner off,' Dawkins said. 'What's the bet he pissed off Southeby as well.'

'How would he do that?'

'Rung him up and harassed him to push for a finding of suicide.'

'While accidental death would suit the company better,' Chris said. 'You'd think it would suit the family better too.'

'Suicide's more shameful.' Now Dawkins's voice contained a hint of satisfaction. 'He was rubbing his sister's nose in it back there.'

'Why does she put up with it?'

'Good question.'

They sat in silence for some minutes, pondering this. Chris tried to relax his hands on the steering wheel, only then realising just how tense he was. The road was straight, the country flat on either side of it, rising to purple-blue hills where the coal mines were.

Dawkins was staring out the window. He turned to Chris and said, 'You were angry when I told you to look for a note in Delraine's room.'

'I knew there wouldn't be one,' Chris replied with his eyes fixed on the road.

'Why?'

'Because if Delraine committed suicide, he'd do so in such a way as to leave it open for the coroner to bring down a finding of accidental death.'

'For his wife's sake?'

Chris thought before saying, 'Yes. And for Brian Laidlaw. Delraine would not have wanted Brian to think he'd taken that way out.'

'Surly old man.'

'Not when you get to know him. When you get to know him, he's loyal and generous. I'll speak to him again, if you like.'

'Do that, while I'm sorting out the phone records. Hopefully they'll be there when we get back.'

Chris revised his opinion of the Sergeant once again. He was unpredictable. Just when Chris believed he was beginning to understand the man, he felt the ground shifting underneath him.

EIGHTEEN

Dawkins had decided to include all the phone companies, not just Telstra, though Delraine had a Telstra phone. If someone had rung him to request a meeting on the evening he died, and the call was from another mobile, they might be with Optus, Vodaphone, or one of the small carriers.

He hadn't run into any trouble; police requests for metadata had become routine. I could be an imposter, he told Chris indignantly, a member of a drug cartel. The idea made them smile.

When the first batch arrived, Chris tried reading from the screen, but felt himself going cross-eyed before half an hour had passed.

He told Dawkins he'd print out a bundle and take it home to read.

Going through phone records was the last thing Chris felt like doing after the long drive back from Hastings. He felt like a walk to stretch his legs and an early night. He told himself he didn't have the luxury.

He made coffee the way he liked it, with the soy milk scalding hot and a sprinkle of cinnamon. Minnie had suggested once that he ought to buy a coffee machine so he could make frothy cappuccino. He'd never told her, because her suggestion had been made in a spirit of friendliness, that he did not like frothy drinks. He preferred his mug filled up with 'solid liquid', though he knew that there was no such thing.

The print-out looked like an indecipherable jumble of letters and numbers.

He would have liked to tell Minnie about the task he'd taken on. A needle in a haystack she would say with a laugh.

Should he ask Olly for help? Chris had great faith in Olly's technical ability. But that would mean telling Anthea and Olly about the 'case', something he would have to clear with Dawkins now that he and the Sergeant had reached an understanding. Besides, it was too late to go knocking on their door.

Chris took too big a mouthful and burnt the roof of his mouth.

He'd left the curtains open. Somehow the darkness outside helped. He got into a rhythm, finding that it was better if he didn't look at any clocks. He took his watch off and put it in his bedroom drawer.

First thing the next morning, Dawkins called David Anstey. He used the station's landline switched to speakerphone.

'Captain Delraine phoned you a week before he died. Why didn't you tell me when Constable Blackie and I came to see you?'

Anstey didn't sound at all flustered or put out, but replied calmly, 'Fred wanted me to talk to Rosemary.'

'What about?'

'She was pressuring him to agree to a divorce and sell the house.'

'And Delraine didn't want to?'

'That's the thing,' Anstey said. 'It would have been better for him if he'd made a decision, got it over with.'

'Is that what you told him?'

'I tried to.'

'Why was Rosemary in a hurry?'

'She told him she wanted it over and done with.'

'Why you? Why did Captain Delraine ask you to intervene?'

'Because of Thelma. He thought that I might have some influence.'

'What did you think?'

'I thought that he was clutching at straws.'

'Did you speak to Rosemary?'

'I was going to, but then Fred died.'

'Did either of her brothers contact you during that time?'

'No.'

Brendan Hearn was on the consultative committee, a public servant with the finance department. Chris had got his name from Optus the night before and had done a background check.

When Dawkins asked why Delraine had phoned him five days before he drowned, Hearn said, 'The Captain was a good man and now he's dead. Nothing I can say will bring him back.'

'I'm trying to find out why he died.'

There was silence on the other end and Chris thought Hearn might have hung up.

Finally he said, 'There's no choice without moral burden.'

'Were they Captain Delraine's words?'

'More or less.'

'What was he referring to?'

'Fred's problem was that he couldn't make a decision and put the alternatives behind him.'

'Was he referring to the choice of site for the new container port?'

'Amongst other things.'

'What other things?'

When Hearn didn't reply, Dawkins said, 'Captain Delraine was on a consultative committee. It wasn't up to him to make recommendations for or against the different proposals.'

'Don't be naive Sergeant.'

'What do you mean?'

'I mean that Fred was a man of influence, not because he played political games, but because people in power respected his judgment and opinions.'

'By people in power, you mean?

'The Premier, for one.'

'Did Captain Delraine speak to the Premier directly?'

'Not that I'm aware of.'

'Did he tell you he was planning to resign from the committee?'

After a short hesitation, Hearn said, 'Yes, he did.'

'What did he say exactly?'

'I can't remember his exact words. Something along the lines of it was too much for him and he'd had enough.'

'What else did you talk about?'

'It was late at night. Fred sounded sleepy and disoriented. I think he rang for some kind of re-assurance.'

'Re-assurance that resigning was the right thing to do?'

'I tried to give him that.' Hearn sounded tired and bitter.

Dawkins asked him which alternative he favoured, Hastings or Bay West.

'For what it's worth, and speaking financially, since that's my area of expertise, I'd say Bay West. Hastings would be more expensive for road transport, but you wouldn't have the bottlenecks you have now. Money would have to be spent on the east-west link.'

'That would be your department.'

'The different proposals are being costed. But it's not in anybody's interests to have that information leaked half-way through the process.'

'Anyone's?'

'Neither the government's nor the opposition's.'

'Did you speak to Captain Delraine after that late night phone call?

'No.'

'If you recall anything you think might be helpful, please give me a ring.'

Dawkins recited the station's landline and his mobile number before ending the call.

Chris said, 'Delraine must have trusted Hearn to ring him late at night like that.'

'After he'd dosed himself on antihistamines?'

'Do you think Hearn knew about them?'

'Possibly.'

Delraine had made two phone calls to the chair of the committee in the days before he drowned. When Dawkins rang to ask about them, Eric Finlay said that Delraine had called him because he wanted to resign.

'What did Captain Delraine say, exactly?'

'I don't – '

'Surely you remember.'

'Health reasons,' Finlay said.

Chris listened carefully to the chairman's tone of voice. It was deeper than he'd expected. For some reason he'd pictured Finlay as a small man with a high-pitched voice. He could still be small, of course, one of those short men who sang bass in a choir. Chris had found a photograph on the Transport Department website, but it gave no idea of Finlay's height. He looked to be somewhere in his early fifties, though his hair was dark, barely showing any grey, and his face unlined.

'Did you know Captain Delraine's health was poor?' Dawkins asked, frowning at the phone.

'I knew he was living at the pilots centre. I knew he had health issues – in general, not the details.'

'Did you accept the Captain's resignation?'

'I told him he could have more time to think about it.'

'Did he ask for more time?'

'No.'

'Why the second phone call?'

'We had a meeting scheduled for the middle of September. Captain Delraine rang to say he wasn't coming. He said he'd send a formal resignation through the post.'

'What else did you discuss?'

'That was all.'

'Did you receive the resignation letter?'

'No.'

'I'll need a list of the committee members.'

'Why?'

'Do you have a problem with that?'

After a short silence, Finlay said, 'I'll email it to you.'

'I'll need their phone numbers as well. And I need to make an appointment to see you in your office.'

When Finlay started objecting, Dawkins said, 'Let's say tomorrow at eleven.'

Chris made coffee and they drank it on the station's back veranda. He felt gritty-eyed from lack of sleep.

Dawkins was jittery and restless, unable to sit still. 'Maybe we should have just turned up,' he said.

'If Finlay wasn't there, or made some excuse not to see us, it would have been a wasted trip.'

Back at his desk, Chris opened Finlay's email and went through the list of names and numbers. There were eight altogether. There was only one match with the numbers Delraine had called, or belonging to people who'd called him, in the two weeks before he drowned, and that was Brendan Hearn.

'Will we go back earlier?' he asked.

'Not yet,' Dawkins said. 'We'll finish what we've got here first.'

Chris hadn't found Brian Laidlaw's phone number in the lists. He'd sat up till he was cross-eyed looking for it. Did that mean Delraine hadn't phoned Brian? Had they met in person? Chris cursed Brian for his secretiveness, at the same time admiring him for his unswerving loyalty. He'd knocked on the door of Brian's cottage after they'd got back from Hastings; but if Brian was inside, then he hadn't responded. Chris had tried phoning him, but his calls had gone unanswered.

Dawkins' next call was to John Bennett. He

introduced himself, then said, 'Captain Delraine rang you the day before he drowned. What did you talk about? What was the reason for the call?'

'I've answered all your questions, Sergeant. You've no right to keep pestering me.'

If Bennett was surprised by Dawkins' information, then he didn't show it. Chris wondered at the CEO's confidence, that he could immediately sound superior and scornful.

'Why didn't you tell me about the phone call when I came to see you?'

'Because it was nothing to do with Captain Delraine's death.'

'What was it about?'

'Captain Delraine was concerned about Captain Robinson's final payout. I told him the matter was in hand and that Robinson would receive the money shortly.'

'Why the delay?'

'It was a technical matter.'

'What else was Captain Delraine concerned about?'

'I've told you the subject of our conversation.'

Chris recalled Bennett as he'd looked at the funeral, and in his office. He knew how to perform for an audience and did so without conscious effort. Chris wondered who he'd worked for before taking up a position with the pilot company, and told himself he ought to have checked this detail.

'Did you know Captain Delraine intended to resign from the consultative committee?' Dawkins asked.

'I heard something to that effect.'

'From Ivan Southeby?'

Bennett hesitated before saying, 'Yes.'

Chris was thinking that Delraine could have made or received calls on the operation centre's landline. But according to the dispatch officers, the pilots didn't do that. Alison Delraine had been an exception. There were too many possibilities and there was no time to explore them all.

'What about Captain Delraine's company shares and his final payment?' Dawkins asked.

'It will be paid to his widow.'

'When a pilot leaves the company, must he withdraw his shares?'

'Leaves?' Bennett repeated coldly.

'Resigns,' Dawkins said. 'Or dies.'

'When a pilot leaves, his shares go with him. He can't continue to draw a dividend when he's no longer working for the company.'

'How soon must he withdraw them?'

'I'm not sure what length of time is stipulated.'

'Look it up, please. I'll wait.'

Bennett made an angry noise, but came back on the line in less than a minute.

'No length of time is specified.'

'When a pilot dies, does his next-of-kin withdraw his shares?'

'That would be the normal practice, yes.'

'Can you give me an example?'

'What?'

'Of that happening,' Dawkins said patiently.

'I can't think of one off-hand.'

'What changes will it make from your point of view

if the government decides to build a new container port at HastIngs?'

'What?' Bennett sounded as though for once he'd been caught off guard.

'Problems of re-location,' Dawkins suggested mildly.

'Whatever the government's decision, it makes sense for the admin office to remain in Melbourne, and for the operations centre to stay where it is.'

'But surely there'd need to be a second operations centre at Hastings? Staff on the ground to deal with the Hastings Port Authority. Somewhere for the pilots to stay.'

'What are you getting at Sergeant?'

'Nothing complicated. There'd need to be additional staff and capital expenditure. Some devolution of authority.'

'There would be more revenue.'

'Of course. There's that side of things to consider too.'

After ending the call to Bennett, Dawkins spoke to the coroner's office and confirmed that assets could be frozen in a case of suspicious death, or when the coroner's report was pending. If the coroner brought down a finding of suicide or accidental death, then Rosemary Delraine would be free to withdraw her husband's shares and sell the Brighton house.

He said to Chris, with a lift of one eyebrow and a wry half smile, that he should have thought to check this detail earlier. Chris shook his head to try and clear it. He felt as though he and Dawkins were running a one-legged race.

He spent a few minutes looking up Bennett's employment history. Bennett had worked for an international shipping company in Singapore and the Netherlands before returning to Australia.

When Ivan Southeby answered, it sounded as though he'd been expecting Dawkins's call. Perhaps Bennett had warned him.

Whatever the reason, the board's chairman had prepared his answers and they ran smoothly off his tongue.

'I think Captain Delraine wanted my assurance that it was okay to resign from the committee.'

'Why then?'

'Excuse me?'

'Why did Delraine ring you two days before he died? He'd already made up his mind to resign.'

'As I said, he wanted re-assurance.'

'What did you tell him?'

'It wasn't necessary to have a pilot representative on the committee.'

'So Captain Delraine's not going to be replaced?'

After a short pause, Southeby said, 'It hasn't been decided yet.'

'Did you discuss the outcome of the government's decision? What it would mean for your company?'

'Not then.'

'But you had discussed it earlier.'

'In general terms. It was too early to be making plans.'

'What about the dredging?'

'What about it?'

'You and Captain Delraine held opposing views.'

'Who told you that?'

'Did you resolve your differences before Captain Delraine died?'

Southeby made an angry noise before hanging up.

Chris suspected he was lying and that the subject of their conversation had been very different, but it was hard to see how Dawkins could get under the board chairman's guard.

Dawkins' next call was to Peter Robinson.

'Why didn't you tell me you'd spoken to Captain Delraine on the phone the evening he died?'

After a short silence, Robinson said, 'I wanted to check that he was alright.'

'Was he?'

'He said he was tired. He hoped to get a good night's rest.'

'Did Captain Delraine say anything about going out?'

'No! It never occurred to me that he'd do that. I told him I'd talk to him again in the morning. I – I wished him goodnight.'

'You should have told me when I came to see you.'

'I'm sorry.'

No, Chris said to himself. I don't think you are. You're a shifty customer, for all your righteous indignation at having been treated badly. Maybe you phoned Delraine because you were concerned about him, but even then it was your own troubles that were at the forefront of your mind.

'Had Captain Delraine spoken to his wife that evening?'

'He didn't tell me if he had.'

Rosemary was perhaps the only person Delraine would have left the centre, drugged and sleepy, in order to meet. But Rosemary's number wasn't on the list. Chris had double-checked, then checked again.

'Did you call anybody else, or did anybody else ring you that evening?'

'You've already asked me that.'

And you lied about it, Chris thought, wondering why Dawkins wasn't being tougher.

'My ex-wife, Celia, phoned.'

'She called you?'

'Yes.'

'At what time?'

'Around seven, maybe ten past.'

'What did you talk about?'

'It was personal. No concern of yours.'

'Did you go out at any time during the evening?'

'I told you when you came to see me. No.'

'Did anybody call in?'

'No!'

'What about Rosemary's brothers? What did Captain Delraine tell you about them?'

'He said they were a close-knit family.'

'Did he talk to you about his wife's share portfolio, the shares she inherited from her father?'

'He may have mentioned it. I can't recall the details.'

'Did he mention companies that would benefit directly if Hastings is chosen for the new container port?'

'I don't remember a conversation of that kind. We mainly talked about the environmental impact and the dredging.'

'What about your payment?'

Robinson sounded relieved. 'It's come through at last.'

Dawkins wiped his forehead with a tissue. Chris was glad it was the Sergeant on the phone, not him. Yet he thought Dawkins ought to be preparing himself better, thinking it through before ringing the next person on the list.

'Will I make tea?' he asked.

'Not yet. Robinson lied about the phone call. If he's innocent, why would he do that?'

'Because he's ashamed he didn't do more, didn't realise what a state his friend was in.'

'State?' Dawkins repeated, frowning.

'Confused,' Chris said. 'Not knowing who or what to believe.'

Dawkins shook his head, still frowning. 'Robinson spoke to Delraine on the phone just after seven-thirty. Plenty of time to get himself to Queenscliff and meet Delraine on the beach.'

'But why?'

'He lied to us about the phone call,' Dawkins said stubbornly. 'Goodness knows what else he's lied about.'

'Sergeant Dawkins.'

Ian Charleton sounded more confident on the phone than he had in person. Chris wondered if Robert was standing beside him, or if he was somewhere on the property alone.

'I'm ringing about a call you made to Captain Delraine on the afternoon before he drowned,' Dawkins said.

Ian answered without hesitation. 'I rang Fred because I was worried about him.'

'Why didn't you tell me earlier?'

'You didn't ask me.'

'Where were you when you made the call?'

'At home.' Ian's tone of voice implied, where else would I be?

'What did you say exactly?'

'I asked Fred how he was going.' Ian still sounded confident, relaxed. Chris decided that he was most probably alone. Robert made him anxious. He would lie more effectively without Robert there.

'What did Captain Delraine reply?'

'He said he was fine.'

'Did Captain Delraine ask about Rosemary?'

'We – Robert and I – were trying to help our sister. We still are.'

'Help her in what way?'

'By offering her a home for as long as she needs it.'

'Did you bring up the subject of divorce?'

'I mentioned it.'

'What did Captain Delraine say?'

'He told me he didn't wish to discuss it just then.'

'Who ended the call?'

'We said goodbye and that we'd talk another time.'

Dawkins put the phone down. Chris said, 'He could have been arranging to meet Delraine that evening.'

'With Robert?'

'They could have come on the *Aeola*.'

The two policemen walked down to the kitchen to make tea. Chris thought with pleasure of drinking his on the back veranda, letting the sun warm him through, leaning back and closing his eyes.

Dawkins said, 'You know the Super warned me about you.'

'What did he say?'

'That you could be a pain in the arse, but you had a working brain.'

'Not at the moment.'

'It's understandable. You've had a late night.'

The jug boiled and Chris watched Dawkins stump away, holding his mug carefully in case it spilt. He walked like a man who'd seen the worst that human beings could do to each other and moved out to the flat country that lay beyond.

Chris took his tea outside, thankful for a few minutes break. He wondered if Dawkins was used to being sat on by superintendents and smiled to himself, thinking of the weight.

NINETEEN

Once upon a time, the Point Lonsdale lighthouse had been staffed twenty-four hours a day. Now George Norris did four twelve hour shifts a week, two at night and two during the day. The rest of the time the lighthouse was operated remotely from Melbourne.

If Captain Delraine had been taken out in a boat and 'persuaded' to go overboard, then there was a chance the boat had been noted, even if there'd been nothing unusual about it.

The night Delraine drowned had been calm and quiet. Chris had checked the shipping schedule for the hours between eleven and six in the morning. The pilots and ships masters who'd been on the bay between 10 pm and 2am had reported nothing uneventful. The next run had been at 4 and by then Delraine was dead.

They watched while Norris checked the radar records. Chris was aware that they should have thought of questioning the lighthouse keeper days ago. His brain was sluggish; each mental step felt like being dragged through sand.

He had a basic general knowledge of the system, mainly from talking to Tom, who, if there was an accident or some other kind of emergency, worked with Norris and the water police.

At night, radio blips called traces appeared on the radar screen and vector marks recorded the course a vessel was steering. On the night of the drowning, Norris told them he'd been keeping an eye on a vessel that didn't have its radio box switched on, but appeared on the radar. There wasn't necessarily anything unusual in that. Boaties did sometimes forget to switch their AIS on, but he'd kept an eye on it.

The boat had twice circled between Queenscliff and Point Lonsdale before leaving Port Phillip Bay through the heads.

'Where was it launched from?' Dawkins asked.

'I can't tell you that. All I know is that it shows up on my screen here.' Norris pointed with a pencil to a spot just outside the heads. 'To find out where it was before that, you'll need to contact the Port Authority directly.'

'It could have been the *Aeola*,' Dawkins said to Chris after they'd left the lighthouse. 'We can check with Hastings harbour. See what boats left from there.'

'You're hoping their CCTV might have something?'

'Or the harbourmaster saw them leaving. Or somebody else did.'

'If it was the brothers, then they'd know about the radar trace. What's to stop them towing the *Aeola* up the coast and launching from a little used ramp somewhere?' Chris suppressed a sigh. It seemed worse than looking for a needle in a haystack.

They bought rolls and wraps for lunch and took them out to the station's back veranda. Chris had never thought he'd enjoy sharing his lunch there with anyone but Anthea. He caught a faint whiff of her perfume on the air, remembering the way the wind blew the hair back from her face as she lifted her chin to the sun.

He realised that Dawkins was looking at him speculatively.

'You don't eat meat.'

'Not for years,' Chris said.

'That doesn't look too bad.' Dawkins nodded at Chris's salad roll.

Chris broke off a piece and handed it across.

He was remembering the time he'd almost drowned, when Jack Benton, who'd killed his wife and hidden her body in the sand dunes, had pulled him underwater, then stood on his back.

'What's wrong?' Dawkins asked.

'Nothing. Not hungry. Do you want the rest of this?'

Dawkins took the remains of the roll and chomped his way through it.

It occurred to Chris that the Sergeant ate as though he was alone. In fact, Dawkins did many things as though he was alone and nobody was watching him. He had to report to Superintendent Walsh in a few days time. If they had no concrete evidence that Delraine had been murdered, the Super would call a halt to their investigation.

Robert Charleton was probably laughing at them. Chris had a sudden suspicion that Robert knew where they'd been that morning, knew they'd spoken to the lighthouse keeper. He could hear Robert's laughter all the way from Hastings.

'I'd like to talk to the Queenscliff harbourmaster again,' he said. 'Aldridge knows something about the *Aeola* that he's keeping to himself.'

'Do that, while I check up on Hastings.'

Evan Aldridge wasn't answering his phone. The Hastings

harbourmaster told Dawkins he'd check his records and get back to him.

Chris rang around his list of Our Bay members. None admitted to having spoken to Captain Delraine in the weeks before he died. He tracked down a phone number for Neil Anstey. Something warned him against ringing the young man's father and asking for it. Neil remembered talking to Delraine at his mother's funeral, but had had no further contact.

'I thanked him for coming, that's all.'

When asked about Delraine's views on the new container port, Neil said, 'The pilots never take a principled stand on anything.'

'I thought Captain Delraine was concerned about damage to the environment.'

'He may have said so privately, but he wasn't prepared to do anything about it.'

The two drivers for the pilot company who'd had shifts on the night Delraine drowned said that they'd been uneventful. They'd both been shocked when Chris first questioned them and shock had rendered them as good as speechless. Chris hadn't had the feeling they were hiding anything. One of the crewmen had been similarly lost for words, but the other had been voluble and angry. It was to this man's house that Chris retraced his steps.

His wife told him that Bill was fishing on the pier.

Chris found the crewman sitting on his bait box, quite a distance from the other fishermen, who nodded a greeting then returned to studying their lines.

'Blackie,' he said gruffly.

'Hello Bill.'

The crewman was close to retiring age. Chris wondered what superannuation arrangements the company made for its seamen and administrative staff and if they'd changed since his father's day.

'Do you remember Captain Delraine taking a call on the launch?' Chris asked.

'Nothing unusual in that.' Bill stared at his feet, but Chris knew he was paying close attention.

'On his mobile.'

'Might have done.'

Bill frowned. It seemed to Chris that he was angry and bewildered, and that anger was making him uncooperative. It was the crews' job to look after the pilots and he'd failed in his duty of care.

'Who phoned him?'

'I don't know.'

'What did Captain Delraine do?'

'I – I asked him if he was okay.'

'He didn't look it?'

'He was as white as a sheet.'

Bill looked up, the lines on his face driven deep. Chris knew what it cost him to make the admission. Bill knew about the anti-histamines, of course he did. The crews and the drivers would all have known; impossible to keep it from them.

Chris pushed on with his questions, concerned that Bill would clam up altogether.

'Who was driving?'

'Otto.'

'How did he react?'

'He – we were worried the Captain might faint. We helped him to sit down.'

'Did you talk about it afterwards?'

'No.'

Chris wondered if he was lying. Surely he and Otto would have talked about the incident. But maybe not; maybe a reticence where the pilots were concerned would have meant they kept their feelings and opinions to themselves. It was, after all, the ethos of the company, one his own father would have vigorously defended.

'What did Captain Delraine say when he took the call?'

'"Yes, I see," and then "All right."'

'He was agreeing to a suggestion or proposal?'

Bill swallowed what might have been a lump of rock in his throat. 'I don't know.'

'When was this?'

The crewman named a date.

Chris called Otto, who wasn't answering his phone. Chris had an address, but hesitated over whether to go all the way to St Leonards only to find nobody home.

Otto might, at that very moment, be steering the launch through the heads, edging alongside a huge tanker or bulk carrier so the pilot could step up onto the ladder.

The thought made Chris feel sick.

He phoned Dawkins, who said he'd get onto the phone companies and ask for records going further back. Chris realised that he'd formed the opinion of Delraine as a brave man, who could not be bought or bribed. He wished he'd had the chance to meet him.

If Delraine had been pushed or thrown into the water, then this had to have taken place too far out for him to swim ashore, and well out of range of any boats that might have rescued him. It had been ebb tide; otherwise, if he'd kept his head and floated, the current might have brought him back. His killers would have watched to see what happened. They'd want Delraine's body to wash up the next day, in order to put an end to searching and to speculation, and they needed the autopsy to show that he had drowned.

Chris called Otto again. The driver agreed with Bill's account of Delraine taking a phone call on the launch. But he refused to be drawn on who had phoned, saying he had no idea.

The previous request for phone data had taken over twenty-four hours. Chris supposed they'd have to wait the same length of time again. He found his feet taking him down the hill.

Tom was leaning over the end of the jetty, not smoking for a wonder.

He swung round, frowning as though he'd caught Chris spying on him.

'The snails are coming back,' he said.

There was a special kind of snail that lived in the seagrass nursery, important food for the baby fish. The lead in the bullets the trainee soldiers on Swan Island fired over the water had been turning all the snails into males, according to one scientific report. After a lot of argument the army had finally agreed to change the direction of their target practice.

'That's good then,' Chris said.

'A small victory for nature. Now all we need is for the canola farmers to lay off the fertilizer and the bay might have a chance.'

Chris recalled reading about the seagrass at Hastings, how it formed the basis of the fish and crustacean nurseries there as well, how the migrating birds relied on it. But he didn't want to be drawn into a discussion about threatened ecosystems.

'Any more news?' he asked.

'Nope.'

Chris forbore remarking that no news was good news.

'I'm too old to be put out to grass, Blackie. So are you.'

There was no answer to this. Chris decided to describe his and Dawkins's visit to David Anstey. He wanted to use Tom as a sounding board.

'Good old Anstey,' Tom said when he'd finished.

'He married Rosemary Delraine's cousin.'

There was a pause before Tom said, 'I didn't know they were related. Thelma was a lovely woman, kind and smart and funny. Dave Anstey was a lucky man. He knew it too.'

It was the first time Chris could recall Tom referring to a married couple in this way. Usually he curled his lip when he heard that someone had got married and said he'd give them six months.

Chris had found Thelma's name on Our Bay's register. He asked Tom if that was how they'd got to know each other.

'She joined up when the dredging started.'

'Have you met Neil Anstey?'

'Thelma's son? Not personally, but I know he's an environmental activist. I saw him on TV once, boarding an illegal fishing boat.'

'How did Thelma die?'

'Brain tumour. It was a dreadful business. Operations. Radiotherapy. Chemo. The drugs made her crazy. And she was the sweetest, gentlest person.'

Chris said, 'You would have gone to her funeral, Tom. Was Rosemary Delraine there?'

'Come to think of it, she was.'

'Was Fred Delraine with her?'

'I didn't put two and two together. About Thelma and Rosemary being related.'

'Think back, Tom,' Chris said in a mild, uninflected voice. 'Was there anything you noticed about Captain Delraine that day?'

Tom shook his head.

'What about Rosemary's brothers?'

'Those thumpers, no. I don't think they were there.'

'What about Peter Robinson?'

'He was there with Celia.'

'Who did you see him talking to?'

'I don't remember.'

'What about other pilots?'

'Their CEO. He'd only just started with the company.'

'Were you surprised by that?'

'Surprised?'

'Did he and Anstey seem acquainted?'

'I didn't notice. I wasn't paying attention to them.' Tom continued, after they'd left the jetty and begun walking towards the coastguard office, 'You know, I shouldn't say this to you of all people, but I'm not afraid of drowning. The worst thing would be if, at the last moment, you changed your mind.'

Chris nodded. He knew, from long experience that Tom's change of subject was deliberate and that he didn't want to answer any more questions about Thelma's funeral.

One thing Delraine's death had done, it had toughened him against his memories. Once his father's bloated face used to appear as though he'd gone into the sea, to his death, only hours before.

Chris pictured the kelp forests, how they'd held his father down, or how, in his imagination, it had been this way. If Delraine had been caught in the kelp, his body might not have been found for weeks; it might never have been found.

'Which is the lesser evil, Blackie?' Tom said bitterly. 'Isn't that what most of life's decisions boil down to in the end?'

'Have you been threatened, Tom?'

'Me? What with? A dead fish?'

'Tell me,' Chris said.

'It's nothing. Just the sack. Redundancy. *Moving on.*'

'Not nothing, then.' Chris said quietly.

'If I'm replaced, there's bugger all I can do about it.'

You can fight it, Chris felt like saying, but he knew the advice would be unwelcome.

'Has Brian been to see you?'

Tom turned to him, annoyed by the question and the implication that he was withholding information.

'Why would he do that?'
'I thought he might have talked to you,' Chris said.
'Snowball's chance of that.'

Dawkins rang Robert Charleton from the office phone.
'You called Captain Delraine on the afternoon of August 19. What was that about?'
'Congratulations, Sergeant,' Robert said. 'You've been doing your homework.'
Dawkins ignored the jibe and repeated his question.
'It was about our sister,' Robert said. 'Rosemary was distressed. She needed to decide things, settle matters. I tried to make Fred see that he had to accept a divorce.'
'And did you?'
'Excuse me?'
'What did you make Captain Delraine see?'
'Nothing.' Robert bit down on the syllables. Chris had a sudden vision of him biting Dawkins' hand. 'You're wasting my time and your own. Fred killed himself because he couldn't come to a decision and he couldn't stand it any more.'
There was a click as Robert ended the call.
Dawkins turned to Chris. 'Delraine might have been hoping for good news.'
'Such as?'
'Such as Rosemary regretting that she'd acted hastily, run away from Brighton.'
'If that were the case, why wouldn't Rosemary ring to tell him herself?'
'True,' Dawkins said.
They'd found no record of Rosemary having

phoned her husband, neither in the first lot of records nor the second.

'We'll go down there tomorrow,' Dawkins said, making up his mind. 'The bastard won't get away with fobbing us off this time.'

Chris thought of driving all the way to Hastings again, but a phone call early the next morning changed their plans.

TWENTY

Camilla was crying on the phone. 'It's Brian! Please come! There's been a terrible accident!'

Half running, half falling down the cliff path, Chris found Camilla kneeling on the rocks with Brian Laidlaw cradled in her arms.

Brian's neck was broken. It looked as though he'd been dead for several hours. Chris put his arms around Camilla, who raised her head to stare at him, eyes blank with shock and disbelief.

Two teenage boys were standing some way off.

'They let me use their phone,' Camilla said when Chris waved them over.

'Brian, how could – ' Camilla's voice broke. She buried her head in Chris's shoulder and began to cry.

Chris hugged Camilla close, then took the boys' names and mobile numbers. One had a dog with him, a kelpie cross, friendly and alert. They said they'd been walking round the headland when they'd heard the lady crying out.

'Is he dead?' the dog owner asked.

'Yes. I'll be around to talk to you, but you've nothing to worry about. Go home now. Go straight home.'

Chris gently eased Camilla away from Brian's body. He looked up at the cliff path.

'I was walking,' Camilla said. 'I looked down and there he was.'

She'd lifted Brian's head and shoulders, but hadn't moved him otherwise. She drew a handkerchief from the pocket of her jacket and wiped her eyes.

Chris made phone calls. 'The ambulance will be here soon,' he told Camilla. 'I've asked Minnie to come. You'll be all right with her.'

Dawkins was on his way. Chris didn't know if he should be involving Minnie. Should he have asked Dawkins' opinion first? He couldn't think of a better alternative; certainly he couldn't send Camilla home to an empty house.

Brian knew every stone of the cliff path. He could have walked safely along it in the middle of the night. He might have had a heart attack. The post mortem would show it. He'd fallen on an unusually rocky part of the beach. A few metres either way and he would have landed mostly on sand.

Chris understood that he would find a time to grieve, though he must put grief aside for now. He would mourn alongside Camilla, and those few people left in Queenscliff who'd known Brian all their lives.

He couldn't move the body, but he knelt down and studied Brian's pockets from the outside. He put on a pair of gloves and examined the rocks.

Dawkins spoke gently to Camilla and nodded agreement to Chris's suggestion that Minnie take her home.

Chris sucked in his breath. A man was dead, a good man. Another good man was dead. He felt his eyes fill with tears.

The two policemen waited while Dr Hammond finished his examination and the paramedics, after negotiating the steep path with their stretcher, drove Brian to the morgue.

Dawkins watched, squinting into the sun, until they'd disappeared.

'How old did you say he was?'

'In his eighties. Brian was – ' Chris had been about to say reluctant to reveal his age – 'a very private man.'

Minnie Lancaster met Chris at her door. Chris hesitated, then moved forward and hugged her.

'I've had a fine time keeping Camilla here,' Minnie said, not reproachfully, merely stating a fact.

'Do you think you could go back home with her, stay there for a while?'

'I could, but – '

'I can't think of anybody else.'

'Julie Beshervase?'

'She'd want to bring Riza.'

Minnie smiled. 'Why not? We'll make history. Two women on guard, plus a full grown camel.'

Minnie's eyes, when she smiled, were as blue as the day Chris had met her, a skinny new kid who'd quickly charmed the whole of grade five.

But then, having spoken lightly, she stared at him, suddenly solemn, and repeated the word she'd used, making it a question. 'Guard?'

'I don't know what happened,' Chris said. 'It might have been an accident.'

'But you don't want to take chances.'

'Not with Camilla. No.'

Camilla was Brian's age and did not mind people knowing it. A few years ago, she'd suffered from a loss of speech that had been a mystery to doctors, therapists, and her unsympathetic son. Her voice had come back, largely, Chris believed, owing to Brian Laidlaw's friendship. Camilla would never get over losing Brian – that wasn't to be expected – but there was no doubt in Chris's mind that she needed support and protection now.

Chris found Camilla in Minnie's living-room, sitting with her back to the windows, bent over with her head in her hands.

He sat down and put his arms around her. 'I'm so sorry. Thanks for doing what I asked. You can go home now. Minnie's going with you, and we thought we'd ask Julie too.'

Camilla raised her head like a startled animal wishing only to escape. 'I don't want – '

'Please.'

Camilla's white hair was sparse. Now it seemed as though the few strands she had left stood in protest round her head. But she allowed Chris to leave his arm around her and to hold her hand.

'How could Brian have fallen?' she asked in a voice just above a whisper.

'I don't know,' Chris said, then realising this was too bleak an answer, added, 'I'll find out what happened. I promise.'

Camilla shut her eyes and nodded briefly.

'Let's get you home,' Chris said. 'Sergeant Dawkins will talk to you soon.'

Chris knew Minnie would treasure a few minutes to herself while she packed an overnight bag and re-arranged her shifts at the Brewhouse.

He remembered how he'd almost proposed, when

Anthea had announced that she and Olly were going to get married. Sometimes he regretted not having seized the opportunity, at others he felt glad he'd saved Minnie the embarrassment of saying no, and himself the disappointment of having to live with her answer for the rest of his life.

Camilla had been for an early morning walk along the cliff path.

'I saw marks on the gravel.'

She'd leant over the edge and recognised Brian straight away.

'Did you see anybody else?' Dawkins asked. They were sitting in Camilla's living-room. The curtains were still pulled across windows, but Camilla didn't seem to notice. Chris got up and opened them.

'Apart from the boys? No,' Camilla said. 'There might have been, but I wasn't looking.'

Chris wondered about those marks on the gravel. If Brian had been pushed, whoever had pushed him had not tried to erase them. Cuts and scratches on Brian's body could be explained by his fall.

'Did you look for Brian's phone?' Dawkins asked.

'What?'

'When you got down to the – to Brian's body – did you think to look for a phone?'

Camilla shook her head. The idea obviously hadn't occurred to her. 'He was cold, so cold,' she said.

Camilla didn't know what direction the boys had come from. They'd both had phones and she'd borrowed one.

'Did Mr Laidlaw have any enemies that you're

aware of?'

A flick of her eyes showed Camilla's contempt for the question. 'No,' she said.

'I understand that Mr Laidlaw was a friend of Captain Delraine's.'

'From his days in the navy.'

When Camilla put her head in her hands and began to cry, Chris lifted his chin in the direction of the door.

Outside, he said, looking Dawkins in the eye, 'I think it might be better if we let Mrs Renfrew recover a bit first.'

'Why? Time is of the essence. I shouldn't have to tell you that.'

'An hour or two won't hurt. Minnie will look after her while we talk to the boys. They might have seen something.'

Dawkins looked as though he was going to argue. Then he gave a grunt and stomped down Camilla's driveway.

After checking that Minnie was on her way and that Julie and her camel weren't far behind, the two policemen sat in Chris's car to talk.

It occurred to Chris that he had not once thought of asking Camilla's son to stay with her, or take her into his home.

Dawkins wound the passenger side window fully down before he phoned the Superintendent. The Sergeant's end of the conversation was made up entirely of monosyllables. After it was over, he turned to Chris and said, 'The post mortem's tomorrow morning.

Walsh says it sounds like an accident.'

'What do you think happened?'

Dawkins laughed without humour. 'That's what we bloody well have to find out.'

Minnie pulled up and a few seconds later Chris's phone pinged.

He looked at the message and said, 'I think we can go and talk to the boys now.'

Before starting the engine, he replied to Minnie's text, saying thank you and that he would not be far away. He added another sentence. 'Don't answer Camilla's landline. Use your phone or Julie's if you want to get in touch.'

The boys were at the older one's house – at least Chris assumed he was older – he was taller and there was a fringe of dark hair on his upper lip, which he pressed down every now and then with his left forefinger.

The other boy, smaller, stockier, still with the treble voice of childhood, seemed more self-possessed.

Dawkins began by asking their ages, and Chris had his supposition confirmed.

'What were you doing on the beach this morning?'

The younger one, whose name was Sam, said 'Nothing.'

They shouldn't be questioning minors on their own. Dawkins had phoned both sets of parents, but was too impatient to wait.

Chris said, 'No one's accusing you of anything. You're not in any trouble. In fact we're glad you were there to help Mrs Renfrew.'

'Is she okay?' asked James, the older one.

Chris warmed to him for thinking to ask.

'Mrs Renfrew's shocked and upset, but yes, she'll be alright.'

'Did the old guy fall off the cliff?'

'His name was Brian Laidlaw. Did you know him?'

'We seen him on his bike.'

'How long were you on the beach before you saw Mrs Renfrew?'

'She was crying,' James said.

'Wailing, more like,' added Sam. 'We was coming round the corner.'

'The corner underneath the lighthouse?'

'Yeah.'

'And where were you heading?'

'Just going for a walk.'

'Not at that time of the morning,' Chris said firmly.

James went red while Sam looked mutinous.

Chris said, 'You know it's illegal to fish there.'

They offered him the identical expressions of young people when adults have said something stupid.

'I'll let it go for now,' Chris said, 'but I'll be watching out.' He assumed the fishing lines were gone, that some time between the departure of the paramedics, Dawkins and himself, the boys had removed them. They would have had to wade out against the tide, but that would not have bothered them.

When Dawkins asked if they'd touched Brian's body, they looked horrified, wide-eyed and quick with their denials.

'Did Mrs Renfrew ask you to help her move him?'

'No!'

'Did you go up the path?'

The boys stared at Dawkins. They would have been terribly ashamed to realise how transparent they were. Of course they'd climbed the path. They'd been shocked, but also curious. They'd already decided to wag school. It wasn't every day that such an excuse came their way, so why not make the most of it?

'Did you see anybody else up there?'

They shook their heads in unison.

'There were broken twigs and stuff,' Sam said.

'What did you make of that?'

Sam's face was once again a practised blank. He shook his head.

Dawkins said he might want to talk to them again, and if they thought of anything they were to let him know.

Brian never locked his cottage. He'd replied gruffly, when Chris had queried this, that he had nothing worth stealing.

The three-roomed cottage – kitchen and living-room combined, tiny bedroom, bathroom that had been added on – was neat and tidy. If the rooms had been searched in the last few hours, then whoever searched them had put back what they'd disturbed.

A short rope clothesline was fixed between the back drain pipe and the fence; an old, worn towel flapped on it in the mild easterly breeze.

Brian had no family to arrange a funeral. He had never married; the last of his siblings had died five years ago, and his parents long before. If there were cousins, Chris had no idea how to get in touch with them. Perhaps Camilla would.

'How long had he lived here?' Dawkins asked.

'Since I was a boy.'

'Where would he hide something if he didn't want anyone to find it?

'Behind a wall? Under the floor boards?' Chris suggested, knowing that Brian would not have picked anywhere obvious.

Dawkins checked his watch. 'We can come back and do a thorough search. Let's just have a quick look round for now.'

They circled the house. There was no space large enough for a grown man to squeeze under it.

Chris was reminded of the gap under the coastguard office, watched over by Tom Maloney, where Bobby and Max had made a nest for a short while.

There was no carpet. They checked the floorboards, but none looked to be disturbed. They searched the cupboard where Brian had kept his few clothes, and the clothes themselves, but did not find Brian's phone. There were a couple of spare beanies, track pants and tops, one suit, a raincoat and thick, serviceable socks. Chris recalled that Brian often wore fingerless gloves in the colder months. They were dark green woollen ones, old and felty from years of washing.

They had not been on his body and they didn't appear to be in the house. Dawkins had felt in Brian's pockets on the beach. They'd been empty except for a handkerchief.

'If Brian had his phone with him this morning, someone's taken it,' Chris said.

'The boys?'

'No.'

Mrs Renfrew?'

'Definitely not.'

TWENTY-ONE

Camilla sat very still, her hands clasped tightly just above her knees, the knuckles white as sea-scoured stones.

'Are those two boys alright?' she asked.

When Chris said they were, Camilla looked up and managed a small smile. He'd asked if he could go back and talk to Camilla on his own and Dawkins, after frowning at him, had agreed.

'It's funny how Brian and I grew up living close to one another and never became friends till we were old.'

Camilla's family had been well off, Brian's amongst the poorest in the borough. 'I think he may have given me my voice back, you know.'

Chris let Camilla re-live her memories and didn't rush her.

Brian was the man to find items that had been thrown into the sea months, years, or even centuries after the event. Once he'd discovered bits of a one hundred and fifty year old shipwreck, another time a cigarette packet containing residues of cocaine. What other man would have picked up an old cigarette packet, studied and smelt it, rather than pass it by, or throw it in the bin?

'When was the last time you saw Brian wearing those old green gloves of his?' Chris asked.

Camilla didn't remember. She looked confused and shook her head.

Chris knew he was in danger of fixing on a single item in order to block out anger and grief.

'Do you know if Brian received a letter from Captain Delraine in the past few weeks?'

'No.' Tears came to Camilla's eyes.

Chris took her hand, speaking gently, 'Remember how you told me Brian saw two men talking to Captain Delraine?'

'Brian thought Captain Delraine and the men were arguing.'

'What made him think that?'

'He didn't say.'

'When we talked about it earlier, you told me Brian spoke to the Captain about it.'

'He was worried.'

'What about exactly?'

'Brian knew the Captain had problems with his health and – and other problems too. If he was arguing on the beach with someone, then it couldn't be good for him.'

Camilla lowered her head, blinking rapidly. She's not telling me all she knows, Chris thought. She's holding something back.

He pulled out his phone and showed Camilla photographs of Robert and Ian Charleton.

'Did Brian describe the men to you? Could it have been these two?'

Camilla shook her head. 'I don't know.'

'Have you ever seen them?'

'At Captain Delraine's funeral. They're – aren't they his wife's brothers? In the church, Brian – I remember him staring at them, but he didn't say anything. We left straight after the service. Brian didn't want company. He wanted to go home.'

Camilla began to cry. 'I'm very tired. I'm sorry. I don't think I can talk any more just now.'

Minnle opened the door quietly. She looked at Camilla and shook her head.

'I'll leave you then,' Chris said. 'Try and get some rest. I'll come back this evening or tomorrow morning.'

Minnie walked outside with him.

'Thank you for doing this,' Chris said.

Minnie nodded. She seemed about to speak, then changed her mind.

If Brian had sworn Camilla to secrecy, she might feel she had no choice but to keep her promise, even now that Brian was dead.

Instead of going straight back to the station, Chris dropped by the coastguard office.

'When did you last see him, Tom?'

Tom blew smoke in the general direction of the window. 'The day before yesterday,' he said.

'Where?'

'At the harbour. I only saw him in the distance. I didn't say hello. Stupid old bugger.' Tom was crying through the smoke.

'Was Brian wearing his gloves? You know, those ratty fingerless ones?'

'What?'

Chris repeated his question.

Tom shrugged, then frowned and shook his head, stubbing his butt out angrily.

Chris moved across and hugged his friend.

Chris knew the young man on duty at the morgue. He'd

lived in Queenscliff with his mother and step-father till he was old enough to leave a home which had been unhappy. Chris had twice steered him out of trouble, and more often than that cooked him a decent meal. The young man smiled and Chris made an effort to smile back, while Dr Hammond nodded a greeting, his face set in hard lines.

When Dawkins asked if he had anything more to say about the time of death, Hammond shook his head.

Chris wondered if it was his imagination, or if the doctor was recalling Dawkins' dismissive attitude with regard to Delraine's drowning. Hammond was sensitive enough to pick up on a change in the Sergeant, but Dawkins was saying little and keeping his expression neutral.

The corpse was Brian, yet not Brian.

Chris whispered goodbye to this man of few words, who did not look peaceful. He wondered what Brian's last word had been – a shout of protest, a cry of alarm, a name? He thought about chance encounters, and missed encounters too. If Brian had begun his walk an hour later, and Camilla an hour earlier, she might have been a witness, prevented a death by her presence on the path. Or else, and it was a frightening thought, there might have been two bodies broken on the rocks.

Dawkins walked round the table, studying Brian's face, neck and hands. When he asked Hammond whether Brian's cuts and bruises were caused by his fall, Hammond said it was a reasonable assumption.

The doctor went over Brian's body, parting the hair to examine his scalp. 'There's some lacerations here as well.'

'Could any of them have killed him?'

'No. I'll be able to tell more once I've opened him up. We'll see what we can get from these,' he said, lifting Brian's right hand.

The knuckles were swollen. Brian had suffered from mild arthritis for years, and it was always worse in the colder months. He pooh-poohed any suggestion of discomfort, but the fingerless gloves had become a habit.

Dr Hammond took samples from under Brian's nails while Chris stared. Was it his imagination, or was there a space from Brian's wrist to his finger joints that was relatively clean?

'Could Brian have been wearing gloves?' he asked.

'What?'

'Brian owned a pair of fingerless gloves. They're missing,' Chris explained. 'If he'd been wearing them yesterday morning you'd expect them to protect his hands to some extent.'

Hammond thought about this, then said, 'He's cut and bruised all over.' He held up Brian's hand again. 'It looks to me as though he tried to break his fall. As for – fingerless gloves you said? I couldn't say one way or the other.'

Carefully he took scrapings from under Brian's nails.

'I'll send these off to the lab.'

'Is there anything to indicate his neck was broken before he fell?' Dawkins asked.

'No.'

'How long could he have stayed alive after he hit the rocks?'

'It's hard to be sure.'

They watched the doctor weighing and examining internal organs. Brian's heart had been good, product of an abstemious diet and regular exercise. Hammond said mildly that he might have been expected to live for another ten years.

'So he didn't have a heart attack?' Chris asked.

'No. He was killed by his fall.'

'I hope the lab results show something,' Dawkins said as he and Chris left the building.

Chris nodded. He was thinking they could go back to the cottage for a more thorough search; but he knew Brian's gloves and phone wouldn't be there. He could check the lists of phone numbers again for Brian's. Could he have missed it? Surely not.

'Do you think Delraine wrote to him?' Dawkins asked.

'I asked Camilla about that. She doesn't know of any letter.'

Chris waited for Dawkins to tick him off for not getting further with Camilla. Instead he lifted his chin in the direction of the bay and said, 'Let's assume for a moment that there is, or was a letter. Where do you think it is now?

'If Brian was pushed over the cliff, then whoever killed him took it.'

'If Laidlaw believed he was in danger, why would he go walking up there? It wasn't even light.'

Chris opened his mouth to say that Brian wouldn't change his routine for anyone. But perhaps this wasn't the right answer. Perhaps Brian had been meeting someone who had dictated the time and place.

He said, 'I'd like to talk to Alex at the workshop, ask him when Brian was last down there, who else was there at the same time.'

Dawkins nodded. 'You can do that while I'm talking to the coroner.'

They were almost at the car. Chris knew that, if he looked up, he could see the glitter of Corio Bay. He did not look up. It occurred to him that his phobia had given him ballast, something to push against. He'd seen it only as a form of weakness; something to be ashamed of and to hide from others.

Now it was less powerful, new possibilities were opening up. He felt something solid at his back. Was it possible that a morgue holding the dead body of his friend could give him that?

The killer or killers – the more he thought about it, the more convinced Chris was that Brian had been murdered – struck him as both coldly calculating and impulsive. Impulsiveness might lead them to act on the decision that Camilla was a risk. On the other hand, two accidental deaths – or one suicide and one accident – might be explicable, acceptable to the coroner – but three?

Dawkins was walking hunched into himself, as though suddenly aware that he was taking up too much space.

He turned to Chris and said, 'Brian must have seemed indestructible to you.'

Tears filled Chris's eyes. He blinked. 'Perhaps because his frailty was there right from the beginning. From the time I was a boy.'

'Frailty?'

'I never saw Brian actually fall off his bike, but there was always the sense that he was about to.'

'You would have laughed at him.'

'We did.'

'And Mrs Renfrew?'

'You think it's wrong? I mean my friends, the camel?'

Dawkins smiled. 'Unorthodox,' he said.

But Chris was suddenly afraid. 'Perhaps we should move her.'

'Where to?'

'You're right. There's nowhere safe.'

When Chris asked Alex Stavros when he'd last seen Brian, Alex replied, 'A week or so ago.'

'Did he speak to you about Captain Delraine?'

'Five words from Brian was a long speech.'

'And those five words were?'

'I got the impression he was watching the Captain's back.'

'What gave you that impression?'

'He said he was worried about a friend of his.'

'Did he name the friend?'

'From his days in the navy. A life-long friend he said.'

'Did Brian tell you why he was worried?'

'I asked him, but he wouldn't say.'

'Did Brian and Captain Delraine ever visit the workshop together?'

'Not while I was here.'

'When was Captain Delraine last here?'

'I told you. He came to ask about an order for some special maintenance.'

Chris pulled a photograph out of his pocket.

'What about these two?'

Alex stared at it, then raised his head to say, 'They were at Captain Delraine's funeral.'

'What about down here?'

'Who are they?'

'Rosemary Delraine's brothers. Ian' – Chris pointed to indicate which one Ian was – 'owns an ocean-going yacht called the *Aeola*.'

'There's so many yachties. This place gets busier and busier.'

It might, but Alex would not have missed the *Aeola*. His expression was wary, bordering on fearful. Someone's got to him, Chris thought.

TWENTY-TWO

Spring turned on an afternoon such as Chris could seldom remember on that windy coast – calm, the sun a gift, light dancing on the water, water drinking light. It was an afternoon to give thanks for life, to rejoice in life. Is that what Brian would have wanted him to do?

Chris told himself that he would be alright so long as he kept his eyes down, that he'd become inured to the cliff path and the view. He told himself he was doing this for Brian, and would not be ashamed of his weakness, or shame himself in Camilla's eyes. When Camilla had said she wanted to go back and see the place Brian had fallen from, Chris had readily agreed.

He raised his head at the sound of a diesel engine. There goes another one, he thought.

Camilla studied Chris along her shoulder, gauging his mood, Chris thought, deciding what to say.

'I walked past Brian's house early this morning. Minnie came with me. She said she didn't think it would do any harm and I badly wanted to.'

Chris wished they hadn't. 'Was there anybody parked outside?' he asked.

Camilla shook her head.

'Anybody in the street?'

'Not nearby.' Camilla hesitated, then said more firmly, 'Nobody I recognised. The sun was coming up. The roof, the guttering – you know, it was getting too much for him, the upkeep, but he never would admit it – all of it was touched by the dawn. All of it was gold.'

Camilla seemed, in the bright sunlight, very pale. She blinked and looked around her. Chris held out a supportive hand. She hesitated and then took it.

'Brian was so heavy. I – I turned his head over and I kissed him.'

'Then what happened?'

'I looked up and thought of the times I'd watched him climb down that crumbly bit.' Camilla lifted her chin and pointed. 'Other people wouldn't, they'd be afraid it would give way. Brian knew where the stones held his weight. If he'd felt himself falling, he would have known how to break his fall.'

Chris followed Camilla's line of sight. 'Are you quite sure there was no one watching you?' he asked.

'I can't be a hundred per cent sure, can I? I mean, there's those bushes, though it's hard to see how anyone could hide behind them. There's the gun emplacement further along.'

Chris nodded. He'd had a look inside. It was full of old, accumulated rubbish. Impossible to tell if someone had stood there watching in the pre-dawn light.

'Brian did tell me something before he died,' Camilla said.

Chris stood very still. I knew it, he thought.

'He made me promise not to say anything. I thought – I thought yesterday that I should keep my promise. If I broke it, it wouldn't bring him back and I'd have to live with the betrayal for the rest of my life. But then, when I walked by his house this morning, it seemed that Brian was speaking to me, telling me it was alright to tell you. You'll think me a crazy old woman.'

'Of course not,' Chris said.

Camilla nodded, accepting the assurance at least for the time being.

'Captain Delraine was very troubled in his mind. He asked Brian what to do. You understand how upsetting that was for him, having Captain Delraine ask him for advice? He would never have told me otherwise.'

Chris pictured the two men meeting out of doors, somewhere they believed nobody would see or overhear them, Delraine at his wits end, confiding in his friend.

'What did Captain Delraine ask?'

'He was on a committee. He wanted to resign. It wasn't just that the extra work was too much for him, though it was. The meetings were in Melbourne, in one of the government offices. One day Captain Delraine went back to the meeting room after it was over and the chairman was there. I mean the chairman of the committee. I don't know if Brian knew his name. If he did, he didn't tell me. The chairman was talking to someone Captain Delraine knew. This person had his back to the door and didn't see Captain Delraine. He wasn't speaking loudly, but Captain Delraine heard him. He said, "I've contacted the titles office. It's all sorted." "How much?" the chairman asked. 'A million and a half," the other man said. Captain Delraine backed away. He didn't go into the room.'

'But the chairman saw Captain Delraine? He was facing the doorway?'

Camilla nodded. 'Captain Delraine spoke to him afterwards, and the chairman said something to the effect that the Captain was mistaken. It wasn't what he thought.'

'And the other man?'

'I don't know if the Captain told Brian who it was. Brian didn't ask questions. He didn't believe it was his place to.'

'When did he tell you this?' Chris asked.

'A week or so ago. Eight days,' Camilla said.

It was perhaps only when Brian believed his own life to be in danger that he'd passed his secret on.

'I told Brian to tell you, but he didn't want to.' Camilla glanced at Chris, her head on one side, then smiled sadly. 'I tried to persuade him. He said he'd think about it. And now it's too late.'

It wasn't just the conversation Brian had had with Camilla; there were those other times, on the beach when Brian had rung him after finding Delraine's body. Why hadn't Brian said something then? And in his cottage afterwards. Brian had been, understandably, in a state of shock. But was this sufficient explanation for his silence?

Camilla said, 'We walked along the back track. You know, the one I used to take to Riza's paddock? Brian said he'd been awake all night. He never told me things like that. You know how brown his face is normally. Well, it was as though a bleach had come up from the inside.'

They turned around and began retracing their steps along the cliff path. The tea-tree was covered with white blossom, like snow, or a wedding.

'Brian loved it up here,' Camilla said, and now her voice had a trace of acceptance in it, that her friend was gone, that she'd never see him again. 'He'd looked up to Captain Delraine since he was a young man, and I think he found it impossible to get his mind around the fact that the Captain was foundering, that he needed help.'

'What about the two men Brian saw Captain Delraine talking to?'

'He didn't describe them to me. I told you yesterday. I've no idea who they were.'

Chris waited. Camilla said, 'I've explained about my promise. I've told you all I know.'

Brian had watched Robert and Ian Charleton at the funeral, walking with Rosemary down the church's centre aisle, returning with the coffin. Chris knew his eyes had been good for a man of his age. If it had been those two talking to Delraine on the beach, he would have recognised them. Chris understood he was in danger of fixing on Rosemary's brothers because he disliked them. He reminded himself that he still had to ask Evan Aldridge about the *Aeola*. If the *Aeola* had been berthed at the Queenscliff marina two nights ago, then the harbourmaster, Aldridge, would know.

If it hadn't been those two talking to Delraine, perhaps arguing with him, then might have been Eric Finlay, the chair of the consultative committee. But then who was the second man? Could it have been Ivan Southeby? Chris reminded himself that Brian had been sitting near the front of the church at Delraine's funeral and had not come to the reception. He might not have noticed Southeby, and Finlay hadn't come to the funeral. Was his absence significant? Chris told himself he should have thought of it before.

They walked on, Camilla concentrating on where to put her feet.

Chris said, 'Captain Delraine had talked to the chairman, Eric Finlay and the chairman had told him that he was mistaken. What about the other man?'

'Brian got the impression that the Captain had talked to him too.'

'Do you have any idea who it was?'

'No. I'm sorry. But it must be someone whom the chairman knew well, mustn't it? Knows well, I mean. To be speaking confidentially like that.'

A close associate, or else someone very confident of his position and his powers of persuasion, Chris thought.

Camilla had broken her promise and could tell herself that it was the right thing to do, but still she looked vulnerable and frightened. There was no strength in her to resist a physical assault. Killing her would be like breaking a twig, or stepping on an insect.

Perhaps Simon Renfrew was right about his mother living alone. Simon had left messages on the station's landline, which Chris had not returned. Perhaps he was being negligent with regard to Camilla's welfare, just as he'd been negligent with regard to Brian's.

'Who are you looking for?' Camilla asked.

'A man, or men, whose plans were thwarted.'

'What plans?'

'Men seeking to make money out of the new container port.'

'There must be plenty of those.'

Chris nodded, picturing again that café in High Street Hastings, the slanting light stopped by Sergeant Dawkins' shoulders as he leant forward to study photographs of expensive yachts.

He imagined the bulk of warehouses still to be built stretching out along the highway and around the port, and heard the ceaseless noise of trucks.

'I've found that many people are greedy,' Camilla said, 'given the opportunity.'

Chris guessed she was thinking of her son.

'Have you heard from Simon?'

'He wants my house, or the money from it. He's wanted it for years. All this has made him even more determined.' After a short silence, Camilla said, 'Thank you for arranging for Minnie. And for Julie and Riza.'

'I know you'd rather be alone.'

'They're kind. And Riza makes us laugh. He knows that he's on guard.'

Camilla looked at Chris out of eyes that were, for a moment, clear and unafraid. 'It's so easy to mock people and their efforts, isn't it? I do wish I'd been a better friend to him.'

She bent her head and studied the stones on the path, outlined in the spring sunshine.

'I don't know why I wanted to come here.'

'To see if it might remind you of a detail you've forgotten?'

When Camilla didn't reply immediately, Chris asked, 'Has it?'

'Not yet.'

Camilla stopped. She'd been walking slowly and Chris had been making a conscious effort not to hurry or outpace her.

Stones shone on the path ahead of them, each one ringed with light.

'Brian wasn't – he wasn't a reflective man. He had a core of independence and self-respect. When that was challenged, his response had always been to withdraw, to walk away. Brian couldn't cope with argument, dissension. He'd never coped with it, not directly.'

Camilla's voice had become progressively softer. Now she said, scarcely audibly, 'I'm sorry.'

Chris knew what she meant. She was sorry for Brian's sake and her own, but for his sake too. He would have to repeat all of this to Sergeant Dawkins, who would be angry that she hadn't told him earlier.

'Have you ever thought about how objects can't be made to be anything other than themselves?'

'I guess poets think differently,' Chris said.

'I don't know. Poets might come across the same intransigence as ordinary folk.'

What was remarkable was that not only the larger stones, but each tiny sliver of gravel was outlined in light, haloed with light.

Chris had sometimes come across Brian staring, it seemed, at nothing. When Chris had asked – when he'd hazarded a question and Brian was in the mood to reply – he would say 'the stones' or else 'the leaves'.

Few words, but Brian had told the truth. Small wonder that the dilemma posed by Captain Delraine's confidences had caused him such distress.

Chris re-lived those minutes on the beach the morning Brian had found Delraine's body, while they'd waited for the detective, the doctor and the paramedics. Brian had been sullen and uncommunicative. Had he been trying to decide whether or not to speak and, if so, what to say?

And then in Brian's cottage afterwards, those few words he'd blurted out before he roughly turned away.

'So,' Dawkins said. 'Delraine told Laidlaw he'd overheard Finlay being offered a bribe.'

'He hints as much in his letter to his sister.'

Dawkins nodded. 'But instead of confronting Finlay, or informing the police, Delraine wrote to Finlay saying he wanted to resign.'

'He may have confronted Finlay. We don't know.'

Dawkins nodded again, impatiently this time. 'Delraine's at the end of his tether for various reasons. He's sick. His marriage is kaput. He writes to his sister, then meets up with his old friend and tells him what he's overheard, tells him in confidence, makes him promise not to repeat it.'

'He wouldn't have to make – '

Dawkins held up his hand to interrupt. 'Point taken. Laidlaw keeps it to himself even after Delraine drowns. Except for Camilla.'

'And made her promise to keep it to herself. Which she did until today. But why push Laidlaw off that cliff, if he was pushed? Why was he such a risk?'

'I agree it seems like an over-reaction.' Dawkins paused for a moment before continuing. I think we're looking for a man, or men, who are motivated by revenge.'

'Who?'

'Let's start from the other end. Who came here the night before last, having arranged to meet Brian on the cliff path before dawn? How did they get here? Did anybody see them? And there's another thing. I spoke to Robert Charleton the afternoon before Laidlaw died.'

'I've been thinking about that,' Chris said. 'It could have been a trigger.'

'Maybe Robert didn't believe we'd find out about that phone call he made to Delraine.'

'He took a chance and lied about the reason for the call.'

'Time to question Evan Aldridge,' Dawkins said.

'He's been avoiding me.'

'Get down to the harbour and see what he has to say.'

'Do you want to come?'

'I think you'll do better on your own.'

The Queenscliff harbourmaster was polite, while at the same time cool to the point of coldness.

He regarded Chris with steady brown eyes and said, 'The *Aeola* wasn't berthed here.'

'I'd like to look at the footage please.'

Aldridge said, 'On the news – the reporter said it looked as though Brian had fallen off the cliff path.'

'It's possible,' Chris said. He didn't want to get into a debate about how Brian had died, but felt he owed the harbourmaster a response.

'It doesn't sound right, falling.'

Chris agreed that it didn't. 'How well did you know Brian?'

'We got on okay. He wasn't much of a talker.'

'When was the last time you saw him?'

'Last week. Tuesday I think it was. I'll miss the grumpy old sod.' Aldridge turned away, but Chris saw tears in his eyes.

'Could you do something for me?' he asked. 'Could you note down the dates and times you remember Brian being at the harbour in the last few weeks? And if you recall him speaking to anyone?'

Aldridge hesitated, then nodded. 'I'll get you the film, then grab a bite to eat. Do you want anything?'

Chris said thank you, no. 'Could I have another look at the night Delraine drowned as well?'

There was no *Aeola*. Though the film quality was poor, Chris believed he would have recognised Ian Charleton's boat. And why would Aldridge lie to him? On the night Delraine had drowned, it was harder to be sure, but still he did not think the *Aeola* was there.

Dawkins was still waiting on the security film from Hastings harbour. It was possible the Charleton brothers had set off from there, or from a launching ramp with no CCTV cameras.

Chris did some gardening as an aid to thought. Putting away his tools, he recalled that it had been windy the morning before last, but nowhere near windy enough to blow Brian over the cliff. Brian had not been a heavy man, no fat on him at all. On the cutting table, he'd looked shrunken, shrivelled up. He'd known how to walk on ledges narrower than the one he'd fallen or been pushed from, where to place his feet and how to brace himself against a sudden gust of wind.

Brian hadn't owned a boat, not even a tinnie. Chris had always found this something of a surprise. The one time he'd asked about it, the only response Brian had given him was to grunt and shake his head.

Anthea rang to tell him she was sorry. Though he longed to unburden himself, Chris didn't say much on the phone. He asked after Aneira, who was thriving and Olly, who was fine.

TWENTY-THREE

Dr Hammond was a golfer. On their way to meet the doctor at the golf club next morning, Dawkins told Chris that he reserved a place at the bottom of his list of detested sports for golf.

Chris turned to him, surprised, but the Sergeant's expression was impassive as he stared out the passenger side window.

Driving over the causeway, Chris recalled the three young soldiers who'd been so drunk they couldn't steer straight and had driven their car over the edge and drowned. Another drowning, though in that case there'd been no mystery surrounding it.

They found Dr Hammond on the third fairway, alone.

He leant on his driving iron and watched them approaching, then turned away and swung the iron slowly back and forth.

When Chris and Dawkins were about a metre away, he looked round and said, 'I sent you the post mortem report. I don't have anything to add.'

Had there been blood on Brian's gloves and had his assailant or assailants got rid of them? Chris had been back to the cottage. The gloves were definitely not there.

Hammond moved his iron from his right hand to his left and tightened his grip.

'What about the scrapings under Brian's nails?' Dawkins asked.

'I sent them to the lab. You'll have to wait for the results.'

'How long?'

Hammond said, 'Brian Laidlaw could have fallen from that path. I have no evidence that his death was anything other than a tragic accident. Nor do I have the authority to push for the tests I've asked for to be completed as a matter of urgency.'

Dawkins could have argued the point, but he decided to change the subject. 'You treated Captain Delraine for his hay fever.'

Hammond's expression changed. He looked sad, regretful. 'Some people complain about hay fever when they sneeze a bit and get watery eyes in the spring. Fred Delraine had a serious allergy. When I tested him, he came up positive to – well, practically every kind of grass.'

'What did you prescribe?'

'If something new came on the market, or there was a trial I read about, I'd let him know.'

'Did you know he was buying diphenhydramine over the internet?'

After a short hesitation, Hammond nodded.

'Did you try and stop him?'

'The Captain was neither irresponsible nor a fool. He'd managed his dependence for years. I don't know who you're looking for, though I appreciate the fact that you are looking. If I had a name to give you, you can be sure I would.'

'Brighton would have been bad for Delraine's allergies as well,' Chris said.

'His wife liked living there.'

'Is that what he told you?'

When Hammond didn't reply, Chris asked, 'Was Rosemary Delraine sympathetic to her husband's health problems?'

The doctor looked out over the line of trees marking the boundary of the fairway. When he spoke, it was as though he was reminding himself of something.

'She told me that he was a hypochondriac – not that she believed he was, or thought he was – she announced it as a fact, the assumption being that, despite my years of training, she knew more about medicine than I did.'

'When was this?' Dawkins asked.

'Six months ago. Maybe a bit more. I rang her because I was worried.'

'Worried that the Captain's addiction was becoming worse?'

'They were still living together then. I thought we might work out a plan, a way of helping him.'

'Wasn't that unusual, to talk about a patient's problems with his spouse?'

'Of course it was. But I needed her co-operation.'

Chris chanced another question. 'Do you think they were her own opinions Rosemary Delraine was expressing?'

'What do you mean?' Hammond looked at him and frowned, then glanced sideways at his waiting golf ball. He's willing us gone, Chris thought, but at the same time he's caught in a dilemma. Perhaps the coroner's been pestering him.

'Could Rosemary have been influenced by someone else, her brothers for instance?' Chris asked.

'I don't know about that. All I know is, when I rang, that's what she told me. I thought it would be better when Fred moved into the pilots centre. I could keep a closer eye on him.'

'What happened?' Dawkins asked.

'He withdrew into himself and refused to talk about his problems.'

Chris thought of the centre's cook, William, smoking in the courtyard. He thought how others had tried to help Captain Delraine and had failed as well.

Heavy clouds began blowing in from Bass Strait. Hammond looked towards them. Chris wondered whether, if it started to rain once they'd left him, the doctor would stay out on the fairway.

Dawkins said, 'Captain Delraine left the centre just after eleven. It's possible he left in response to a message or a phone call from someone asking for a meeting. Though he'd taken his tablets and was getting ready for bed, it was important enough for him to go out. Have you any idea who that person might be?'

'I'm sorry. No.'

Chris had another thought. They knew Ian Charleton had phoned Delraine on the afternoon he died. What if that had been to arrange a meeting? It had never made sense to Chris that Delraine had agreed to a meeting and then taken his anti-histamines. But what if he'd decided not to go, and then changed his mind?

TWENTY-FOUR

Chris left Dawkins at the station, making phone calls, muttering to himself and scratching notes on bits of paper.

He found his feet taking him towards Swan Bay.

Anthea opened her front door, flushed and excited.

'Oh, it's been too long!'

Chris hugged her, then pulled back, holding her at arms' length. 'You're looking well.'

Anthea leant forward and kissed him on both cheeks. She studied him, becoming serious.

'I'm sorry about Brian.'

Chris nodded.

'Camilla?'

'Bearing up. She's got Minnie to help her, and Julie and Riza.'

'I know. Julie phoned.'

Of course she did, Chris thought. 'How's Aneira?' he asked, smiling at Anthea's glowing face, her graceful, unaffected movements.

'Just gone to sleep. Olly's got a deadline. We can talk in here.'

Anthea led him through to the back of the house. The afternoon sun through west facing windows picked out baby things – high chair, nappies brought inside to finish drying out of the damp air.

'Sorry for the mess.'

Chris felt a sharp pang of envy, and turned away

so it wouldn't show. Perhaps I've been staying away for my benefit, not Anthea's, he thought, and then, I've put wanting this behind me, surely. Ten years ago I might have made a father, but not now.

Anthea poured chilled Moriac white for them both. She was dressed in loose pants and a pale green jumper, which suited her colouring.

Chris reminded himself that she'd been away from police work for almost a year, living at a rhythm and a pace that was centred on Aneira and Olly, homely concerns and pleasures.

'Sergeant Dawkins?' she asked.

'He's running to the starting line.'

Anthea lifted an inquiring eyebrow.

Chris explained how the investigation into Delraine's death had begun, how Dawkins had changed. He kept his explanation brief, wondering if it was wrong to complain. But Anthea would never gossip; anything he said was safe with her.

He sipped his wine and took a deep breath. 'I don't think it was an accident.'

'Brian? Or Captain Delraine?'

'Both.'

Anthea said, 'Tell me what you do think.'

She listened without interrupting. When Chris had finished his account, she asked thoughtful, intelligent questions.

'Accidental death will suit everyone,' Chris said.

'Except you.'

'And Sergeant Dawkins now.'

Chris thrust his chin up and felt the muscles harden in his neck. The gaps in his knowledge had become increasingly obvious to him as he was speaking, the guesses with which he'd tried to join the dots desperately thin.

He felt grateful for Anthea's calm insight, her ability to peel away the outer layers of a problem. He wanted to tell her how much he missed her, but that would not be fair. And besides, she knew anyway.

'I'm so terribly sorry,' Anthea said again. 'For you and for Camilla.'

'It was like – I don't know how to describe it. I never thought about it consciously. Brian was always there.'

'Can I help with Camilla?'

'Thank you. I'll let you know, but I think we've got it covered.' He hesitated before saying, 'Captain Delraine got quite a lot of phone calls in the days before he died. He made a lot as well.'

'Could someone have been offering him information?'

It was an obvious line of inquiry. Chris felt ashamed that he hadn't pursued it.

'They could have. I suspect someone rang him on the evening he died, and he went out to meet them, but I can't be sure. A boat could have been moored off-shore and he was persuaded to board it.'

Anthea looked doubtful. 'Why would he do that?'

'He was doped up on diphenhydramine, disoriented, possibly even hallucinating.'

'And once on board he was overpowered?'

'There were no signs of a struggle, according to Doc Hammond. But given the state he was in, it wouldn't have taken much to push him out.'

'But he was a pilot.'

'Yes. He'd climbed up and down rope ladders in the worst of storms. That's the terrible irony in all of this.'

'That Captain Delraine had built a career as a navigator, yet was all at sea?'

Chris nodded, smiling wryly. 'All at sea,' he repeated. 'Floundering.'

'And his wife knew it. I think the key must be there, you know, in his failed marriage and his in-laws.'

'I've thought so too, but there are other aspects, other men involved.   Captain Delraine overheard someone offering Finlay money. Finlay, that's the chair of the consultative committee I was telling you about. Delraine describes it in a letter to his sister and he told Brian about it too. But if he said who the other man was, then Brian didn't pass it on.'

Anthea returned to her earlier point. 'If someone rang offering Captain Delraine information, that's another reason isn't it? I mean for him to go out late at night.'

Chris nodded. 'I believe Delraine had decided to resign from the committee, walk away from the problem. Perhaps he was contemplating resigning from the pilots service too. But yes, it's possible.'

He thought of all the traipsing round he'd done, the talks with Tom Maloney, Alex at the workshop, the drivers and the crewmen, those visits to Hastings, Brighton and North Melbourne. He thought of Brian's broken body on the rocks and their fast-approaching deadline.

Anthea said, 'If it was Ian – Rosemary's brother? – if it was Ian's boat, the *Aeola* you said? Delraine would have recognised it.'

'Perhaps he was expecting the *Aeola*. Perhaps he believed Rosemary was on board.'

Rosemary asking for a meeting made some sense at an emotional level. But Rosemary hadn't rung him, or if she had, the call wasn't recorded in the data they'd received. Ian could have said that they'd be bringing Rosemary, and perhaps Delraine had believed him.

'It's a big boat, you said, ocean-going? How close to shore would it have been able to come?'

'Delraine could have been rowed out in a dinghy.'

Anthea nodded, acknowledging this. Then she said, 'Brian and Captain Delraine sound as though they were very much alike.'

'I think so. Of course, Delraine was a master mariner and Brian a retired able seaman. But the difference in rank had ceased to matter, if it ever did. I think they were both loyal and, in the end, quite simple men.'

'Camilla?'

'Camilla was important to Brian, but in a different way.'

'What about you?'

'With me it was never like that. Brian tolerated me. If there had to be law enforcement officers, then I would do.'

'What if Captain Delraine was protecting someone?'

'Who? I can't think of anyone who would matter that much to him, apart from Rosemary.'

'That Peter Robinson you talked about?'

'It's possible, but somehow I don't think so. You know, Brian said something to me, right at the beginning, just after he'd found Captain Delraine's body – about a lodeman, about the meaning of the word. I didn't press him at the time. I didn't press him hard enough about anything.'

'Don't blame yourself.'

Anthea reached across and squeezed Chris's hand. Chris wanted to withdraw it because he didn't feel he had the right to her sympathy, but felt comforted by the gesture all the same.

After a few moments, he said, 'Brian was a very literal man, normally. He expected the things he said to be taken literally, and that's what he expected of other people too, that they meant what they said, that they'd be direct with him.'

'But for some reason he couldn't when it came to Captain Delraine?'

'That's right. You know, it stuck with me, that word lodeman. It's somehow more meaningful than pilot.'

'Navigator?'

'That comes closer. When you think about what the first Port Phillip pilots did, in the days of sail.' Chris lifted his chin in the direction of the sea. 'Rowing out there, through the Rip.'

'George Tobin?'

'And others like him.'

'Navigating in a more philosophical sense?'

'Yes. Then there's lodestar, which is an ancient word for the North Pole star. And lodestone, a naturally occurring magnet.' Chris felt embarrassed, as he had when explaining to Sergeant Dawkins that Aeolus was keeper of the winds. But this was Anthea, he reminded himself.

Chris thought again of the laws of Oleron and the

brutal punishment. How often had it been carried out? He imagined the beheading of an unpopular pilot, the execution carried out without hope or chance of appeal. He pictured another situation, in which the unfortunate pilot, perhaps steering falsely, giving false directions, through a simple mistake, or through no fault, really, of his own, begged for mercy.

If Fred Delraine's death was a punishment of some kind, for what misguidance or failure of right steering was he being punished?

They spoke about this for a few more minutes, then Anthea changed the subject, homing in again on Delraine's wife.

'Did you meet Rosemary at the funeral?'

Chris recalled how small she'd looked. He remembered the hieratic formality of the church; Robert, Rosemary and Ian walking down the centre aisle to take their places at the front. The brothers' size, the way they'd loomed over their sister, had not seemed out of place then; but it had been different at the operations centre. Robert had been determined to get Rosemary away.

Chris recalled Rosemary's anxious glance behind her. Had he been afraid that she would say, or do something? Is that why they'd left in such a hurry?

He described the scene to Anthea, who said, lifting her head and looking both at Chris and beyond him, 'Perhaps Robert Charleton is the sort of man for whom family is everything.'

Chris was about to reply when Olly came in. Olly said hello, not coldly, but there was something guarded in his manner.

He bent and kissed Anthea. She smiled and kissed him back, poured him a glass of wine and asked how it was going.

'Slowly,' Olly said. He looked from Anthea to Chris and back again, a slight frown between his eyebrows.

'I'm sorry about Brian Laidlaw. I heard he was up on the cliff before dawn. Did he miss his footing? What happened?'

'I don't know yet,' Chris said. He didn't want to get drawn into talking any more about it with Olly there. 'It's been nice catching up, but I should get going.'

Anthea didn't press him to stay.

Chris spent an hour delivering summonses for failure to pay fines. Normally he hated delivering summonses, but that day it was a relief. He mulled over his conversation with Anthea as he drove around familiar streets. Just the fact of having been with his old assistant, talked to her, made him feel different, lighter somehow and less anxious, with less of a feeling that the weight he carried was too much.

At dusk, he made his way to Camilla's house.

They made a formidable quartet, the three women and the camel – so used to human company, and his owner's close affection, that he seemed to understand his role was to help look after her friend. And Riza had his own bond with Camilla, remembered from a calf.

Julie had walked Riza along the beach, past the sign saying no horses, and that dogs must be on a leash.

'I'm waiting for the Council to add a picture of a camel with a cross through it,' she told Chris, who smiled and shook his head.

Julie still cultivated a reputation as a wild girl. Those she counted as her friends knew her to be brave and loyal. Her red hair stood on end and she grinned at Chris though bright red matching lips.

Camilla's house had acquired such a solid presence that Chris was surprised to find the physical structure no larger than the last time he'd been there. The chimney was no taller, though too much smoke was coming out of it, which suggested that it needed cleaning; the steps to the front door were the same number as before.

He raised his hand to knock and heard laughter echoing along the corridor. He did not want to spoil the mood and suddenly wished that he might slip away.

'Who's there?'

It was Minnie's voice. Chris gave his name, feeling foolish.

'We're fine. Everything's fine,' Minnie said after she'd shut the door behind him. 'Have you had eaten? Julie's made some soup.'

'Thank you. Later, maybe. I need to ask Camilla something.'

Minnie stood aside, her expression instantly tighter, buttoned down.

'I'm sorry for all this,' Chris said.

Minnie looked at him severely, then she smiled. 'When it's over, you can take me out to dinner.'

'Done.'

'No one's tried to break in. We've had no threatening phone calls.'

'You'd tell me at once if – '

'Of course I would.'

'Thank you for staying here.'

Minnie made an impatient movement with her hand as if to say that wasn't what concerned her.

'She's just so sad, and there's nothing I can do.'

'Someone could have been watching when she found Brian, watching to see who found him.'

'I know. Don't worry. Riza's a celebrity already. Look at this.'

Minnie found photos taken by the neighbours and uploaded to Facebook. Was Camilla more at risk, or less, with her house the focus of attention?

Minnie thought it was amusing and he didn't want to frighten or upset her by repeating his fears.

Chris sat next to Camilla on her living-room couch. Both had their backs to the window, but Chris was aware of the last of the spring sunshine fading into twilight, the blossom that covered the tea-tree till there seemed no room for anything other than that feast of white.

He shrank from drawing Camilla's attention back to Brian's death, and took her hand as some kind of apology.

'Did Brian say anything to you about a yacht called the *Aeola*?'

Camilla returned the pressure of Chris's hand, but her own felt frail, bird-boned.

She said in a soft voice, 'I seem to recall Brian mentioning a boat of that name and that it was a beauty.'

'Do you remember if Brian said where he saw it?'

'Queenscliff harbour, I think.'

'What about the night Captain Delraine drowned?'

'Do you mean did Brian see the *Aeloa* that night? If

he did, he never told me.'

Chris thought of all the different possibilities. If Brian suspected the *Aeola* had been moored off shore the night Delraine had drowned, surely he would have said something. It wasn't the same as breaking a promise not to repeat what Delraine had told him.

Would Brian have recognised Ian Charleton's yacht? If he'd seen it even once before, Chris thought the answer to this question was yes.

Camilla turned her hand over. Chris loosened his fingers in case she felt restricted, but she left her hand in his.

'How can fear be an emptiness and at the same time fill you up till you can scarcely breathe?' she asked.

'Fear of what?'

'Of failing him. Which is stupid, since I already have.'

'No, you haven't. Don't ever think that.'

Camilla shrugged, but then she inclined her head so that it was almost resting on Chris's shoulder.

'You know,' she said softly. 'I keep coming back to the fact that we didn't become friends till we were old. Think how different it could have been.'

Chris heard a noise, low voices in the kitchen, Minnie and Julie getting the soup ready most likely.

'You were good friends,' he said.

It was a silly thing to say, inadequate, Chris thought, yet she knew him well enough to understand that he was trying to offer what comfort he could.

Camilla raised her head and looked at him sidelong.

'I should have pressed Brian more. I know that. Or

spoken to you myself. But Brian was like – I don't know, an echidna, I suppose. If you badgered him, he put up his spikes and shuffled off into a hole.'

Chris smiled at the description. Julie called out to say the soup was ready, and he gave Camilla's hand a final squeeze.

TWENTY-FIVE

Evan Aldridge said hello when Chris knocked on his door early the next morning. Chris was sure his visit was unwelcome, but the harbourmaster wasn't going to complain, or initiate any kind of conversation until pressed to do so.

He'd checked the *Aeola* for the times Chris had asked about, but not for any other date or time.

'When was the last time the *Aeola* was berthed here?' Chris asked.

'A while back, as I recall.'

'Check please. I'll be back in twenty minutes.'

Aldridge looked as though he was about to object, then changed his mind. Chris decided to spend the time paying Tom another visit.

Tom greeted him with the first line of a poem.

'It was a dark and stormy night.'

Chris quoted the next lines. 'The rain came down in torrents. There were brigands on the mountains.'

'Not only on the mountains, Blackie!'

Tom's grim expression was exaggerated by the desk lamp. It was overcast and threatening rain, dark inside the coastguard office.

'What's the matter?'

Tom's answer was to reach behind the door and grab the crowbar propped there.

'If they come, I'll be ready for them!'

'Have you been threatened, Tom?'

'They won't get me!'

'Who? Who won't get you?'

Tom laughed without humour. 'Don't worry. Jumping at shadows. Crowbar handy. I'll make us a cuppa.'

Chris watched while Tom put the jug on, frowning and patting his shirt pocket. For once, he didn't pull out his cigarettes.

'When was the *Aeola* last berthed here?' Chris asked, thinking it would be interesting to see if Tom's memory tallied with the harbourmaster's records.

Tom screwed up his face in a parody of a man trying to remember. 'Christmas is the last time I recall.'

Something in his expression prompted Chris to ask, 'What happened?'

'There was a bit of a flap. A girl fell in the water.'

'Fell? From the *Aeola*?'

'No. From Tony Parry's yacht. She's a beauty, that one. It was no big deal. She was drunk. She admitted that it was her fault. A couple of guys jumped in after her.'

'Were you there?'

'Me? God no. You know what I think of yachties' parties.'

'Why didn't you tell me this before, Tom?'

'Didn't think it was relevant. Nothing to do with Captain Delraine, or with Brian.'

'But if the *Aeola* was here, Captain Delraine might have been involved.'

Tom looked stubborn. What if Aldridge had warned Tom to keep quiet about the party? Tom would have laughed, or refused. But Tom was facing the threat of replacement. What if Aldridge had something to do with that?

'Why did Parry choose to have his party here?'

Chris was thinking that he and Dawkins should have prolonged their visit to Hastings and talked to the head of the Development Group as well as the harbourmaster.

Tom snorted. He had an array of snorts that went up and down the scale. 'If you're looking for someone flashing their money around, you couldn't go past Parry.'

'Who told you about it?' Chris asked.

'Rumours were flying round. You know how it is. Wal Gilchrist complained.'

'Why wasn't it reported to me?'

'I don't think Evan saw the need.'

Evan Aldridge knew he had to keep the yachties sweet. It wasn't just the money that they paid for berths, it was word-of-mouth recommendation. If he got a reputation for being heavy-handed, they'd stop coming.

Chris set aside the question of why Tom hadn't told him about the party, though he was disappointed and it made him wonder what else his friend was keeping to himself. He also wondered why Tom had been in such a strange mood when he arrived, but he didn't have time to think about that now.

'Were any of the pilots at the party?'

Tom thought before he said, 'I don't know, Blackie. Here's your tea.'

Chris phoned Dawkins, who suggested paying Wal Gilchrist a visit before returning to the harbourmaster. Dawkins also said to wait for him, that he wanted to be present at the interview.

Superintendent Walsh had given them a week's extension. The Sergeant sounded pleased.

Wal Gilchrist was a retired commercial fisherman with a permanent berth at the marina's western end. It wasn't the first time the peace of the harbour had been destroyed by one of Tony Parry's parties, Gilchrist said sarcastically. And he didn't think it would be the last.

'Evan Aldridge isn't doing his job?' Dawkins asked.

'I wouldn't say that. Wealthy yachtsman are the marina's bread and butter.'

'A balancing act then. Did Parry apologise?'

'To me? You're kidding.'

'But you did complain.'

'Might have said a word. I bet Parry never got more than a rap over the knuckles, if that.'

Chris could see that Wal was used to being laughed at behind his back, and sometimes to his face. 'Was Captain Delraine at the party?' he asked.

'I didn't see him.'

'But you know what he looks like? You'd have recognised him if he had been there?'

'The deck was crowded. There were lots of people.'

'What about other pilots?'

Wal Gilchrist shook his head.

'Did you see the girl fall in the water?'

'Heard the kerfuffle, shouting and carrying on. It was late by then, nearly midnight. Trying to sleep, wasn't I? Not that there was much hope of that.'

Dawkins made a sympathetic face. Chris didn't believe Wal was taken in by it, but he was too keen on telling his story to be bothered one way or the other.

'So you heard shouting. What happened then?'

'Someone fished her out, didn't they?'

'Who?'

'A couple of young guys.' Gilchrist sounded as though they might have been waiting for just such an opportunity.

'Where was Parry?'

'Search me.'

'Could the girl have been pushed?'

'Jesus! How should I know?'

'Did you take photographs?'

'What?'

'Photos,' Dawkins repeated patiently. 'On your phone.'

'It was last Christmas.'

'But you'd still have them.'

'Maybe,' Wal Gilchrist said.

'We'll be in the harbourmaster's office for a while,' said Dawkins. 'Then we'll be coming back. I expect you'll have found the photos by then.'

Evan Aldridge confirmed from his records that the *Aeola* had booked a place at Queenscliff the previous Christmas, but not since then.

He said coldly, in response to Dawkins's question about the security system, 'The entrance to each boardwalk is locked and requires a pass key.'

Dawkins said, 'I assume that's how Tony Parry let his guests through, with a key?'

Aldridge nodded. His expression was impassive, as before.

'Which way do the cameras face, the ones at the entrance to the boardwalks?'

'Seaward.'

'So any record of guests arriving would have been of their backs.'

'We only keep the film for a month.'

'I understand that. You would have checked at the time, though, after that girl fell overboard.'

'There was an incident. We handled it.'

'Who's we?'

'Mr Parry and myself.'

'Did you interview the guests?'

'I spoke to Lauren, the girl who fell, and the young man who jumped in after her.'

'I thought a few jumped in.'

'The one who grabbed her. Nick, I think his name was.'

You know perfectly well what his name was, Chris thought.

'You interviewed Wal Gilchrist too,' Dawkins said.

'Wal – '

'He complained.'

'It takes all kinds, doesn't it?'

'Meaning Mr Gilchrist has a right to a berth here, just the same as Mr Parry, even though Gilchrist is a nuisance and you think all this is a storm in a teacup. Let me remind you that two men are dead and if you're withholding information to protect a wealthy customer, any of your customers, then I can charge you with obstructing a police investigation.'

Aldridge said nothing to this, but his gaze was stony.

'Do you recall seeing Brian Laidlaw at the harbour when either the *Aeola* or Parry's boat, the *Destiny*, was berthed here?' Dawkins asked.

'Brian was often down here.'

'Do you remember specific occasions? Last Christmas for instance?'

Aldridge shook his head.

'Was Mr Parry's yacht here the night Captain Delraine drowned?'

'Blackie here checked the CCTV footage.'

Chris opened his mouth to speak, but Dawkins was quicker. 'I know that Mr Aldridge. Just answer the question.'

'No.'

They left the office, Dawkins red-faced and annoyed. Yet the glance he threw in Chris's direction, once they'd turned the corner, was half apologetic.

'I know. I know. But he got under my skin.'

'Let's go back to Wal,' Chris said.

'How long have you been living at the harbour, Mr Gilchrist?' Dawkins asked.

'Almost eight years.'

'You don't find it restrictive, living on a boat?'

'Restrictive?' Wal repeated, as though the idea had never occurred to him. 'Not at all.'

'What about those photos?'

Gilchrist mumbled a reply. Chris and Dawkins waited while he made a show of finding them, then looked over his shoulder as he scrolled through laughing groups of young people.

'Wait,' Chris said. 'Go back.'

The midsummer sunset was golden and enticing. Figures were clearly outlined against the railings and the mast. Eric Finlay had his head back, laughing. Tony Parry, standing next to him, was grinning. Both were holding champagne glasses. In a corner of the frame was Rosemary's older brother, Robert. He looked amused and, for a man standing to one side, somehow in control.

Chris copied the photo, while Dawkins moved a few steps away and phoned Finlay's office, where he was invited to leave a message.

Then he phoned Tony Parry at the Hastings Development Group. He left a message there as well.

'Would you have expected Ian to be in the photo?' Chris asked as they walked around the harbor to where he'd parked the car.

Dawkins looked thoughtful. 'You mean because the brothers stick together and would have come on the *Aeola*?'

Chris was thinking that Ian could have been elsewhere on the *Destiny*, but he hadn't recognised Ian in any of Wal's photographs. It was possible that Ian stayed on the *Aeola* and not gone to Parry's booze-up. It was possible he'd had other business in Queenscliff that night.

'Do you think Gilchrist is lying about Delraine being at the party?' Dawkins asked.

'I don't see why he would.'

'Because someone's got to him and warned him.'

'Then why didn't he destroy those photos?'

Chris thought of Tom. He didn't like the idea of a

shadowy figure threatening witnesses.

'What about Ivan Southeby?' Dawkins asked. 'Would you have expected Southeby to be there?'

'Not necessarily. If Southeby's in favour of Hastings, and we don't know the answer to that question, he may not have wanted to be seen partying with Tony Parry.'

'Finlay didn't mind.'

'Ah, yes. Finlay. He looks happy in that photo, wouldn't you say?'

'Happy or triumphant,' Dawkins said.

He smiled that smile with a hint of wolf in it, though his voice was light.

'Do you think it was Southeby Delraine overheard offering Finlay a bribe?' Chris asked.

'It could have been. But why would the location of a new container port matter that much to Southeby? The pilots stand to gain either way.'

Chris nodded in agreement. 'It's personal gain we're looking for. Someone looking to make millions for themselves.'

'Southeby may have invested in land around Hastings or Bay West.'

'I can look,' Chris said, thinking he should have done so before. 'What about the girl falling in the water?'

'Tomorrow we can find out what she has to say for herself.'

The sun was setting. Night changed things; things looked different in the darkness. Well, that was the cliché to end all clichés, Chris said to himself.

He thought again of Tom, alone in the coastguard office. Did he have his crowbar handy? What was Tom thinking, sitting smoking under the No Smoking sign?

He could take Dawkins there now, turn up unannounced. But he knew Tom wouldn't forgive him if he did that, put him on the spot like that.

Dawkins would be immediately suspicious of Tom, and suspicious of Chris for keeping his long association with the coastguard officer a secret. That's how Dawkins would view it, though there'd been nothing deliberate about it. Not consciously so; but Chris acknowledged to himself that he'd kept Dawkins away from Tom.

Gilchrist had known about that photo all along, but had taken his own time to produce it. Chris felt the fisherman's churlishness like an itchy second skin. I could become like that, he thought, if I stay here, retire here. Not on a boat, of course; but in my cottage, grumping at the neighbours. I'd poke my nose into other people's business then complain about them.

They were lucky that Wal Gilchrist did have a long nose. But still, Chris shuddered to think of that second skin tightening, becoming one with his own.

In the gathering darkness, with the harbour lights behind them, Dawkins seemed to have both grown and shrunk in size.

Chris thought of Evan Aldridge, who'd been unapologetic. Aldridge had spoken as though the security cameras, their placement and their functioning, had never been questioned before, and it was an insult to him that they were being questioned now.

'When you're down here in the dark,' Dawkins said, 'you realise how easy it would be to sneak in and out.'

'You mean the *Aeola*?'

'Or the *Destiny*.'

'Someone would have seen them.'

'Wal Gilchrist?'
Chris said, 'Aldridge would have known.'

TWENTY-SIX

'Brian Laidlaw was a friend of Captain Delraine's from his naval days,' Chris said. 'Did Brian ever visit the captain here?'

'The old man who fell off the cliff?' William's voice was flat. He'd made it clear that Chris's visit was unwelcome. 'I don't recall seeing him.'

It was next morning. Chris had left Dawkins at the station haranguing the Hastings harbourmaster over why he was taking so long to produce the CCTV footage.

He'd found William in the pilot centre's kitchen, chopping vegetables for soup. The cook had looked up as Chris came in, but hadn't stopped what he was doing, and hadn't invited him to take a seat. He'd had his hair cut though, and it fitted his head like a neat brown cap.

'Did Captain Delraine ever talk to you about Brian Laidlaw?'

'No.'

'Who are you protecting?'

'No one.'

'Come with me.'

'I'm busy.'

'You can spare five minutes,' Chris said.

Captain Delraine's room smelt stale and closed up. His clothes had been removed, but no one else had slept there, William told Chris.

The cook stood in the middle of the room with his arms loose by his sides. 'I should have stopped him,' he said in a different voice, sad and almost sobbing.

'How could you have done that?'

'I was worried. I shouldn't have gone home.'

'Worried more than usual?'

'You asked if I came in here that night. I lied when I said I hadn't. I came to say goodnight. Captain Delraine was sitting on the bed with his head in his hands.' William looked at the bed and blinked rapidly. 'It was just before nine. I was tired, ready to go home. I asked him what was wrong, if there was anything I could do. He shook his head.'

'The anti-histamines?'

'I knew he'd taken some. He said he was going to sleep, that he'd be okay. I shouldn't have gone home. I should have stayed.'

'Why did Captain Delraine go out?'

'I don't know.'

'You had dinner with the Captain. He told you what was worrying him.'

'I've already been over this.'

'Sometimes people don't recall everything the first time.'

After a few moments, William spoke again. 'Captain Delraine didn't complain, but he said he wished his wife hadn't gone back to Hastings.'

'Did he say why?'

'He said she was too much under the influence of her brothers.'

'What do you think he meant?'

'I'm not sure, but I think they were pressuring her to insist on a divorce.'

'Would the Captain have gone out late at night to

meet his wife?'

'I don't know. How would she get here?'

Chris wasn't going to try and answer that. He thought it was interesting that Delraine had told William he wished Rosemary had not gone back to the family property.

'Do you recall a party at the Queenscliff marina last December?' he asked.

'No.' William shook his head.

'I put it to you that you do recall that night,' Chris said, losing patience. 'I think you remember it in detail.'

William's resistance collapsed. It was as though he'd been waiting to be pushed that extra step, and now he'd taken it he no longer cared about repeating what had been said to him in confidence.

'I spoke to Captain Delraine the day after.' William was still standing with his hands by his sides, but now his fists were clenched. 'We sat outside in the courtyard and had a cup of tea.' Chris wondered how often they'd done that – sat outside so the cook could smoke while they talked. 'Captain Delraine looked exhausted. He'd shaved erratically and there were bits of stubble on his chin. He asked me if I made a habit of going to Christmas parties. I laughed because it was embarrassing. I'm not the party type.'

'Neither was Captain Delraine.'

'I know,' William said abruptly. 'The Captain said he'd gone to meet a wealthy yachtsman with the hope of talking to him sensibly, but it was neither the time nor the place.'

'Who was the wealthy yachtsman?'

'Captain Delraine didn't say.'

'Did you ask him?'

'It wasn't my place to do that.'

'Did he tell you what he meant by sensibly?'

William shook his head.

'Did he repeat any of the conversation?'

'Not directly. He said he'd tried to explain that he must remain impartial, and that this had made the yachtsman angry.'

'Impartial?'

'Captain Delraine didn't go into details, but he mentioned that committee he was on. I knew he was worried about it.'

'Why would the yachtsman be angry about that?'

'I don't know.'

'But you must have wondered about it.'

Chris waited. When William said nothing further, he went on, 'I saw you talking to the Captain's sister, Alison, at the funeral.'

'Ms Delraine was tired and anxious. She didn't want to be there.'

'I could see that she appreciated what you said to her.'

William smiled, a small, wan smile, but a smile just the same. 'She seems like a nice person,' he said.

'And your opinion of Rosemary Delraine, has that changed?'

William didn't reply immediately. He seemed unsure what to say. 'At the funeral – '

'Yes?'

'I thought she might be ill.'

'Her husband had died.'

'Not that so much. I couldn't really believe that

she was grieving for him,' William said. 'I thought she looked scared.'

Chris sat on the bench under the black lighthouse. Out of the corner of his eye, he watched a pilot launch expertly pulling in to the jetty in front of the operations centre, and a man step out. At this distance it was impossible to identify him. The pilots continued to do their job, day and night, around the clock, their movements and routines so familiar that the townsfolk – him included – hardly noticed them.

When a man felt himself embattled and beleaguered, when he felt his enemies closing in, but at the same time did not feel he could seek help, was it any wonder that he jumped at shadows? Or dosed himself on diphenhydramine.

Dawkins was still busy on the phone. Chris began searching for evidence that Ivan Southeby had invested in land or businesses around Hastings, but drew a blank. He decided to pay another visit to the pilots workshop.

'What do you know about a party last Christmas on Tony Parry's yacht?' he asked Alex Stavros.

'Yachties are always having parties.'

'A girl fell overboard.' Chris was careful to keep his voice neutral.

Alex stared at Chris in silence for a few moments before saying, 'I heard about that.'

'What did you hear?'

'She was drunk, wearing those stiletto heels. She tottered too close the railing and lost her balance.'

'Who told you?'

'I don't remember now.'

'Have there been other incidents?'

'Like I said, yachties are always having parties.'

There was something in Alex's expression that reminded Chris of William. 'What do you know about Ian Charleton?' he asked.

'His yacht's fantastic.'

'You'd like to own one like that?'

'Who wouldn't?'

'Do you remember the *Aeola* being here last Christmas?'

Alex said carefully, 'It was a long time ago.'

'What about Ian's brother Robert? When was the last time you spoke to him?'

'I don't remember exactly.'

'Come on Alex. Think.'

When Alex refused to be provoked, Chris tried a different tack. 'What do you know about Eric Finlay?'

'I know he works for the government. In the Transport Department.'

'Is he often down here?'

'I wouldn't say often.'

'Did Captain Delraine mention his name to you?'

'No.'

Chris reflected that he seemed to have lost the knack of getting under people's guards; if he'd ever had it. The men who worked at the harbour formed a close-knit group. Alex's loyalty was to the company that employed him. If he needed advice about something, who would he turn to? Jim, the workshop mechanic who'd left suddenly? Fred Delraine, who'd surely had enough troubles of his own.

'Captain Delraine was on a committee chaired by Finlay,' Chris said patiently. 'They may have had a disagreement.'

'How would I know about that?'

'You work here. You get to hear things.'

'Not about some committee in Melbourne I don't.'

'You might have heard if Captain Delraine got into an argument with Finlay,' Chris said firmly.

'Well I didn't.'

Alex began walking quickly towards the front of the workshop. Chris had been careful to stay back in the shadows up till then. Now he followed Alex, no longer caring who saw him questioning the mechanic again.

'Have there been any more bills for special maintenance?'

'No.' Alex turned over his shoulder to reply. He sounded relieved by the change of subject.

'What happened to the bill?'

Alex stopped at the huge double doors. 'What do you mean?' He looked out over the water, not at Chris.

'You told me Captain Delraine came down here asking about a bill for special maintenance that you knew nothing about. What happened to the bill? Who paid it?'

'Head office, I suppose.'

'Was it an error?'

'What are you getting at?'

'Reasons why Captain Delraine might have made himself unpopular.'

'The Captain was well liked.'

'Here and at the operations centre. What about head office?'

'You'll have to ask them.'

'But you never heard anything to the contrary?'

Alex shook his head.

Chris allowed himself to sound exasperated. 'You must have wanted to know. You might have been accused of claiming false expenses.'

'I told you, Jim handled all the paperwork.'

'Jim might have been accused then.'

'He left, didn't he?'

Suddenly Chris had had enough. 'Brian's dead too,' he almost shouted. 'Don't forget that. Brian's dead too!'

Chris banged on Wal Gilchrist's door, aware that he was allowing his frustration to get the better of him.

Gilchrist looked affronted when Chris said he wanted to copy all of the photos the fisherman had taken of the Christmas party.

Back at the station, Chris went through them carefully. None included Southeby.

'Which doesn't mean he wasn't there,' Chris told Dawkins, who nodded, pre-occupied with his plans for another visit to Melbourne.

TWENTY-SEVEN

After going through the security procedures, Chris and Dawkins were taken up to Eric Finlay's office. Finlay was sitting behind a large desk and did not stand up when they came in. Chris had the unsettling feeling he'd been waiting there, holding that pose, for several minutes.

Finlay was a small man – Chris's guess about this was confirmed – who initially seemed dwarfed by his desk, which was made of beautiful dark wood. Other items of furniture also seemed personally chosen, far from standard office issue, such as the bookshelves, made from wood matching the desk, fitting neatly under the window, the abstract oil painting on the opposite wall. The very cleanliness of the windows, with their expensive-looking curtains, marked this as the room of a man who held himself in high regard and could afford to indulge his personal tastes. Chris had no trouble picturing Finlay being wined and dined by Tony Parry. He would consider it no more than his due.

Though he didn't invite Dawkins or Chris to sit down, Dawkins positioned a straight-backed chair in front of the desk and Chris did the same.

Finlay moved his right hand closer to a full in tray, as though to emphasise the fact that he was a busy man. Clearly, they were going to be made to feel that their visit was a time-wasting intrusion, and that Dawkins could just as well have asked his questions over the phone.

Dawkins said without preamble, 'Captain Delraine

told you he wanted to resign from the consultative committee. What reason did he give?'

Finlay stared at Dawkins, ignoring Chris, who noted that the hand next to the in tray was stiff and tense.

'I've already told you that. Medical reasons.'

'And?'

'And what, Detective Sergeant?' Finlay made Dawkins's rank sound like an insult.

'What was your response?'

'I understood that Captain Delraine might find the committee burdensome.'

'Why was he appointed in the first place?'

'He volunteered.'

'Were you looking for a pilots' representative?'

Finlay moved his right hand, brought his fingers and thumb together, then released them. Chris wondered if he'd once been a smoker. 'It seemed like a good idea,' he said.

'It's odd that Captain Delraine was appointed just because he volunteered,' Dawkins replied, patiently pursuing his line of inquiry. 'Did you consult with Mr Southeby?'

'We spoke about it, yes.'

'What was Mr Southeby's opinion?'

'You'll have to ask him that.'

'I will. But for now I'm asking you.'

Finlay frowned and looked annoyed. 'Mr Southeby made no objection,' he said.

'It suited him?'

'I didn't say that.'

'What about Captain Delraine's resignation?'

'I informed Mr Southeby of Captain Delraine's intention.'

'Surely Captain Delraine had informed Mr Southeby personally?'

'He – yes, he had.'

'What was Mr Southeby's response?' Dawkins asked patiently.

'We didn't discuss the details.'

'Did you discuss a replacement for Captain Delraine?'

'The committee has almost finished taking submissions.'

'When will you be reporting to the Premier?'

'In a few weeks.'

'Which proposal will you be recommending?'

Finlay smiled. 'I'm sure you realise I can't tell you that.'

He wasn't bothering to hide his dislike or his condescension. He was laughing at both of them, although, as a uniformed constable, Chris knew he scarcely merited the bureaucrat's attention.

Dawkins pressed his lips together, then, it seemed to Chris, made a conscious decision to try another tack.

'Did you travel to Queenscliff to speak to Captain Delraine?'

'Why would I do that?'

'I'm not asking for your reasons, Mr Finlay. Not at this point. I'm asking if you did.'

'Fred and I spoke when he was up here for the committee meetings.'

'Please answer the question.'

'No.'

'So all your conversations with Captain Delraine took place here or on the phone?'

'That's right.'

'What about Tony Parry's Christmas party? The one at Queenscliff marina?'

'Was Captain Delraine there? I didn't know.'

It seemed to Chris that Finlay could well be lying, but unless they found a witness who'd seen Finlay and Delraine together that night, they would never prove it.

In response to further questions about Parry and the relationship between them, Finlay said that he was keen on sailing, though he didn't own a boat. He'd made a trip to Erith Island with Parry the year before.

'Don't you see that as a conflict of interest?'

'No.'

'You're chair of a committee advising the government on the location of a new container port. Mr Parry clearly has an interest in that location being Hastings.'

'Mr Parry put in a submission, just as anybody is entitled to.'

'But you don't go sailing with just anybody.'

'I'm acquainted with a number of the people and organisations who've made submissions. I associate with them. It's part of my job.'

'How did Captain Delraine get on with Tony Parry?'

'I don't know. I'm not aware that they were acquainted.'

'Going back to the Christmas party, did you know the girl who fell in the water?'

Finlay hesitated before replying. 'No.'

'Did you see what happened?'

'I wasn't nearby. I heard a splash and a scream.'

'Where were you precisely when it happened?'

'I – on the other side of the deck, the landward side.'

'What was the joke about?'

'What joke?'

'Parry's. You were laughing. Robert Charleton was in on it too.'

For the space of a few seconds, Finlay sat very still. Then he forced another smile.

'It was Christmas, Sergeant, a time of good cheer.'

'Were you offered money to slant your committee's findings in favour of Hastings?'

'What?'

'You heard me, Mr Finlay.'

'That question is an insult.'

Finlay seemed to realise that blustering was not the way to go. When he spoke again, he had his voice under control.

'Whoever told you that is lying.'

'What did you say, yes or no?'

'No one offered me money.'

'Because they didn't need to?'

Finlay's voice was still controlled, but with an icy undertone. 'My committee's job is to collect submissions and to pass them on.'

'But you talk to people, the Premier for one.'

'I have no power to influence the Premier one way or the other.'

'Did Captain Delraine know about the bribe?'

Finlay frowned again and said, 'There was no bribe.'

'What did you think of Captain Delraine?'

'I respected him. I liked him.'

'Did you believe he was capable of doing his job?'

'His job as a pilot? I'm not qualified to answer that.'

'His job as a member of your committee.'

'He said he intended to resign. I've already told you that.'

'That wasn't what I asked you.'

'Captain Delraine was perfectly competent.'

'But?'

'But I thought he was right to pull back if he was finding it too difficult.'

'Is that the advice you gave him?'

'He didn't ask for my advice.'

Dawkins went on asking questions for a few more minutes, then he and Chris got up to leave.

Finlay didn't say goodbye. His hands were clasped on the desk in front of him, the skin across his knuckles pulled so tight Chris would not have been surprised to see it split.

'Of course he denied it,' Dawkins said sourly as they walked to where Chris had parked the car.

They only had Camilla's word about the offered or potential bribe, a word that had been passed from Delraine, to Brian, to her. Delraine's letter to his sister referred to corruption, but the wording was vague.

They could apply for a warrant for the committee's minutes, and the application might be granted, but the minutes would tell them nothing, Chris was sure. Besides, the application would take days, and by then their time would be up.

'Finlay couldn't be sure that Delraine would keep

his mouth shut, Dawkins said.

'So he took steps to make sure?'

'If Finlay was only offered money, if he didn't accept it, where's the danger?' It seemed to Chris that Dawkins was arguing with himself.

'The danger to Finlay was in keeping quiet about it, Chris said. 'We can try and find out if he reported it to his superior.'

'But you don't believe he did?'

'No, I don't.'

'Who tried to bribe him?' Dawkins asked.

'It could have been Robert Charleton, or Ivan Southeby.'

'Or Tony Parry. What about Ian Charleton?'

'I don't think Robert would have trusted Ian with the job.'

'Nor do I. What were the odds on Delraine going back to the committee room?'

'It may not have been chance.' Chris had given this point a good deal of thought. 'He may have suspected and that's why he went back.'

It occurred to Chris that there was something of a sea creature about Dawkins, something narrowly focussed on its next meal while avoiding being eaten in turn. Chris had watched a documentary once – the large predators circling, the small fish swimming to escape. He pictured Delraine's drowned body drifting in to shore and remembered that there'd been no marks of violence at all.

Walking, Dawkins kept his head down, staring at his feet, only occasionally glancing at Chris while their exchange of views took place. Chris knew Dawkins was going back over his interview with Finlay, berating himself for not having got more out of the committee chairman.

Finlay had known they were coming and had been prepared for them, prepared to be questioned about the offer of a bribe. He'd known he had only to sit tight and deny it.

Ivan Southeby was unavailable to see them. Dawkins spoke to him on the phone, sitting in the car's passenger seat with the window down.

He'd talked it over with Chris before making the call. They'd agreed it was possible that Finlay would have phoned Southeby once they'd left his office, in which case they would lose the advantage of surprise. But Dawkins thought he'd come straight out with what he called 'the big question' anyway.

'Did you offer Eric Finlay a bribe to put in a recommendation favourable to Hastings?'

'Of course not!' Southeby sounded suitably outraged.

'Do you know who did?'

'No!'

'What did Captain Delraine tell you about a bribe?'

'Nothing. These questions are ridiculous.'

Chris felt that he and Dawkins were in a very windy place and were about to have their feet blown out from under them. Southeby was a skilled tactician, just as Eric Finlay was. Neither man could have risen to the position he occupied without having learnt to silence opposition, to manoeuvre and control.

'Could you describe your last meeting with

Captain Delraine?'

'It was – we were - 'Southeby began, then seemed to change his mind. 'Captain Delraine phoned to talk to me about resigning from the committee.'

'How did the Captain seem?'

'I've already been through all this.'

'Just answer the question, please.'

'He – Fred sounded very tired.'

'Did you think he'd been drinking?'

'Oh, no.'

'How can you be sure?'

'Captain Delraine didn't drink, or only very sparingly.'

'You knew about the anti-histamines?'

After a slight pause, Southeby said, 'Yes.'

'Did you believe Captain Delraine capable of piloting ships?'

'He was perfectly alright in the daytime.'

'And you knew that the dispatch officers only gave him day shifts. But the situation couldn't continue. Your company couldn't continue to employ a man who was addicted to tablets that affected his ability to work. Captain Delraine could have caused an accident. Surely you must have been aware of that.'

The word accident reminded Chris of Peter Robinson, and Robinson's anger that Southeby had failed to support him.

Southeby said in a different voice, regretful, almost apologetic. 'I did try and talk to Fred. I suggested that he take a few months off until he'd sorted out his personal problems. He said his doctor was helping him. It was better for him to keep working, with a few day shifts, rather than having nothing to do.'

'But you knew the situation couldn't continue. What would your next step have been?'

When Southeby didn't reply immediately, Dawkins said, 'You would have forced Captain Delraine to resign. You couldn't take the risk of allowing him to pilot ships. And you haven't answered my question. When was the last time you saw Delraine face to face?'

'It was only briefly. At the harbour, at the workshop. I came down to see the new beak hull. Fred was there, talking to Jim and Alex.'

'How did Captain Delraine seem that day?'

'We didn't really speak. We just shook hands and said hello, then Fred left.'

'Did you ask Jim and Alex what Captain Delraine had been talking to them about?'

'The new hull. Everyone was proud of it.'

'What about a bill for special maintenance?'

'Excuse me?'

Dawkins explained, going over the points Alex had raised with Chris, then asking why Delraine would have visited the workshop in order to query it.

'I don't know.'

'Did Captain Delraine raise the matter with you?'

'No.'

Southeby hung up.

Chris realised something that he hadn't put into words for himself clearly until then. With the possible exception of William and the drivers and crewmen he had known for years, he didn't trust anyone who worked for, or was associated with the pilot company.

He reminded himself that the pilots were used

to washing their dirty linen behind closed doors, presenting a united front. Southeby's submission in favour of dredging had not provoked any public opposition.

Peter Robinson had made as much fuss as he could over the injustice done to him, or the perceived injustice. He'd enlisted Delraine's help, though he must have known that Delraine was beset by problems of his own. But in the end Robinson had had to accept his dismissal.

'Do you think Southeby threatened Delraine with the sack?' Chris asked.

'Southeby had a right to sack him,' Dawkins said. 'What if he'd collapsed? Begun hallucinating? It was a disaster waiting to happen.'

Chris recalled Peter Robinson again. 'Sacking Delraine wouldn't have been easy. What if Delraine knew something that Southeby would rather keep quiet?'

'Like?'

'Bribery,' Chris said.

'You think Southeby's lying about that?'

'We're looking for men doing deals while other men turn a blind eye.'

Dawkins looked thoughtful. 'Then along comes Delraine who won't turn a blind eye. But all they had to do was deny it. Delraine's word would have been easy to discredit. All they had to do was bring up his drug dependence. They didn't have to kill him.'

When Dawkins phoned Jim, who'd left the pilots workshop suddenly, Jim was taciturn to the point of rudeness. Yes, Captain Delraine and Mr Southeby had said a few words to one another the day they'd come to see the new beak hull, but neither had raised his voice nor appeared upset.

When Dawkins asked about the bill for special maintenance, Jim replied, 'We got it sorted. There was nothing "special". The computer systems on the new launches require a different kind of maintenance, and that took a bit of getting used to. It took a while to get the billing sorted out.'

Dawkins put the phone down. He turned to Chris and said, 'Look for a transfer of land to Eric Finlay. Try the titles office first.'

'Surely it would have been too much of a risk to lodge the title publicly,' Chris said.

'I agree, but we have to eliminate the possibility.'

It didn't surprise Chris that he drew a blank with the titles office. Finlay was divorced. Chris searched for his ex-wife's name and the names of his three children. He could widen the search, but in whose name if not those of his immediate family?

It was possible that a gift of land had been promised in return for future favours. Why pay in advance might have been the reasoning of whoever had offered the bribe. He would pay when Finlay had demonstrated that he'd done the favour, not before. Yet whoever it was had been taking an enormous risk. What if Finlay claimed he'd tried to influence the government's decision, but had been unsuccessful? What would happen to the promise then?

But the title search had not been wasted. Chris discovered that Tony Parry had been buying land around Hastings, not just a few blocks, but extensive property. Parry had put the profits from his hardware business into land.

TWENTY-EIGHT

Chris lay awake that night and thought about it. Normally he liked to sleep with the bedroom curtains closed, not even a sliver of night sky showing through, but that night he left them open and lay looking at the stars.

Why had Brian been killed? In spite of the fact that they still had not found concrete evidence, Chris was sure that Brian's death hadn't been an accident. Was it just because he'd seen two men talking to Delraine, and they'd seen him? Had something happened at Delraine's funeral? Had Brian spoken to one or other of them after the service at the church, waited after saying goodbye to Camilla and telling her that he was going home? Had Brian arranged that pre-dawn meeting on the cliff top? But no, surely his murderers had done that. They had sought him out and got him to agree.

But why had Brian agreed to a meeting which he must have known was dangerous? Chris thought it must have been for Delraine's sake. Brian felt guilty and ashamed for not having protected the Captain. If there was anything he could do to alleviate that guilt, to make some recompense, then he would do it.

As for himself, perhaps Brian hadn't cared all that much whether he lived or died. He was ashamed and grieving, and must have known that he couldn't go on living independently forever. A swift death might have seemed, if not an attractive alternative, then not one to be afraid of either, not one to be shunned.

Chris wondered if he should go and knock on Camilla's door, make sure she was alright. But it would be stupid to go there at night; he would frighten Minnie and Julie, for one thing. Riza would stamp and snort. Did camels snort? Even if they didn't normally – Chris smiled in the dark, in spite of himself – there could always be a first time. Should he find somewhere else for Camilla to stay? She would hate to leave Queenscliff and might refuse outright; still, her safety must come first.

Chris slept badly and woke tired and gritty-eyed. The sea yawned behind him as he walked up the hill. He felt it like a human yawn and shuddered. Then he told himself that at least his worst fear was behind him; he'd made some progress in conquering it and he wasn't going backwards now.

Beside him, in the station's front office, Dawkins sat hunched into himself like an old grey currawong.

They'd gone as far as they could with Finlay and Southeby for the present. The last thing they needed, Dawkins said, was for either man to ring up Superintendent Walsh and complain.

The Hastings harbourmaster's failure to produce the CCTV footage now seemed deliberate. Dawkins said grimly that it had probably been destroyed.

Tony Parry's properties were on the opposite side of Hastings to the Charletons. Chris reminded himself how long Hastings had been touted as a container port, and for how long Parry and others like him had been lobbying and scheming. Parry was fifty-three. He'd grown up with the hope that the place where he'd been born could become an international centre for trade and industry. Parry hadn't been born wealthy like the Charleton brothers. He'd earnt his wealth by hard work and invested in the future.

If Delraine had opposed Parry, accused him of attempting to exert undue influence, where would the evidence be and how could he and Dawkins find it?

Chris began the laborious task of checking with Parry's party guests. Evan Aldridge had taken contact details. Almost all had stayed on deck for the whole time they'd been on board the Destiny. He found a couple who had gone below, or had started to; when Lauren screamed, they'd turned around.

He'd almost given up when he had a bit of luck. A young yachtsman, very keen on sailing, but unable to afford his own boat – he told Chris this on the phone, volunteered the information in a wistful voice – had taken himself on an exploratory tour of the *Destiny*.

It was before Lauren had fallen in.

'How long before?' Chris asked.

'Fifteen minutes? Ten? I wasn't paying attention to the time. I heard raised voices and recognised Tony's.'

'The other one?'

'I don't know. I don't think I'd ever heard it before. But he was upset. His voice was shaking. He was accusing Tony of something, and Tony was denying it. "No, no," Tony said. "You've got it all wrong."'

'And the other man?'

'He said, "I'm going to have to report it. You've gone too far."'

'What happened then?'

'I heard shouting. I ran up the steps.'

'Mr Parry?'

'I didn't see him come up, though he mustn't have been far behind me.'

'Do you have any idea who it was?'

'I've told you, I don't know. If he followed Parry, then I didn't see him.'

The name of the girl who'd fallen overboard was Lauren Bloomberg. On the phone Lauren sounded breathless, willing to help but afraid she couldn't really.

She couldn't remember anything much about that night at all.

'You don't recall falling overboard?' Dawkins asked.

'Not *how* it happened. But feeling terrified, water rushing in my mouth and ears, yes, I remember that.'

Lauren took a breath. Chris thought that there were some people – some young women in particular? – who sounded as though they'd run up three flights of stairs before getting a word out.

'I was lucky Nick was there.'

'That would be the young man who jumped in after you?'

'He saved my life,' Lauren said.

Chris guessed that Lauren was in her early twenties, glamorous and used to pulling men.

'Had you known Nick before?' Dawkins asked.

'I only met him that night. But as I said, most of it's a blur.'

'Have you seen him since?'

'Once. We met for coffee. I wanted to say thank you. But, well – Nick's engaged.'

'Was his fiancée on board that night?'

'No, she wasn't.'

'Does Nick work for Mr Parry?'

Lauren hesitated before saying, 'I believe so.'

'Have you seen Mr Parry since the party?'

'He was very upset about what happened. He sent me a lovely bracelet. Had it delivered by a courier, with flowers.'

'That's generous.'

'I told him it was too much, that it wasn't his fault.'

'Where was Mr Parry when you fell overboard?'

'Below decks I believe.' Lauren sounded uncertain, but there was no hint of suspicion in her voice, no hint that she might have been warned not to say what her host was doing.

Parry had given Lauren an expensive present; Chris believed he'd gone to some trouble to make sure Evan Aldridge let the matter drop.

'Was Captain Delraine a guest that evening?'

'I don't remember anybody of that name.'

'What were you drinking?'

'Bloody Marys.'

'Not the best choice.'

'Oh, I know!' Lauren giggled. Dawkins made a sympathetic noise. He thanked Lauren for her time and rang off.

In photographs, Parry's face appeared coarsened by alcohol, rich food and high living. At Delraine's funeral, he'd been a tall man in an expensive suit.

Now his clear blue eyes regarded Chris and Dawkins with polite goodwill. The muscles in his arms were hard. He looked fit and alert.

When asked about the Christmas party, Parry said, 'Everything was fine until poor Lauren – '

He hesitated as if unsure how to describe what had happened.

'Where were you when she fell overboard?' Dawkins asked in a neutral voice.

'In my cabin.'

'What were you doing there?'

'Talking to a guest.' Parry frowned slightly, but his voice was still low pitched, agreeable.

'Who?'

'Captain Delraine.'

Apparently, Parry had chosen to disarm them with frankness. Chris decided that he'd made the trip to Queenscliff with precisely that in mind.

'What did you talk about?' Dawkins asked.

'The future of the pilot service.'

'What about it?'

'How the company could expand, benefit by the development of Hastings as a container port.'

'You were attempting to persuade Captain Delraine that Hastings is a better option than Bay West?'

'It is.'

'Captain Delraine would have been familiar with your arguments. He would have read your submission to the committee. Why did you feel the need to make a personal appeal?'

'It was a rational discussion. It wasn't an appeal. The development of Hastings would give the pilot service an opportunity to expand. They'd keep their operations centre at Port Phillip and build a new one. The company could double in size.'

'What about Bay West?'

'It can't work in the long term.'

'Why not?'

'Congestion is one of the reasons. Too much traffic in too small a space.'

'You mean Port Phillip Heads?'

'Not only that. The site itself.'

'What happened when you finished your discussion?'

'Captain Delraine left.'

'Left the cabin or your party?'

'Both.'

'You had an argument?'

In spite of Parry's good intentions, his top lip curled in a sneer. 'You never met him, did you? If you had, you'd understand what I'm about to say. Fred Delraine didn't argue. If he disagreed with something, he politely withdrew.'

'Were you concerned that there might be an argument? Is that why you staged an incident?'

'Don't be ridiculous! Lauren falling overboard had nothing to do with my talking to Fred Delraine. It was pure co-incidence.'

Chris reflected that it didn't take much to wipe away the helpful veneer. He glanced from Dawkins to Parry and back again. Dawkins was looking pleased with himself, as though he'd calculated how long it would take to wind Parry up and his calculation had been right.

'When do you think the government will make a decision?'

Parry looked relieved. He made a sideways

movement with his hand.

'Before the election or after it?' Dawkins asked.

'It will have to be before.'

The change of subject was calculated in advance. Dawkins would let Parry stew over the business of Lauren falling in. Parry couldn't know for sure what Lauren had told them, or how much she'd given away without intending to.

Hearing again Lauren's breathy, eager voice, Chris doubted if there was any more to learn from her. She'd drunk too much, she'd tottered on her too high heels and fallen overboard. Delraine had used the opportunity to leave without being noticed. He would have been filmed entering and exiting the boardwalk, but the film was long gone.

Dawkins said, 'The Opposition's in favour of Hastings, but the government seems to be about 50/50. Is that your assessment?'

'All we can do is put our arguments clearly and persuasively and trust that the right decision will be made.'

'Is that why you invited Eric Finlay to your party, to put your arguments to him?'

'I did that when I made my submission.'

'Then why did you invite him?'

'Mr Finlay and I share a love of sailing.'

'Did Finlay speak to Delraine that evening?'

'I don't know.'

'Did you ask him?'

'Other things were happening.'

'What if Mr Finlay were persuaded to recommend Hastings?'

'Persuaded?'

'Offered money, or a gift of land.'

'That would be a criminal offence.'

'Did you promise Eric Finlay a gift of land in exchange for favouring Hastings?'

'Of course not!'

'Mr Finlay had been on sailing trips with you to the Bass Strait islands. You were closely associated and had common interests.'

'I'm closely associated with many people. And sharing a love of sailing is hardly a crime.'

Parry's voice was scornful, but Chris reminded himself that he couldn't be sure who Delraine had spoken to, or how much the police knew.

He wondered if he was looking at, not only Delraine's killer, but Brian Laidlaw's as well. He had no doubt that Parry was ruthless enough to kill for what he wanted, but Chris thought Brian would have recognised Parry as the proud owner of the *Destiny*.

Was it possible to smell greed? Was there a distinctive smell that attached itself to people for whom greed was second nature?

Of course Parry would not admit to being greedy. He would say he'd earnt what he had by hard work, and that claim would be true.

'Was Ivan Southeby a guest at your party?' Dawkins asked.

'No.'

'You sound very certain, Mr Parry. Is that because you and Mr Southeby did not see eye to eye?'

'I'm certain because Mr Southeby would not have turned up without an invitation.'

'Did you discuss the new container port proposals with Mr Southeby?'

'Not directly.'

'Indirectly?'

'I gained the impression the pilot company would welcome the opportunity to expand.'

'Did Mr Southeby give you that impression?'

'It's in the company's interests.'

'The Bay West option would also provide opportunities.'

'Not to the same extent.'

Chris thought Dawkins might press Parry on that point, but instead he asked, 'What about Ian Charleton?'

Parry looked momentarily confused. 'What about him?'

'Was he at your party?'

'No.'

'You seem very sure. Yet for part of the evening you were below decks talking to Captain Delraine.'

'Ian wasn't there,' Parry said coldly.

'So Robert came without him.'

'They may be brothers, but they're not joined at the hip.'

'How well do you know Rosemary Delraine?'

'Not at all. I wouldn't have met her more than a couple of times.'

Chris caught a hint of cruelty around Parry's mouth and behind his eyes.

'Since coming to stay with her brother?' Dawkins asked.

'Mrs Delraine seems to be a very private person. She keeps to herself.'

TWENTY-NINE

After Parry had left, Dawkins breathed out with relief. There were stray bits of stubble on the Sergeant's chin, that he'd missed while shaving. His face was grey with fatigue.

Chris couldn't help feeling that Parry had come out ahead. He wasn't above playing with them, mocking them, and that's why he'd turned up in person. Perhaps he was already boasting on the phone to Finlay, advising the committee chairman to keep stone-walling, telling him that they did not have long to wait.

They had a snack, washed down with hot, strong tea, then Dawkins rang Brendan Hearn, who'd been on the committee with Fred Delraine.

'I don't believe you were completely frank with me the last time I spoke to you, Mr Hearn.'

'What do you mean?'

Chris was afraid that Dawkins was making the same mistake he had before, putting a potential witness on the defensive when they needed his cooperation.

'Captain Delraine would not have phoned you at the time he did unless he had something specific to tell you, or to ask of you.'

Hearn was silent for a moment. When he spoke, it was reluctantly. 'Captain Delraine told me he wouldn't be attending any more committee meetings and asked if I'd note any mention of his brothers-in-law, and Tony Parry.'

'The minutes – '

'He didn't mean formal minutes. He meant conversation, casual remarks.'

'What was your response?'

'I told him I'd try.'

'Did you have information for Captain Delraine? Did you contact him again?'

'He died! He drowned!'

Dawkins repeated his question.

Chris thought Hearn might hang up, but he controlled his voice and said, 'I didn't contact him again because I wasn't sure I had any useful information. There were a couple of submissions still to come in. I mean everyone knew the deadline, but there were a couple of organisations that were working on submissions and had asked for an extension. One was the Hastings Yacht Club. Ian Charleton's name came up in connection with that.'

'Has that submission been released?'

'Not yet.'

'Do you know if it will be made publicly available?'

'I guess so. We've only had one meeting since Captain Delraine died. Mr Finlay dictated a message of condolence to the family.'

'When you spoke to Captain Delraine on the phone, what did he say about his brothers-in-law?'

'He didn't say anything directly, but Robert's been harassing the committee. He's always ringing up, wanting to know when the recommendations are going to the Premier, who else will see the submissions.'

'Have there been complaints?'

'Not formally, or none that I'm aware of. But it's exasperating.'

'What does Eric Finlay say?'

'He says the Charletons have to take their turn.'

Chris recalled again the photograph Wal Gilchrist had taken against the setting sun. He remembered Eric Finlay with his head back, laughing, Tony Parry with a big smile on his face, Robert Charleton off slightly to one side, amused, sharing the joke; or perhaps he'd just made it. Finlay hadn't looked exasperated then.

Dawkins's next phone call was to David Anstey.

'I'd like some information about who was at your wife's funeral, please.'

'What information?' Anstey sounded as though the subject was unwelcome, but he was prepared to help.

'Tony Parry. He's – '

'I know who Parry is. He's a development cowboy. Why would he be at Thelma's funeral?'

'To show his respect perhaps, even though they were on opposing sides.'

'Respect? I don't think Parry knows the meaning of the word. He didn't care tuppence for Thelma. Or any of our family.'

'But was he there?'

'Thelma wasn't religious. We hired a room at North Melbourne Town Hall. It wasn't big enough. People stood outside. I suppose Parry could have been part of the crowd. But I can't imagine why.'

'Did friends came back to your place afterwards?'

'Tony Parry has no shame and no conscience. But even he would not have shown his face inside my house.'

'You dislike the man that much?'

'He insulted Thelma. When he learnt of her involvement with the groups opposed to the Hastings development, he rang her up and abused her. He called her a gullible fool. He insulted our son Neil as well. That didn't matter. Neil could take it, but Thelma, she – she'd already been diagnosed by then.'

Anstey's voice broke, then he rallied. 'I rang Parry and gave him a piece of my mind.'

'Was Rosemary Delraine at your wife's funeral?'

Anstey sounded surprised by the question, but he answered readily enough. 'Yes, she was.'

'And her husband was with her?'

'Yes.'

'What about her brothers?'

'They were there too. Why do you want to know?'

'Did you speak to them?'

'I said hello.'

'That's all? Just hello?'

'That's all I remember. You'll appreciate that my mind was on other things.'

Dawkins ended the call looking thoughtful. Anstey had described a side of Parry that had been there under the surface, a propensity for angry outbursts and a determination to get his own way.

While Dawkins was making more phone calls, Chris googled the Hastings yacht club. It was small, not much bigger than the Queenscliff one. He wondered what their submission would be like, and if they'd taken the trouble because they didn't want their bit of foreshore swallowed up. He also asked himself why their submission was late. Ian Charleton was listed as a member, but not Robert.

Was it possible that Ian's loyalties were divided between the money his family stood to gain from port development, and a reluctance to see the amenities he enjoyed ruined from an environmental point of view?

Chris did an online check on Parry's yacht, telling himself it was something he ought to have done before.

'Worth eight million,' he told Dawkins when the Sergeant took a break and put the jug on for more tea. 'It's registered in the Cayman Islands.'

Dawkins snorted. 'Tax avoidance. Well, he's far from the only one.'

'A lot of people donated money to the Hastings Development Group,' Chris said. 'They'd be pissed off if they thought Parry was taking a cut for himself.'

Chris wondered if Fred Delraine had discovered that Parry was spending other people's money on an expensive yacht and if he'd confronted Parry with this on the night of the Christmas party.

In retaliation, what if Parry had threatened to go public regarding Delraine's addiction, claim he was no longer fit to work as a pilot, that he was a danger and should be dismissed?

And if Parry had made those threats, what had he done about them?

THIRTY

Chris and Tom walked to a different part of the harbour, close to where the coastguard boat was moored. Tom wasn't smoking. He said he had a cold. Chris has a sudden premonition of Tom seriously ill. He thought of William at the operations centre, fastidiously collecting his cigarette butts, and wondered if he'd ever tried to quit.

Chris brought Tom up to date on their conversations with Wal Gilchrist.

'Wal likes to poke his nose into other people's business,' Tom said. 'But he's a softie inside.'

'He seemed to enjoy complaining about Tony Parry.'

'Parry's the sort of showy extrovert who gets his goat.'

'Yours too, Tom.'

'I dislike what I've seen of him, that's true.'

'But?'

'But I wouldn't confront him personally unless I was very sure of my ground.'

'Do you think that's what Delraine did?'

'You're asking me, Blackie? How the hell should I know?'

Tom seemed to regret having responded snappily. 'You're trying to find out more about the party?' he said in a conciliatory voice. 'It doesn't sound like Delraine to pick a fight with a man on his own yacht.'

'Maybe he was desperate,' Chris said.

He knew he shouldn't be talking so openly to Tom, but he couldn't help himself. He had to talk to someone apart from Sergeant Dawkins.

'You lock your door at night, Tom?'

Tom laughed, his expression incredulous. 'What good would that do?'

Chris nodded, accepting Tom's reproof, recalling Brian's 'accident'.

'Don't take the launch out alone.'

Tom laughed again. 'What if some fool weekend fisherman gets into trouble? What if I get a call?'

'Take me with you.'

'Oh, right, Blackie. They – whoever they are – will throw us both overboard.'

Tom was determined to make light of danger, his own included, his own most of all.

Chris recalled Delraine's funeral – the genuine mourners and those whom duty or hypocrisy had brought, to stand and sit and sing a hymn – Rosemary Delraine with a brother at either elbow. And Peter Robinson, who'd arrived late and was sitting at the back, perhaps ashamed, knowing that everyone there recognised him as the pilot who'd been forced to leave the service. Robinson had sat bolt upright, solitary, apart from the others, his face a mask.

Chris and Tom walked back to the coastguard office.

Tom stared morosely at the tattered No Smoking sign. Chris asked what the matter was.

'You mean more than usual? I don't know, Blackie. Since I got threatened with the high jump – you know how it is – '

Tom had to go on proving himself as a volunteer. Whereas, for as long as he drew a salary, Chris could tell himself that somebody at least thought he was worth employing.

He glanced at the wall again, at the photograph of Bobby McGilvrey. Was it real and present to Tom, more than just a picture? Or did his eyes glance over it the way they glanced over the No Smoking sign? Surely the former, Chris thought. If he was looking for the beginning of a change in Tom, there it was. Tom had never been the same since Bobby died.

Chris's phone rang. It was Dawkins and he sounded pleased. The Hastings harbourmaster had finally got back to him with some dates and times. Ian Charleton had used one of the launching ramps to load the *Aeola* onto a trailer on Tuesday September 11. He'd said that he and Robert were going up the coast for a few days.

'I can guess what happened,' Dawkins said. 'They didn't want anybody seeing where they launched from, or on the road for that matter. Ian parked the boat at their property. They waited until dark, then set off for the launching ramp. They could be confident that nobody would see them.'

Chris said, 'And there was plenty of time to sail in through the heads and pull up off-shore not far from the pilots centre.'

'Where Delraine met them.'

'We should question Ian Charleton again about that phone call on the Tuesday afternoon,' Chris said.

Dawkins nodded. 'I'll do that.'

Julie went back to her caravan and Riza to his paddock.

Lifting his large, gentle feet, Riza turned to look back along his hump at the humans he was leaving behind. If you hadn't known him as a calf, you might have called his expression haughty.

Chris and Minnie said very little to each other. An exchange of glances reassured them that there'd be time to talk. Minnie would make up her shifts at the Brewhouse, covering for the waitresses who'd covered for her.

Camilla turned to Chris once her guards had gone. She looked both relieved and weary.

'Someone rang Simon and told him there was a camel in my garden.'

'Someone?'

'He thinks I'm suffering from dementia. Well, you know how my son is.'

Chris nodded. 'Did Simon know that you and Brian were friends?'

'I didn't – I never – he wouldn't have approved.'

'Do you want me to talk to him?'

'Thank you, but for the moment, no.'

When Camilla began to walk back into the house, Chris followed. At least I'll see her to the door, he thought.

Camilla turned and said with a self-deprecating shrug, 'I feel Brian's trying to tell me something. I know that sounds weird.'

Chris saw by her expression that she'd been working her way up to this.

'Something to do with the men he saw talking to

Captain Delraine?'

'I don't know.' Camilla stood disconsolate in the middle of the driveway.

Chris knew that she was observant and intelligent. She'd been slow to tell him what she knew, but he'd believed, after their last talk, that she was holding nothing back.

He wondered which of her neighbours had told Simon about Riza. Simon's plan to get his mother into a retirement home might have been put on hold, but he hadn't given up. Though they'd met only a few times, Chris found his memories surprisingly detailed, his dislike of Camilla's son fresh and undiminished.

'Ring me please, if something occurs to you. It doesn't matter when, or how small a detail.'

Camilla said she would.

Chris and Minnie sat companionably at Minnie's kitchen table. Chris looked around the room, reflecting how like his own it was, and yet how different too. The layout was the same, the basic furniture, yet this was unmistakably a woman's room.

Watercolours on the wall opposite the window were by a local artist. Chris did not dislike them, but he would never have hung them in his house. The bowl of spring blossom at the far end of the table – again, it would never have occurred to him to pick and place it there. Yet he grew flowers and enjoyed doing so.

'Nobody came near us,' Minnie said, 'except Camilla's neighbours.' She allowed herself a small, complacent smile.

'You saw them off, Min.'

'Nosy parkers.'

'And nobody phoned? Nobody out of the ordinary, that is.'

'Nobody Camilla didn't know. Her son phoned twice a day.'

Minnie knew that Chris had a low opinion of Simon Renfrew and why.

'Did she talk to him?'

'You mean, was I listening? She said, "Hello Simon," so I knew who it was. She didn't talk much. After he'd hung up, she looked tired and sad.'

'Simon hung up on his mother?'

'It looked that way, but we didn't quiz her. We thought, if she wants to talk about it, then it's up to her. Julie said he sounded like a drop kick.'

Chris pictured Julie huffing out the words and smiled.

They ate leftovers from the Brewhouse, with a baguette Chris had picked up on the way.

Chris asked Minnie how her first day back had been. He knew she wouldn't complain, any more than she'd complain about the inconvenience of staying at Camilla's.

Minnie laughed at herself. 'Boring, which is good,' she said.

Chris would have loved to go on sitting in her kitchen, pretending that there were no unanswered questions, no unexplained deaths.

He got up abruptly and left. Too many innocent people had already been drawn in.

THIRTY-ONE

'Where are you?' Dawkins was shouting down the phone.

'At the Bays hospital.' Rosemary Delraine's voice was very faint.

'We're on our way.'

Chris drove. It had taken them three hours to get to Hastings last time. Robert and Ian would be looking for their sister. How had she managed to escape?

Rosemary looked both shocked and enormously relieved. It was just dawning on her that she'd done the impossible. The light of that dawning was in the rings around her eyes, her tangled hair, the scratches on her hands.

Dawkins had phoned Superintendent Walsh from the car; he'd arranged for her brothers to be questioned.

Dawkins switched on a tape recorder and placed it by the bed. 'Tell me what happened on the night your husband died,' he said.

But Rosemary started further back in the story. 'I knew that they were planning something,' she said softly. 'One evening Ian pulled up at the front door and Robert went to meet him. They weren't speaking loudly, but I caught the word Shoreham. It didn't mean anything to me.'

Shoreham launching ramp, Chris thought.

Purple bruises on Rosemary's hands and legs were badges of triumphant courage. Her face, lifted to them under the penetrating hospital lights, was a face from which panic had been washed away.

'Robert took my phone when they locked me up. I was allowed to make calls, supervised of course. It would have looked suspicious if I didn't. If someone rang me, it went to voicemail, and Robert decided if and when I was allowed to return the call. He sat next to me while I made it.'

'Always Robert?'

'He didn't trust Ian to be – to be tough enough. When I was handed my phone, I tried to check the history, but I was never given enough time to do more than make a call. Robert sent text messages for me. I knew when they left the house together because they shut me in a storeroom with no windows. When one of them was there, I was allowed to stay in my old bedroom. The storeroom has no toilet.' Rosemary shrugged as if to say the point was an obvious one. 'Once they shut me in there all night. They left me a – a receptacle.'

'The night your husband died?' Dawkins prompted.

'They didn't tell me what they planned. It was early in the morning when they got back. I didn't have a way of telling the time, but I knew by the position of the sun. Ian came to let me out. When I asked him where they'd been he wouldn't say. He refused to look me in the eye. I became ill after that. I could have picked up a bug, or else it was exhaustion and stress. Ian brought me food and clean clothes, and made sure I had plenty to drink.

Robert only came in once. He had my phone with him. He said that Fred had walked into the sea and drowned and that the police wanted to speak to me. He told me what to say. He stood over me while I said my lines.

I had nothing to do but lie there and worry. I could hear the landline phone ringing downstairs, but I couldn't hear what was said. I thought you – I mean the police – might want to talk to me again, and if that happened, I must find a way to let you know that I was being kept a prisoner. But there was nothing until Robert came back one morning and told me to get dressed up because we were going to a funeral.

I collapsed after the funeral. I couldn't think at all. I lay there day after day knowing that I'd missed my chance. At the church, at that reception, I should have shouted, run to you, asked for your protection.'

'You were terrified of Robert,' Dawkins said.

'Since I was a small child. Our childhood was mainly spent apart, at boarding school, but in the holidays – ' Rosemary's voice, still low-pitched, sank even lower. 'But it's not only that. I was angry with Fred. Some days I felt eaten up with anger. Fred had never tried to be a proper husband to me.'

'Why didn't Captain Delraine go down to Hastings and talk to you in person after you left Brighton?'

'Robert put him off.'

Rosemary put a hand to her bruised face.

'Do you want some water?' Chris asked. 'Here.'

He leant across and steadied the glass for her while she drank.

Dawkins' phone rang. He answered it, said, 'Good' and then, 'I see.'

'Was that about my brothers?'

Dawkins nodded. 'They're at the station. The officer in charge is interviewing them. Please go on. What about the day when we came to question you?'

'Robert had kept me up late the night before, coaching me, making me repeat what I had to say.'

'It might have been better if we'd turned up unannounced.'

'I doubt if Robert would have let you see me. He would have said I was ill.'

'That would have made us suspicious.'

'But I was ill. Sick with worry and fear. Robert planned everything. He thought of everything in advance, except that I would overcome my fear of heights.'

'Of heights?'

'Oh, yes. I've been afraid of heights since I was a child. I could never go up on a Ferris wheel or anything like that. I was too upset and confused to think of escaping when I realised it was Robert's intention to keep me a prisoner, but I made sure they were aware that I stayed away from the window, that I was afraid of looking down. Robert used to look at me with a smile of satisfaction, and I thought, it's not nearly as bad as it was when I was young, but I'll pretend it is. I'll fool you in that one small thing.

After that, whenever they were in the room with me I kept my back to the window. I closed the curtains too. Robert would open them when he came in and I'd catch a cold, malicious glitter in his eye. I never argued with him. But after Ian had taken away my dinner tray, I would sit on my bed and watch the evening light leave the trees and think how I might escape. The bedroom windows were well secured, and Robert and Ian checked them every time they came in, just as they checked the door to make sure I hadn't tried to force the lock. But the bathroom window was a different story.

They checked the bathroom window the first few days as well. I was careful to shrink back and pretend to be afraid. And it was small. It looked too small for me to climb out of, even if it hadn't been for the drop down to the ground. Robert watched me, measuring my size against the window. For a careful planner and a dominant personality, Robert's thoughts were sometimes transparently obvious.

I had no tools. Of course they saw to that. I only had my hands. The one thing I had was time, long hours when I was left alone. Robert planned to take me to a doctor who'd recommend psychiatric treatment. Then he could apply for power of attorney. I overheard them talking about it one night. Robert raised his voice. Ian never argued with him, but I think he was asking him to wait.

Once I was safely locked up in a psychiatric hospital, Robert would have made sure I was drugged on tranquillisers, then ignored me.'

'Ian?'

'Ian might have visited. Guilt might have brought him that far. On the other hand, he might have convinced himself that forgetting about me was the better course.'

'You don't think much of your brother. Either of your brothers.'

'Robert hates me. Hate is his ruling emotion. It dictates everything he does.'

'And Ian?' Dawkins asked again.

'Ian's weak, and has always lived in Robert's shadow. When I began working at the lock, I didn't know whether I could squeeze out of the window or not. I told myself I wouldn't worry about that. I must face one problem, one hurdle at a time, or else I would be overwhelmed and accomplish nothing.

I couldn't think of a way to cover up what I was doing except with the blind. It didn't reach all the way to the bottom of the window and I just had to hope that neither Robert nor Ian would notice.

I found a hair clip, the old-fashioned kind. When I straightened it, it was like a piece of thin, strong wire. Ian had cleaned out the bathroom cabinet and emptied the shelves. I had some soap and tooth paste, shampoo, a towel and face washer, that was all. I searched everywhere, behind the toilet bowl, in the corners where the shower recess met the wall. I found the hair clip underneath the cabinet. It was such a tiny space! If the clip had been further back, I wouldn't have been able to feel it, let alone pull it out. I don't know how many times I've given thanks to that woman, whoever she was, who dropped her clip and forgot to pick it up.

Of course a small length of wire wasn't a key, and I didn't know the first thing about picking locks. But I treasured it. It became much more than a tool to me.'

Rosemary produced a small piece of wire from a folded handkerchief and held it out on the palm of her hand. It shone as metal does when the sunlight catches it. Light followed the bobbles and hollows of its uneven surfaces.

Chris was aware of Sergeant Dawkins braced and impatient beside him. He thought back to that evening at the Brewhouse, when he'd been surprised to find Dawkins changing, so it seemed, before his eyes.

Dawkins nodded at Chris, who took an evidence

bag out of his jacket pocket.

'Take care of it,' Rosemary said.

Some of the old Dawkins had come back. He'd said he wanted Rosemary to tell the story in her own words, but Chris knew half of the Sergeant's mind was at the station, wondering if Robert and Ian had had time to destroy the evidence of their sister's imprisonment.

He recalled a child's tea cup and saucer he'd once found under a water tank, precious possession of at least one vulnerable child. He remembered thinking how such a possession could take on magical significance.

'Your make-up at the funeral?' he asked, not quite sure why he was bothering with that detail now.

'I forgot to fix it. You noticed that. I could see you taking note.'

Rosemary jumped ahead in her story and began describing how, after she'd escaped, she'd waved down a motorist in the rain. The driver had skidded. He'd braked and skidded to a stop.

She'd asked to be taken to the nearest hospital. She'd apologised for taking him out of his way and offered to re-imburse him for petrol once she had some cash.

The motorist, wary but polite, had done what she asked.

Dawkins moved Rosemary back a few steps.

'I began working on the bathroom window and Ian didn't notice. Before the funeral, I wasn't allowed to use the bathroom without one of them locking me in and standing outside the door. The lock was old. Once I found the hair pin I began to try and loosen it. I left the shower running and Ian didn't call me out, or tell me time was up. I took that as a good sign. I began talking to Fred. I stopped being angry and just felt sad. I said I hadn't been the best wife to him – not a good wife at all, in many ways – but now I was doing something for him. I'll never forget what it felt like when I finally forced the lock. A moment of great joy. Once I'd done it though, I knew I couldn't wait for long.

I balanced on the cabinet and pushed the window as far as I could. I was terrified of getting stuck half way. If that happened and I had to call for help, I would have lost my chance forever. I was shaking and sweating. I tried to slow my breathing, concentrate on breathing out. I had my torn sheets ready. I couldn't find anywhere to tie them on the outside of the house. I tied one end to the cold tap in the wash basin. I've never been any good at knots. I'd lost weight since being kept a prisoner and that helped. I let the sheets down, thankful they were soft and made no sound against the wall. I got my shoulders through and managed to twist my lower body out. I bumped against the wall and bruised and cut myself.' Rosemary held up her right arm. 'I let go too soon and landed in a heap. Then I got up and ran.

I thought I would break my leg, or both legs. For hours in my room I'd pictured that window, how far it was from the ground, how Robert would never have let me use the bathroom if he believed I could escape. I'd never been any good at sport. It was Robert who'd won all the sporting trophies. And I thought how that was a help, that they didn't believe me capable.

My bed sheets – once a week I stripped the sheets off my bed and handed them to Ian, who gave me fresh ones. The night I finally forced the lock, I tore my sheets up. I used my teeth to make a start. I thought I was never going to be able to manage it, but then I told myself I'd managed the lock somehow and I'd manage this.

On my way down, I felt the sheets tearing, moving apart. It's true what they say, that something that takes seconds seems like hours. I fell the last bit, but I'm glad I did. Falling brought me to my senses. I knew I had to start running at once, and as fast as I could. The rain was a blessing, cold and hard and sharp. I opened my mouth and let the rain hit the back of my throat.

The first car that passed me on the road I waved down. The driver wasn't local and that was another stroke of luck. He was from the opposite end of Victoria. He drove me straight to the hospital and from there I phoned you.'

THIRTY-TWO

Robert's eyes were steely. He sat stiff and upright in his chair. If Rosemary's account was to be believed, he'd allowed an obsession to rule his life for years.

Chris was glad he and Dawkins had been invited to sit in on the interview, but glad as well that he'd taken a seat at the back of the room, in what shadow was available. He felt himself drawn to the light of Robert's scorn, and was ashamed of this.

Robert didn't look at anyone, but through them. Yet his stare was just as much turned inward as outward, to the place where his anger and hatred were fed, and to the fuel that fed them.

'What did you say when you met Brian Laidlaw on the cliff path?' Detective Sergeant Flanders asked. Flanders was a tall man, thin, with the beginnings of a stoop.

While Robert and Ian were being questioned, a forensic team was going through their house. The property was so large and there were so many places where evidence could be hidden that a proper search was going to take days.

'I said good morning,' Robert replied confidently.

'Did you push Mr Laidlaw off the cliff?'

'The old man over balanced and we tried to help him.'

Chris lived those seconds on the path as though he'd been there. He saw Brian tumbling in slow motion, yet quicker than an eye flash.

'Why did you take the gloves?' Flanders asked.

'What gloves?'

'The ones Mr Laidlaw was wearing.'

'I didn't take them.'

If Flanders' tactic was to try and rattle Robert, who'd probably believed he was going to start by questioning him about Fred Delraine, then it wasn't working.

'When Mr Laidlaw realised you were going to push him over the edge, he grabbed hold of you.'

'Mr Laidlaw lost his footing. I reached out and grabbed hold of him.'

'Why didn't you go straight to the police?'

'Mr Laidlaw's death was a tragic accident, but I didn't think I would be believed.'

'Why not?'

Robert looked up. His eyes met Chris's briefly.

'The other officers suspected me, Sergeant Dawkins and – and his assistant. I knew they wouldn't give me a fair hearing.'

'You expect me to believe you now.'

'I'm telling you what happened.'

When Flanders changed the line of his questioning and asked about Rosemary, Robert's reply was scornful.

'My sister's crazy. Her story is the fabrication of a crazy mind.'

'Mrs Delraine ripped her sheets and knotted them together to make a rope. She picked the lock on the bathroom window and climbed out. She flagged down a motorist.'

Now was the time for Flanders to say they'd tracked down the motorist and confirmed Rosemary's story. But she hadn't noted the registration number, and no one had come forward.

Robert smiled, a small, satisfied smile. 'That lock's been broken for years. I never got around to fixing it. My sister went to pieces after her husband drowned.'

His voice was calm and reasonable. Chris wondered why he hadn't insisted on having a lawyer with him. Perhaps because he thought he made a better show of innocence without one.

'We tried to persuade Rosemary to see a counsellor, but she refused. Our sister wasn't capable of looking after herself. We did our best.'

'What did you do with the sheets?' asked Flanders.

'What sheets?'

'The ones Mrs Delraine tied together.'

'I did nothing with them. I've been trying to explain. My sister suffers from hallucinations. She imagines things.'

'How do you explain your sister's cuts and bruises?'

'She fell while she was running away.'

'So you do admit she ran away?'

Robert shrugged as though to say, we wouldn't be here otherwise.

'We tried to look after Rosemary since she wasn't capable of looking after herself. But she needs psychiatric help.'

After the first rush to find their sister, bring her back, the brothers' next thought would have been the sheets, the bathroom lock.

Chris pictured them speeding through the rain, Robert shouting, blaming Ian, driving like a maniac. Ian would have been frightened, his vision blurred by fear. Had he taken the sheets to the nearest public bin, made up his sister's bed with fresh ones?

Robert's voice became peremptory, demanding that Rosemary be given a full psychiatric assessment. Chris wondered what it would take to break him, and wished that Flanders could find the right words, hit upon the means.

Rosemary was sitting in a chair by the window of her hospital room, wrapped in a green cotton blanket. She looked comfortable, but the clear light from the window highlighted the purple and green bruises on her face and hands.

There was only one other chair in the room. Dawkins moved it closer to the window and sat down. Chris stood by the bed.

Dawkins asked Rosemary how she was and she replied that she was fine, looking at him keenly, eager for news.

They'd driven straight to the hospital from the police station. Flanders had said he had no objection to them talking to Rosemary again, but that he'd be arranging a psychiatric assessment. Of course he'd questioned Rosemary himself in the time between Chris and Dawkins' first visit and the interview with Robert Charleton.

'Robert says you made up the whole thing, that you were never kept a prisoner,' Dawkins said, after making sure the tape recorder was working.

'Of course he would say that.'

Rosemary's eyes were clear and unsurprised. She was sitting with the light behind her. Her hair was freshly washed and framed her face in soft waves. In spite of her bruises, she looked well rested, younger than Chris had ever seen her.

'They'll have gotten rid of the evidence,' Dawkins said, 'but there may be some detail that they've missed. Think back carefully. Did anybody else stay at the house while you were there?'

Rosemary looked over her shoulder, staring out the window. She didn't think anyone else had slept in the farmhouse since she had arrived. There'd been very few callers.

She described how her brothers had been sympathetic when she'd first moved out of Brighton, helping her with practical details, offering her a home for as long as she wanted it, but wanting her to start divorce proceedings as soon as possible, suggesting she should use the family solicitor.

'Robert said I should have got in touch with him months ago.'

Their control over her had tightened gradually.

When Chris told her about the proposed psychiatric assessment, Rosemary said, 'I'll just have to do my best.'

When Dawkins asked about the container port proposals, it took her a while to focus on the question. Finally she said, 'Robert and Ian wanted Fred to speak in favour of the Hastings option. They couldn't see anything wrong with that. The development of the area would benefit the whole family, and they thought that surely Fred could express a point of view. But he was angry. He said that he should never have agreed to be on the committee in the first place, but that now he was on it, he must remain impartial.'

Chris reflected that another kind of man would have gone along with the suggestion, paid lip service to it, told Robert and Ian that he'd done his best. But Robert would never have accepted that excuse. It would not have ended there.

'Robert blamed me for not handling Fred better, persuading him to do what they wanted. When he realised that Fred wasn't going to change his mind, he was furious.'

'What happened then?'

'They never told me what they planned, never took me into their confidence, but I overheard things. I heard Robert and Ian arguing one night – or not so much an argument, you couldn't argue with Robert – but Ian was upset. It was about money, something about money and the chairman of the committee. Robert has no patience with committees and bureaucracy. He thinks it's all red tape to be cut through. He learnt that from our father and grandfather. I was too young to remember Granddad, but Robert remembers him well. After Dad died, Robert talked about Granddad more and more. I think they kind of ran together in his mind, men he respected and looked up to, tough men who would never take no for an answer. For generations, the men in my family have got their own way.'

'When was this, that you overheard them?'

'I don't remember exactly. It was hard to keep track of the days. I remember Robert shouting at Ian. He was shouting on the phone as well.'

'Could that have been to Captain Delraine?'

'I didn't hear Fred's name. I only knew that Robert was angry. I mean more than usually. He was always angry to some degree.'

'Did you talk to Robert about it?'

'Oh, no! I wouldn't have dared.'

'Ian?'

'I tried to. Ian wouldn't talk. He looked unhappy and shook his head.' Rosemary said sadly, 'There's another reason Robert disliked Fred. He blamed him for the fact that we never had children. Robert disliked Fred even before we were married. He tried to talk me out of it. Fred was used to being respected and looked up to. He couldn't understand what Robert had against him. Dad was still alive then. I miss him, you know. Dad kept Robert in check. Once he was gone, there was nobody to do that. Then when Fred turned out to be, well, stubborn I suppose you might say, Robert blamed me. He'd wanted me to marry someone local.

Fred bought that house in Brighton. He thought I'd like to live in the city – well, I thought so too. I was excited about it, starting a new life. But I didn't realise what it would be like to be on my own so much. Fred was hardly ever home. He was on the water, or at the pilots centre. It didn't matter at the start. I thought I'd get pregnant, have a baby. We wanted at least two children. But I couldn't conceive. I kept on expecting it to happen, but it never did. We had tests. Robert believed it was Fred's fault, but the tests were inconclusive.

Fred's response was to withdraw further into his own world. He didn't blame me, any more than I blamed him. But he was against adoption.

Then his health started to deteriorate. His hay fever got worse. He took strong anti-histamines and became addicted to them. We argued about it. I should have been more understanding. I know that now. Perhaps there were friends amongst the pilots he confided in, but after a while he refused to talk to me.'

Chris waited to hear Brian's name, or William's. But he didn't think Delraine would have talked to Rosemary about his friends. He might have spoken about Peter Robinson, but that would have been with reference to Robinson's troubles, not his own.

'After the funeral they were more relaxed with me. I mean Ian was. I hardly saw Robert. I think he was away from the house a lot. Ian felt guilty, but when Robert was there, he would do whatever Robert told him because he was more frightened of Robert than of the police.'

'Did you try to talk to Ian about your husband's death?'

'Oh yes, several times. When he brought my food, and stood hesitating by the door, almost as though he wanted to apologise, I said, "You killed him, didn't you?" He looked stricken, but he always denied it.

I didn't give up. Out of my sorrow I might speak, I told him. And out of your sorrow you might tell me the truth. You are my brother, after all. Don't you think I feel guilty too? If Fred and I had stayed together, none of this would have happened.'

Dawkins' phone rang. 'Yes,' he said, and then, 'Thank you, sir.'

He motioned Chris outside.

It had been Flanders on the phone. In one of the paddocks furthest from the house they'd found the remains of a recent fire. In it were charred fragments of wool.

'Brian's gloves,' Chris said.

Dawkins frowned. 'Why bring them back?'
'Maybe they were in a hurry.'
'They could have tossed them overboard.'
'Maybe they forgot,' Chris said.

THIRTY-THREE

Ian Charleton looked as though he'd shrunk ten centimetres. When he walked into the interview room to take his seat, he stumbled like an old man.

'You've admitted to pushing Captain Delraine overboard. Why did you do it?' Flanders asked.

'For the family,' Ian said. His voice was low, but calm; not shaky as Chris had expected it to be.

Chris remembered Anthea's conviction. She'd been right.

'Did Robert coerce you, force you, threaten you at any time?' Flanders asked.

'I'd like to say yes. The truth is he didn't need to. But that night, I thought – I thought we were just going to talk to Fred.'

'Is that what Robert told you?'

'Robert said that we had one last chance to bring him round.'

'Why one last chance?'

'We had Rosemary to bargain with.'

'You'd threaten to harm your sister if the Captain didn't do as you said?'

'It was just a threat. Robert wouldn't really have hurt Rosemary.'

'So what happened that night?'

'We – I – neither of us realised what a state Fred was in, how doped up he was.'

'You knew about the anti-histamines.'

'Yes, but not that they'd make him so disoriented.

He could barely see where he was going.'

'Why did he take them if he was planning to meet you?'

'I don't know. Maybe he was in two minds about the meeting. Maybe he took them because it was a habit. It was simply what he did each night.'

'How did you arrange the meeting?'

'I rang Fred that afternoon. That other sergeant asked me about it. I told him I'd rung to ask Fred how he was, but that wasn't true.'

'Why did you think Captain Delraine would agree to meet you late at night?'

'I told him we were bringing Rosemary.'

'Did he believe you?'

'I don't know. Like I said, I think he may have been in two minds.'

'How did you get him on board the *Aeola*?'

'With great difficulty. Robert went to get him in the dinghy. We both helped him on board. We were lucky he was used to climbing ladders, otherwise it might have been impossible.'

'What did Captain Delraine do when he discovered that Rosemary wasn't there?'

'He didn't twig, not really. He asked where she was and then he, well, he kind of collapsed.'

'When did you push him overboard?'

'Robert did that. We were already half way to the heads.'

Ian started to cry. It was terrible to hear. Still, Chris couldn't believe that Ian hadn't known Robert intended to kill his brother-in-law.

'Did you make any attempt to rescue Captain

Delraine?' Flanders asked. He's as unimpressed by the tears as I am, Chris thought.

Ian shook his head. When he spoke again, it was almost in a whisper. Flanders asked him to speak up and to say yes or no, rather than nod or shake his head.

'I couldn't bear it that the *Aeola* was implicated. She was my friend, my pride, my comfort. Now she was contaminated. I couldn't bear to take her out, or even look at her. Left to herself, the *Aeola* would have turned around, would have circled till she found Fred alive.'

Flanders said dryly, 'I doubt whether Robert thinks like that.'

'It's impossible to have a discussion with my brother. Robert's only a few years older than me. I kept believing I could catch up. Rosemary was too far behind. I never gave much thought to her when we were small. Then we were sent to boarding school. I never really knew my sister.'

'Your family's fortunes weren't at risk if the Hastings development didn't go ahead. You and your brother would still be wealthy men.'

'It wasn't just that.' Ian took a breath and moistened his cracked lips. 'Things would have been different if either of us had had a son.'

'There's still time for that.'

'In Robert's mind, time is running out. He blames his ex-wife for failing to produce an heir, but he also blames me and, even more than me, Fred Delraine. Rosemary wanted children. When time went on and she didn't fall pregnant, Robert decided that it was Fred's fault. Rosemary wanted to adopt, but Fred was against it and Robert hated the idea that someone not of his blood might inherit even part of what his father and grandfather had built.'

Chris tried to imagine what it would be like to believe that the continuance of a family bloodline, along with a family's material fortunes, over-rode all else. Sitting in the small, close room with Ian Charleton, Robert's obsession became more – not forgivable, it never would be that – but more present and therefore more understandable.

'If an heir's so important to Robert, surely he would have produced one himself?'

'My brother's ashamed of not having done so, but he won't admit to shame. He's angry that the prospect has receded with the passing years. He believes that if he'd been born into an older generation, his grandfather's or his father's, his wife wouldn't have left him. She would have considered it her duty to stay married and to have his children. But his wife did leave him and he's never been able to persuade another woman to take her place.'

'What about yourself, Mr Charleton?'

'I – marriage never seemed possible for me.'

'Did Robert try and talk you into it?'

'Oh, yes. He tried.'

It's said of someone undergoing great stress that they age quickly, years in a matter of minutes, but Ian Charleton in his extremity seemed ageless to Chris, or else his face was at once that of an old man and a child.

'Did Robert try to bribe Eric Finlay to recommend Hastings as the new container port?' Flanders asked.

'It didn't work.'

'Why not?'

'Finlay stalled.'

'Stalled?'

'He played for time, didn't say yes or no. Robert was furious.'

'But Captain Delraine did overhear Robert making the offer.'

'Of all the people to come back to the committee room at that moment, it had to be Fred.'

'Did Captain Delraine challenge Robert about it?'

'He tried to. Robert denied it, said Fred was mistaken. When Fred asked Robert what he was doing in the committee room, Robert lost his temper and called Fred a drug addict and an impotent fool.'

'What did Captain Delraine do then?'

'He backed down. He told Robert he was resigning from the committee and he just wanted to be left alone.'

'Why couldn't Robert accept that?'

'Because he was too angry. He really hated Fred by then.'

'Would you have let your sister out if she hadn't escaped?'

'I like to think so,' Ian said.

Chris wondered about the saying that if you dropped a frog in boiling water, it would try to jump out, but if you put the frog in cold water then heated it, the frog would stay there, cook to death. It was a horrible saying, cruel, a horrible idea. Chris didn't like to think of it at all, yet supposed it might apply to Ian.

When you go on doing as you've always done, or have done for as long as you can remember, it doesn't seem peculiar. You just move step by step, and feel pleased that you can do that much. Surviving becomes a goal in itself. Even so, it must have happened sometimes that Ian stepped outside the hold his brother had on him, that he caught a glimpse of what life might have been like, might be like, without Robert. The feeling would have been quickly squashed because it was too painful.

'What about Tony Parry?' Flanders asked.

'We donated twenty grand to the development group. Of course Tony was lobbying the committee too. Robert kept on saying that if we could only get to the right people then it would be in the bag.'

'Right people?'

'The Premier.'

'Did Robert talk to the Premier himself?'

'He tried for a meeting, but they put him off.'

'What about opposition on environmental grounds?'

'Robert said there were always going to be environmental protesters. There are over the Bay West option too.'

'Parry paid eight million for his yacht. It's registered in the Cayman Islands.'

Ian nodded as though this was old news. 'I wondered about that, whether campaign donations went to pay for it. But Parry is a wealthy man.'

'What does Robert think?'

'If he had his suspicions then he didn't tell me. Robert's much closer to Tony than I am.'

'They certainly seemed to be getting on well at Parry's Christmas party. The one he threw at Queenscliff marina.'

Ian looked confused for a second then he said, 'Robert told me about it afterwards. A girl fell in the water, but no one came to any harm.'

'Did Robert tell you about Parry's discussion with Captain Delraine that night?'

'He said Tony tried to talk to him, but Fred was as stupid and stubborn as ever.'

'Where were you that night?'

'I don't like parties,' Ian said. 'I knew it would be noisy. I booked myself a room at the Queenscliff Inn, went for a walk and had an early night.'

There was a pause before Flanders changed the direction of his questions. 'What happened to Captain Delraine's phone and wallet?'

'Robert threw them overboard.'

'You mean he took them from the Captain's jacket pocket?'

'He threw that overboard as well.'

'And the Captain let him?'

'I told you. He was terribly disoriented. He could hardly see.'

'What did you think?'

'I said it might look better if they'd been left on the beach. Robert said too bad.'

Chris thought that if Captain Delraine's death had been treated as murder from the start, there would have been a proper search. It was possible that some of his possessions would have been found.

Ian was still speaking. 'You do understand, don't you, that Robert will never give in? He'll hire the best lawyers and fight to the end. Backed into a corner he'll blame me for everything.'

'What about Mr Laidlaw? Had either of you met Mr Laidlaw before?'

'No. Robert spoke to him on the phone. The old man was at the funeral, but he didn't introduce himself.'

'And the phone conversation? Were you present? Did you hear what Robert said?'

'No.'

'What did Robert tell you? Try and remember his exact words.'

'He said we needed to pay a visit to a friend of Captain Delraine's. When he told me we were meeting him on the cliff path, I still didn't understand.'

Because you didn't want to, Chris said to himself.

'Why do you think Mr Laidlaw agreed to meet you up there?'

'He didn't look frightened. It was a private place to talk.'

'So you had a conversation?'

'No. Robert held out his hand to shake Mr Laidlaw's, but instead of letting go, he swung the old man off balance. Mr Laidlaw was stronger than he looked. He grabbed hold of Robert round the neck. I tried to separate them. Robert gave him another push.'

'And sent him over the edge?'

When Ian didn't reply, Flanders said, 'And climbed down to make sure he was dead. There was blood on the gloves and that's why you had to remove them from the body.'

'Robert did that.'

'Why didn't you throw them overboard?'

'I forgot. Once I'd pulled up the anchor all I could think of was getting the *Aeola* home. When Robert told me to burn the sheets after Rosemary escaped, I put the gloves on the fire as well.'

THIRTY-FOUR

After the interview was over, Dawkins spoke briefly to Flanders, then he and Chris found somewhere to have a quick meal.

Dawkins had lost weight; the adjective burly no longer suited him. Chris recalled again that evening at the Brewhouse, when the Sergeant had taken off his jacket and the muscles underneath his white shirt had tensed and then relaxed.

He wondered if they'd keep in touch. Would it be up to him? And would it involve meeting in a pub or a café in Geelong, making small talk? Neither of them would want that. Already their collaboration seemed to belong to a past that couldn't be re-visited. Robert and Ian would be charged with the murder of Fred Delraine and Brian Laidlaw. Ian was probably right in saying Robert would fight the charge with every means available to him; but as for the part he and Dawkins had played, that was very nearly over.

They had never used each other's first names. Though Chris had seen Dawkins' written down, it had not seemed to belong to him. And Dawkins had called him Blackie, which many people did. He'd barked the word out at first. Chris might have said he had a history of being ordered around by detectives, but he hadn't said this. Instead he'd gone behind the Sergeant's back.

Contempt had grown, dislike on both sides; but then something had changed. Chris thought of his father's first name, John; of course sons didn't call their fathers by their first names, but it seemed that suddenly, in his memories, he might be able to.

Dawkins said, some of his old barking manner returning, 'What will happen to her?'

'Rosemary Delraine?' Chris had to shake himself in order to return to the present.

Dawkins nodded. Chris recalled the mingled shock, hurt and triumph in Rosemary's eyes that first day they'd spoken to her in the hospital.

'Is there a word for killing your brother-in-law?' Chris asked. 'Not fratricide, but something like it?'

Dawkins shrugged. 'Rosemary will be rich, but that mightn't help her. I wonder if she'll visit them in jail.'

Chris thought how hospital lights leached colour from a person's face and how Rosemary's bruises had been marks of courage.

He said, 'It will help her, knowing she escaped. She didn't just sit there, waiting passively, a prisoner.'

'She knew her brothers had murdered her husband.'

'She was frightened, but she acted. That's the important thing.'

Dawkins shrugged again and said, 'You know, I never liked my first name.'

'Why not?'

'I was named after my uncle, who was a piece of shit.'

'What happened to your father?'

'He left when I was three.'

'And you've had no contact with him since?'

'Bugger all,' Dawkins said. 'Edward. Eddy. Awful.'

'And your Mum?' Chris asked.

'Oh, she's still there.'

Dawkins sounded as though continuing existence was an achievement, which Chris supposed it was.

'I prefer my second name. Edward Charles Dawkins. Charlie I wouldn't mind being called.'

'Charlie it is then,' Chris said.

They sat in companionable silence for a few moments, then returned to the subject of Rosemary Delraine. Chris said he'd like to visit her again.

The psychiatrist made his assessment. Rosemary was of sound mind. There was no reason why she should undergo psychiatric treatment, no reason why she shouldn't manage her own affairs.

She gave Chris a hug, which he returned, thinking of Camilla.

'Oh, that I should be free of them!' she said.

Chris wondered if he'd ever felt such immense, uncluttered relief. Rosemary could leave hospital as soon as she'd arranged for somewhere to stay.

'Ian said they did it for the family.'

Rosemary's face clouded over. Chris didn't want to make her sad again, but there was something about the explanation that troubled him, that wouldn't let him go.

'For a myth about our family,' Rosemary said softly.

Chris thought again of Anthea, how Anthea had homed in on Delraine's in-laws, had seen the black heart of the matter. He said, 'My assistant constable understood that.'

'Who?'

'Former assistant constable.' Chris smiled. 'Her name's Anthea. She's on maternity leave.'

'A boy?'

'A girl. Aneira. Welsh for snow.'

'That's good. You know, I always secretly wanted a girl.'

'There's – '

Chris had been about to say that there was still time for that. But it wasn't true. He asked, 'How well do you know Alison Delraine?'

'Not well at all.' Rosemary seemed only mildly surprised by the question. Perhaps she was still thinking of daughters. 'Alison only visited Australia once before – while Fred and I were – she came to our wedding. I think she's a very private person.'

'But she and your husband were close.'

Chris hadn't said anything to Rosemary about the exchange of letters between Alison and her brother, and he didn't think it was the right time to raise the matter now. But a hope at the back of his mind was beginning to put out small green shoots.

'Did you ever think of making a trip to England?'

'Fred mentioned it from time to time. To see his sister and a bit of the country. I had no objection, but his life was full here. By full I mean routine, you know – his work, the pilot service. After we'd given up hope of having children, we might have gone, I guess. Fred and Alison spoke regularly on the phone.'

Chris waited. Rosemary said in a flat, almost indifferent voice, 'Alison must have thought it strange that I hardly spoke to her at the funeral.'

Perhaps she did, Chris thought. But it was more likely that Alison had been pre-occupied with her brother's letter and her guilt at not having contacted the police before.

Rosemary smiled again and Chris felt a warmth inside him. It was as though there was inside each person a small hidden warmth; every person, no matter what faults they had, or what they had to endure.

'I've never been to England,' he said. 'I set out for Europe once and got no further than the Nile.'

He could have told her then, about the river and the sea. It occurred to him that she would understand. Chris thought of Minnie. He recalled Minnie ringing him on Julie Beshervase's phone and saying in a stage whisper, 'All quiet at number 10.'

Chris saw, in his mind's eye, Alison and Rosemary visiting galleries and museums together, dressed in comfortable, loose-fitting clothes and sensible shoes. They would look alike, would grow to look alike.

He could see the two women as clearly as though they were walking down a street in front of him. From the back they might be taken as sisters, which they were, joined by marriage. At the same moment, they would grow tired of their outing, turn aside from painting or historical exhibit, fetch their bags from the check-in. Alison was frugal, used to living on a modest income; Rosemary was wealthy. In this, too, they found common ground. Sometimes they'd make sandwiches at home, which they'd eat sitting on a park bench in the dappled light; sometimes Rosemary would pay for lunch in a café.

All the friendships that might have been, or that existed and then were cut short before their time, were somehow present in Chris's imaginings, in the picture of two women whom violent death had brought together.

Who else did he know who possessed courage and a generosity of spirit? Camilla Renfrew and Minnie Lancaster, of course.

The investigation was over. He could draw a line under it – wasn't that the popular expression? But what Chris felt now was different from other murders he'd become involved with, been drawn into, though that implied reluctance on his part. He had been reluctant, but then other emotions, other needs and decisions had taken over.

Chris didn't believe he would ever 'get over' Bobby McGilvrey's death, ever stop feeling guilty and blaming himself.

Brian had been an old man, and his guilt over Brian's death was different. But still, Chris thought, he could and should have seen it coming. Camilla would need help; he must be careful how he offered it. Camilla guarded her independence fiercely from her son. If she thought there was a danger that he, Chris, wanted to encroach on her independence, she would shut him out. He would keep an eye on Camilla unobtrusively. They could go for walks together, not along the cliff top unless Camilla particularly wanted to; but inland, to Riza's paddock, through and underneath the Moonah's fugitive yet reliable shade. The oldest of the Moonah – the grand old men and women of the Moonah tribe – pre-dated European settlement. Their biggest branches rose and fell and rose again in fantastic shapes. Once most of the coastline behind the sandhills had been covered with them. Now there were just a few pockets left.

That could be their way, their canopy. It was where

Camilla had broken her leg, on one of the humped, tree-root-laden paths. But Chris did not believe the memory would deter her. She would walk there; they would walk together. Sometimes they would speak of Brian.

THIRTY-FIVE

Chris and Camilla were sitting in Camilla's living-room, curtains open to a morning that was all the spring, warmth in the air that was like no other warmth before or since.

'It's the rain we've had,' Camilla said, seeing where Chris looked.

'You can tell Brian,' Chris said hesitantly. After a short pause, he continued, 'After my mother died I talked to her, in the house when no one else could hear.'

Camilla said without turning her head, 'None of that was your fault.'

Chris said firmly, 'Neither was what happened to Brian your fault.'

'No?' Camilla said fiercely. 'If I'd made him go to you, if he'd told you everything he knew – '

'You couldn't have made him. We've been through all that.'

Camilla looked sceptical and stubborn, prepared to hang onto her responsibility. Then her face cleared a little. 'This house is a crucible,' she said.

Brian could be falling always and forever and that could be a link between them; but this was not, after all, how feelings and how memory worked. So long as Camilla had good friends, so long as he did not let her forget that, then Chris thought she'd be alright.

He recalled the party after Julie and Riza had been re-united – the first case he had worked on with Anthea as his new recruit – the case of the stolen camel.

Brian had waited on Camilla with her broken leg, and how those who knew him had watched with dropped jaws and staring eyes because never before had Brian brought anyone a sandwich on a plate, or a cup of tea.

Camilla asked how Minnie was. 'Thank her for me the next time you see her.'

Chris said that he would.

The feeling he'd carried with him for years, that he'd let Minnie down, failed to fill the gap left by her dead husband, fell away. In its place there was a lightness. The past could not be re-lived and put right, but neither did it need to shadow all a person's days.

He would ask Minnie to marry him. Perhaps she'd been waiting for him to say the words for years. But no, Minnie wouldn't wait passively like that. She was braver than he was, at least where feelings were concerned. It could simply be that she didn't want him, not in that way, not for life. But it was time to ask the question and to face her answer.

He would take the risk, now that it had presented itself to him as one that could no longer be avoided. Rosemary Delraine had lost her husband, and Camilla her dearest friend. Why had he believed that there was plenty of time, that he could put off doing what needed to be done?

Camilla was watching him, alertly, not unkindly.

Chris said, 'I've just made a decision.'

'That's good then. That's good.'

Chris stopped himself from adding that he'd made a decision to act before it was too late. The sense of urgency he felt in relation to proposing to Minnie somehow transferred itself to the woman sitting opposite him. He thought of courage in all its different forms. Even Robert's actions could be considered as a form of courage; refusing to brook opposition, refusing to take no for answer. But then, if you accepted that, courage as a concept and ideal ceased to have any link with morality or goodness.

When, years ago, he'd talked to Minnie about travelling overseas, Minnie had asked what he'd be coming back to. It had been a typical Minnie question, both gently expressed and perceptive.

He could not recall his exact reply, but that didn't matter. I'll be coming back to you, he could have said. But it didn't matter either, that he'd missed that opportunity. Now he wanted to shout, rattle the rafters, shout until there could be no doubt at all.

He knew Minnie was working late and that he couldn't propose to her in the middle of her shift. He was in a fever till it finished. He ran up and down the street four times, then furiously weeded around his vegetable seedlings.

Chris and Tom Maloney walked from the Point Lonsdale front beach to the cemetery. Chris had picked some flowers from his garden and Tom was carrying a small blue stone. He'd said, when Chris had asked him where he'd got it, that it was the sort of thing Bobby would have noticed and picked up. To the best of Chris's knowledge, Bobby and Brian Laidlaw had had nothing to do with one another, though they would have known each other by sight since they'd both spent a great deal of time out of doors. He thought that Brian would have respected Bobby's independence and approved of Max.

Because Brian had been murdered, his funeral had been better attended than would have been the case had his heart stopped one night while he was asleep.

Camilla had been calm and dignified. Minnie had stayed by her side, unobtrusively, but there if Camilla needed her. Minnie had looked dignified in her own way, bright hair under a grey scarf shot with lines of blue. The memory brought Chris a feeling of affection and gratitude.

Tom was rubbing the blue stone as though to rub some life into it. Sometimes sadness was a weight a person didn't want to lift because the effort of lifting was too much. But it didn't have to be that way; that's what Chris wanted to tell his friend.

They were standing in front of the mound of new-dug earth before they spoke again.

Chris said, 'It was Camilla's idea to bury him. There was nothing about it in his will.'

He bent to arrange his flowers. Tom was clutching his stone as though he wasn't sure, now they were there, whether to leave it or take it home with him.

'It means that she can visit him.'

'There is that I suppose,' Tom said.

'Do you think Brian was ready to go?' Chris asked.

'What?' Tom turned sharply, frowning.

'He was still living independently but he couldn't keep that up forever. And he would never have gone into a nursing home.'

'Camilla would have helped look after him.'

'For as long as she could, yes.'

'Who did he leave his house to?'

'A charity for sailors.'

'Not Camilla?'

'No.'

'You know it's funny,' Tom said. 'I still see Bobby sometimes, in that red kayak of his. And I hear Max barking, just when it's beginning to get dark.' Tom squinted into the sun, his frown dissolving. 'Think of me sometimes, Blackie. A thought now and then.'

'Tom?'

'I'm retiring. Not before time. You don't need to say it.'

'I wasn't – '

'Go before you're pushed. Isn't that the message?'

'I didn't – '

'Because you didn't need to. I may be a stubborn old bastard, but I'm not a complete fool.'

'Where will you go?'

'I haven't worked that out yet. I won't stay here though. Too many memories.'

Chris didn't say, you'll take them with you. Of course Tom understood that.

'New blood,' Tom said, his voice neither impatient nor bitter. 'And you, Blackie?'

'I'm getting married.'

Chris half expected Tom to respond sarcastically. Even now, he more than half expected that.

'Jesus,' Tom said, then grabbed his Chris's hands. 'Good for you.'

He bent down so Chris could not see the tears in his eyes.

It was like a painting, Chris thought. He seldom went to exhibitions, or thought much about paintings, and would have quickly replied, had anyone asked him, that he hadn't much idea of form or composition. But the flowers he'd brought were blue, and the blossom of the tea-tree hedge so white that its purity was an invitation to stop and look more closely, and then wonder and take in a breath of gratitude. He wanted to shout for the rightness of it.

Tom had finally decided on a spot for his stone. The earth was all new-turned, but the stone lay on a moister, darker circle than the earth immediately surrounding it.

Tom stood looking down at where Chris pictured Brian Laidlaw's feet might be. He thought of the promise he and Tom had made, that they would toss each other's ashes off the cliff top, whoever was reduced to ashes first. He wondered now if that would be possible, supposing Tom moved far away. But surely he and Tom would keep in touch.

Tom stood with his head still bowed. He might have been thinking about moving his stone to a better position, fearful that some passer-by would take it. For the dead can scarcely lay claim to possessions, and even if they do, are unable to enforce their claims.

We must do that for them, Chris thought, but then the idea, and the thought behind it, passed. Its going was like the softest breath of wind.

The galahs were noisy, calling to each other, feeding on the grass between the graves.

Chris reflected, as he had before, that galahs weren't as common as they used to be, and that he mostly saw them these days in the park behind the Queenscliff pier.

He looked up. Winding ahead of him was the Moonah walk, studded with memorial plaques. People had chosen to remember their loved ones with a few words engraved in metal, set in stone, as indeed they'd done for many centuries. It was an alternative to taking up the room for a whole plot. Chris glanced across at Tom, who had shuffled forward and was almost kneeling on the broken earth. He didn't believe it would suit either of them to be remembered on a plaque.

Along one edge of the Moonah was a row of sage bushes. Someone had planted the first few and they'd augmented themselves year by year. Or else the first few had seeded from bird droppings. Impossible to tell. They'd been there as long as Chris remembered, and nobody had pulled them out. Herbs were hardy, surviving hot dry summers one after the other, and that was just as well.

Now the sage added its purple-blue tribute to the spring.

Chris thought of saying something, pointing out the continuity to Tom – blue stone, sage flowers – above them the pale, newly-washed sky. But he hesitated in the face of his friend's concentration.

The sage was flowering as though there could be no tomorrow, and all must be accomplished in a single morning. Chris thought of Brian Laidlaw riding his bike slowly along Hesse Street, heedless of the traffic building up behind him.

He wondered how he would be remembered – digging in his garden, or walking, back turned resolutely to the sea? Or perhaps finding new courage. Is that how Minnie would remember him?

Chris took Tom's hand and helped him up, and together they left the cemetery.

ACKNOWLEDGEMENTS

With grateful thanks to all those who have supported me in the writing and publication of this novel, especially Jen McDonald and Barbie Robinson – Jen as the founder of For Pity Sake Publishing and Barbie for her cover and internal design. Thanks to Kim Blain for the map design.

Many people have helped with my research for *The Lodeman*. I'd like to thank everyone in the Queenscliff area and further afield whom I consulted while writing this book.

My appreciation to Paul Malone, Maureen Cashman, and David and Rina Bayne for reading early versions of the manuscript and to Rosemary and Bill Brown for their careful proof reading.

Thanks to Karen Barker and Paul Forrest of the Point Lonsdale Newsagency for their enthusiastic promotion of my books and to Hilary Stennett, branch manager of the Queenscliff library for many years of encouragement and help. Thank you to Matt Davis and Jayne Tuttle, owners of Queenscliff Bookshop for continuing support.

Finally, a big thanks to my family.

Also by Dorothy Johnston

Sea-change Mysteries:

Through a Camel's Eye
The Swan Island Connection
Gerard Hardy's Misfortune

The Sandra Mahoney Quartet:

The Trojan Dog
The White Tower
Eden
The Fourth Season

*****

Tunnel Vision
Ruth
Maralinga My Love
One for the Master
The House at Number 10
Eight Pieces on Prostitution (short story collection)

The Swan Island Connection

'All children were a mixture of innocence and guile, Chris Blackie thought, but the innocence had been squashed out of Bobby McGilvrey unnaturally young.'

A shocking murder rocks the quiet coastal Victorian town of Queenscliff, a place were police work usually entails minor traffic infringements and the occasional Saturday night drunk.

Local senior constable, Chris Blackie and his deputy Anthea Merritt fully expect a murder investigation to be handled by the Criminal Investigation Unit based in Geelong. But they're blind-sided by the interest shadowy figures from the secret military training base on nearby Swan Island take in the case.

Consigned to the edges of the investigation and fearing an imminent wrongful arrest, Chris and Anthea defy their superiors and follow their own lines of investigation – at great personal risk.

Gerard Hardy's Misfortune

According to local legend, the historic *Royal* hotel in the Victorian coastal town of Queenscliff is haunted. Having served as both a mental asylum and a morgue in the early days it could hardly fail to be, but a bizarre murder in the hotel's basement puts a decidedly eerie spin on things.

The victim is an academic, obsessed with spiritualism, the tarot and the town's most famous literary resident, Henry Handel Richardson.

From the outset, the local knowledge and unorthodox methods of Queenscliff's police officers, Chris Blackie and Anthea Merritt, are ridiculed by the bull-necked Detective Inspector Masterson from Geelong's CIU. And yet, hard-nosed police investigation practices seem ill-equipped to counter the otherworldly influences at play.

What DI Masterson believes is an open and shut case turns out to be anything but.

Dorothy Johnston was born in Geelong, Victoria, and lived in Canberra for thirty years before returning to Victoria's Bellarine Peninsula where her 'sea-change mystery' series is set, comprising *Through a Camel's Eye*, *The Swan Island Connection*, *Gerard Hardy's Misfortune* and now *The Lodeman*.

She is the author of thirteen novels, including a quartet of mysteries set in Canberra. The first of these, *The Trojan Dog*, was joint winner ACT Book of the Year and runner-up in the inaugural Davitt Award. *The Age* gave it their 'Best of 2000' in the crime section.

Two of Johnston's literary novels, *One for the Master* and *Ruth*, have been shortlisted for the Miles Franklin award.

She has published many short stories in journals and anthologies, along with essays in Australia's major newspapers.

For more information about the author, please visit her website: http://dorothyjohnston.com.au